The Golden Goal

ANNAH CONWELL

Copyright © 2024 by Annah Conwell

All rights reserved.

No part of this publication may be reproduced, distributed, or transmitted in any form or by any means, including photocopying, recording, or other electronic or mechanical methods, without the prior written permission of the publisher, except as permitted by U.S. copyright law.

The story, all names, characters, and incidents portrayed in this production are fictitious.

Book Cover by Alt19Creative

*To my secret society of ladies in waiting, my sisters in Christ: Beth,
Baylie, and Kathryn. This book, this series, is for you.
Thank you for the inside jokes, millions of voice messages, and prayers.
Ps. Let the record show I don't love Anakin the way Beth and Baylie
(and Sutton) do. I'm convinced no one does.*

The Golden Goal: When two opposing teams are tied at the end of the game, they enter into a sudden-death match. The game ends when a goal is scored.

Contents

Content Warnings	VIII
1. Sutton Jones	1
2. Shaw Daniels	8
3. Sutton Jones	19
4. Shaw Daniels	29
5. Sutton Jones	41
6. Shaw Daniels	50
7. Sutton Jones	60
8. Shaw Daniels	67
9. Sutton Jones	75
10. Shaw Daniels	83
11. Sutton Jones	89

12.	Shaw Daniels	98
13.	Sutton Jones	104
14.	Shaw Daniels	112
15.	Sutton Jones	119
16.	Shaw Daniels	132
17.	Sutton Jones	141
18.	Shaw Daniels	149
19.	Sutton Jones	157
20.	Sutton Jones	166
21.	Shaw Daniels	171
22.	Sutton Jones	179
23.	Shaw Daniels	187
24.	Sutton Jones	195
25.	Sutton Jones	203
26.	Shaw Daniels	207
27.	Sutton Jones	213
28.	Shaw Daniels	224
29.	Sutton Jones	231
30.	Sutton Jones	242
31.	Shaw Daniels	250
Epilogue		258
Bonus Epilogue		264

Author's Note	268
Acknowledgements	270
Also By Annah	272
About the Author	273

Content Warnings

This is a closed door romance with some steamier makeout scenes.

The book does mention alcoholism and drug addiction, but it is not a focus of the book. Since hockey is played in the book, there are mentions of blood, injuries, and game-related violence.

Chapter One

Sutton Jones

If I were a guy, none of this would matter. Do men think about their appearance when they're on their way to see their enemy? Probably not. I guess I don't know that for sure, but it seems unlikely based on the fact that the men I know barely put any thought into their clothing *ever*.

"Which top says *I'm amazing at my job* while also saying *I'm better than you at everything*?" I hold two tops up in front of me for my best friend, Ariel, to see over our video chat. One, a silky red blouse, the other, a black wrap top.

I need to make a good first impression on the entire staff of the Alabama Rockets, but I also want to feel confident facing Shaw for the first time since Christmas two years ago. Yes, even my own childhood home isn't safe from him since he's my twin brother Brock's best friend. It was a beautiful gift that he didn't attend last month's festivities.

Shaw Daniels is the razor burn of men. Irritating beyond belief and impossible to avoid. Ever since we were kids, growing up together in the same tiny town, he's gotten under my skin. All I wanted to do was be the best in my class, but Shaw always came along and managed to beat me without even trying. He'd skip class, go to parties, not study for a second, and still outscore me on tests. It drove me up the wall.

Not to mention, he was–and is, though I'll never tell him to his arrogant face–an incredible hockey player. Which is why I'll be seeing him today because he's the star player of the Alabama Rockets, the NHL team whose staff I'm joining as a physical therapist.

"You really shouldn't care about what Shaw thinks about you," Ariel says. "But go with the red. Red always looks good on you."

"Thank you," I say with a smile and throw the red top on my bed. "And you don't have to worry about me when it comes to Shaw. I plan on ignoring him as much as possible. I'm so over the whole rivals thing."

Ariel gives me a disbelieving look. She's been my best friend since high school, and we roomed together in college. But after I scored this amazing job with the Rockets, I moved to Alabama, leaving behind my North Carolina roots and my best friend. So almost all of our interactions happen through a screen now. But even over video chat, I can tell she's not buying what I'm selling.

"You said that before your family Christmas party a year ago, and you ended up with *bruises* from sled racing him."

"I would have raced anyone, you know how competitive I get. It wasn't about him."

I'm lying, and we both know it. It was about him. It's *always* been about beating Shaw.

"Just remember that you wanted this move to be a fresh start."

"It will be. I'm done with hockey playboys."

"See, I still don't get why you won't just work somewhere else. If you don't like hockey boys, *don't work around them.*" She says it like it's obvious.

And on the outside, it is obvious. But she just doesn't understand. Hockey is in my blood. My whole family eats, sleeps, and breathes it. It surprised all of us when my brother decided to become a sports agent instead of going pro. He had the talent, it just wasn't his dream. So, I can't work anywhere else. The goal has always been hockey for me. Even if being *close* to a player burned me in college.

"You're not a hockey person, you don't get it."

She sighs. "You're right about that. I just want you to be happy. The last year of college was rough."

Memories crawl like ivy up the walls of my mind. I spray them down with weed killer. I'm done moping around about what Mason did to me. He made his choice, and it wasn't me. It doesn't mean I don't deserve to be chosen. At least, that's what my mom said when I showed up on her doorstep in tears.

"I'm not going to let that happen again. You don't have to worry about me. The old Sutton burned in the same fire as Mason's jersey."

"Good. I've got to get back to work, but let me know how today goes."

"Thanks, love you."

"Love you too!" she says before hanging up.

I grab my phone off the phone stand that I use whenever I chat with Ariel or my family. My introduction to the team is in a few short hours. That should be plenty of time to be ready to face an entire team of professional hockey players, the coaching staff, *and* the one man who always manages to throw me off kilter, right?

Wrong. My red silk blouse is going to look burgundy from my sweat by the time I work up the courage to walk inside. When I left the house I felt confident. The entire way here I played my pump-up playlist and envisioned myself walking in and owning the whole building. But now that I'm in the arena parking lot, I'm positive of only one thing: I am not ready to meet all of these people.

Shaw is the least of my worries right now. It's actually a comfort to know that he'll be there, if only because he's a familiar face amongst the strangers. That's the only comfort he could *ever* bring, and I regret even thinking of his name and that concept in the same sentence.

When I can't stall any longer, I get out of my car and hope that the frigid January temperatures will press pause on my nervous sweating. I don't even bother to put on my coat, instead opting to sling it over my arm. I need the icy air to sharpen my senses.

My heels click in a steady rhythm as I walk to the door of the practice facility. This is likely the only time I'll be seen in an outfit of this caliber, but I wanted to show them what I look like outside of the athletic attire and sneakers I'll wear on a day-to-day basis. That way the team can see how professional and passionate I am about this job.

I pause with my hand on the door. *Oh no.* I've set myself up to only go down from here. Why didn't Ariel mention this when I spent an hour going over my outfit choices? If she wasn't my only best friend, I'd demote her in the ranks for this. She should have known better, she's the one with an eye for fashion. Seventy percent of why I chose my profession was because of my passion for hockey, but the other thirty? That was because I'd get to wear comfortable clothes and shoes every day.

Now everyone is going to see me at my very best and then feel underwhelmed when I show up for my first day. I think I have a spare set of clothes in my car for emergencies, and I did drive in tennis shoes. But I'll be late if I go change now–

"You pull the door, not push." The familiar teasing lilt of Shaw's voice makes me tense up. This is *not* the way I wanted him to see me for the first time in two years.

"I know that, Daniels," I snap, letting go of the door handle and turning to face him.

I'm caught off guard by how attractive he looks. His dark curls are tousled like he's been running his hands through his hair. And he's wearing a matching Alabama Rockets hoodie and sweatpants in heather gray. He should look lazy and messy, but he looks like he belongs on a billboard. It's disgusting and it only makes me dislike him more.

"Nice to see you again, Jones." He smirks, looking me over. His eyes are twin blue flames, scorching a trail over my skin. "They didn't tell me we were getting a doorman. Or is the proper term, doorwoman?" He looks up as if he's actually considering which term to use.

"Funny," I deadpan. "But actually, I'm the new physical therapist."

He looks down at me, because *of course* he also gets to be taller than me. I'm not short either. At 5'11" I'm tall for a woman, not to mention the extra height of my heels. But that's no match for his 6'6" frame.

"I know, Brock told me last week that you got the job."

Can't a woman tell her twin brother anything without him telling his best friend? I told Brock not to tell anyone, but he thinks Shaw isn't a part of that category. And if I told him specifically not to tell Shaw, he'd go on some long lecture about how we need to *bury the hatchet* and let it all be *water under the bridge*. I don't want to do that though. I want to use the hatchet to hack at the bridge and then burn it to ash.

My arms start to feel frozen in the winter weather, so I cross them as a subtle way to warm them.

"Great, so glad you're still friends and you haven't had a tragic falling out caused by him realizing how arrogant and annoying you are." I give him a saccharine smile.

"That's awfully specific. How often do you think about that scenario?" He reaches around me and opens the door. I walk inside the thankfully warm lobby. It's filled with Rockets memorabilia and no people. I can't decide if I'm thankful no one is here to hear Shaw's and my conversation, or wishing someone was to force us to tone things down.

"Every night before I go to sleep."

"You're thinking about me in bed, Jones? And here I thought you were different from every other woman I've met."

"You're disgusting." I glance down at my smartwatch. "And unsurprisingly, late to practice. I guess you haven't given up your slacker ways."

He shakes his head then starts to back away, duffel bag over his shoulder and a smirk on his lips.

"Much like a party, practice doesn't *really* start until I walk in. See you later, Jones. Save an ice pack for me."

He winks before turning around and jogging toward the locker rooms. I'm left feeling flustered and way too warm. When I studied the Rockets' schedule, I thought choosing this time to arrive would ensure I didn't run into Shaw before I was ready. I should have accounted for the fact that he's never been on time for anything in his life.

My charm bracelet rattles as I shake out my hands. I won't let him get in my head or under my skin. This is my dream job. Not even Shaw Daniels can ruin that for me.

Chapter Two

Shaw Daniels

Something is seriously wrong with me. I sigh as I drop down onto the bench in our locker room after practice and start to unlace my skates. I had a plan for when I saw Sutton. That plan was to meet her at the door–which I accomplished by waiting in the parking lot for her–and tell her she looked beautiful. Then I was going to open the door for her and say I wanted to start over and ask for a clean slate. But when I saw her standing there I just couldn't help but tease her. Something about seeing her brown eyes narrow at me gets my blood pumping.

Unfortunately, that rush of adrenaline didn't lend as well to practice as one might think. I was beyond distracted the entire time. I kept looking around the rink to see if she was going to show up. The first time I missed a pass, the guys on my line made fun of me. The second time, they asked if I was okay, and if I maybe stayed out too late the night before. The third time ... they weren't happy.

And on the topic of angry men, Brock is going to be so mad at me. He wants more than anything for his twin sister and best friend to get along. It's not like I don't want that either. In fact, I'd like even *more* than that, as in her wearing my jersey on game days and jumping in my arms when we win. That's what I'd like, but unfortunately, I've been sabotaging myself for *years*.

In elementary school, competing with Sutton was fun. She'd get all mad and her face would scrunch up. Brock and I would make fun of her. But once we got to middle school, things started to change. Suddenly, we weren't just racing each other on the playground. Guys started to notice just how pretty Sutton was. The Jones' genes are blessed, that's for sure. I'm convinced she never had an awkward stage, even if she says otherwise whenever she looks through photo albums with her mom.

So when the other guys started to notice, I did too. But she's Brock's *twin sister*, so I just ignored it. Until he asked me to help him intimidate one of her jerk boyfriends in eighth grade. Apparently, he was talking to other girls behind Sutton's back. That was the day everything changed. We confronted the idiot and he had this smug look that I punched right off his face only for Sutton to round the corner when I did.

She did *not* like that I hit him, and instead of listening to my explanation or Brock's, she just got angry and walked her lying boyfriend to the nurse's office. Ever since that day, we went from rivals to true enemies. I never stopped trying to protect her from her terrible taste in men, and in retaliation, she sabotaged my dates as well.

I never cared though, because I've only ever wanted her. I just have no idea how to show it. We speak in sarcasm and quips. I know the woman like the back of my hand but none of that matters if she won't stop fighting me long enough for me to show her that I'm as in love with a person as you can be without actually being in a relationship with them.

"Is everyone decent in here?" Coach Fowler's voice booms through the locker room.

A symphony of affirmative grunts answers him. I look up from my skates to see Sutton enter the room, making my eyebrows shoot up. I was expecting a burly hockey coach, not my beautiful enemy. She's pulled on a coat over her red top, which doesn't surprise me. Growing up she lived in hoodies and sweaters because she was always cold. I'm grateful she decided to put it on because if the guys saw what I saw earlier, their current reactions would be even worse.

Why is she wearing red, anyway? Our team colors are black, white, and gray. Is it because she's set on making every man in her general vicinity drool over her? I'm convinced that the color is what made me say what I did earlier. I was drawn to it like a bull in the ring.

The ruckus of equipment being thrown to the side and guys talking about practice begins to die down as everyone notices Sutton.

"Team, this is Sutton Jones. She's joining our staff as a physical therapist," Coach announces after walking in, gesturing to where Sutton is standing, hands clasped in front of her and a wide smile on her face.

One of our rookies, Danny, decides to take his shirt off right after Coach introduces her. As if he doesn't know Sutton is in the room, when he clearly does. He's only nineteen, though, so I'll cut him some slack for his lack of decorum. Sutton's eyes widen slightly before diverting to the opposite corner of the room. Unfortunately for her, that's where I am. I shoot her a smirk and I can tell she's resisting the urge to roll her eyes.

"It's so nice to meet all of you. I'm looking forward to working with y'all. Hockey is my favorite sport, and sports medicine is my passion," Sutton says with the kind of polish that only comes from practicing the words in front of a mirror.

"I might fall down next practice just to go see her," Mac, a defenseman, says under his breath to my left.

"I wouldn't mind if she gave me a little *massage*, that's for sure," Paul, another defenseman, says back.

I can tell Sutton hears this line because of the way her smile tightens and her back stiffens. My muscles tense up too, and it takes every ounce of restraint in my body to not launch myself at the two idiots to my left.

"Be respectful or I'm going to shove your face into your locker so hard you'll need more than a little physical therapy to recover," I warn in a low voice, making them eye each other. They quickly shut up.

As the first-line center with a few years of experience on my side, I've garnered enough respect to throw around in moments like this.

"Sutton will be starting with us this week and will be a familiar face soon enough," Coach says.

"But hopefully not *too* familiar," Sutton adds with a smile. "Let's keep the injuries to a minimum."

A few of the guys chuckle, and Coach grins like he's already half in love with her.

"All right, we'll let you get back to what you were doing," Coach says and Sutton nods before following him out.

When the door shuts behind him, chaos ensues. A whistle rings out and everyone starts laughing and talking about how gorgeous she is. Everyone except the guys in a relationship–and the two defensemen I threatened.

"Hey!" Liam, our captain and the oldest veteran on our team, yells. The room falls silent. "You can go to a bar if you want to talk about women. If it's not about hockey, leave it at the door."

His command gets everyone to shut up, but I know it won't last long. Sutton will be the main topic of conversation for at least a few weeks. I'm grateful nonetheless, and I hurry to leave the locker room before Liam does, knowing that once his intimidation is gone they'll resume their conversation. I don't need to connect myself to Sutton any more than I already have by my threat. And if I hear one more guy talk about her long legs or what her blonde hair might indicate about her personality ... I might end up in a brawl.

My hair is still damp from the showers and I can hear my grandma scolding me about how I'm going to get a cold from going out with wet hair in the winter. It reminds me that I need to call her; it's been a few days and I know she'll worry if I don't. She's the only blood relative who checks on me without expecting money in return, so I try to make sure I'm taking care of our relationship.

Sutton is in the first row of parking spaces when I leave the facility, balancing on one stiletto while she puts a sneaker on the other. Only she could make an act like that look graceful. She's always been poised, likely from her time as a figure skater. That's one of the many reasons it's so fun to mess with her. There's something delicious about seeing a woman so dignified and composed become completely undone by my words alone.

It makes me wonder what it would be like if we were together. This is where my mind becomes a minefield of desire. It's a dangerous, dangerous place to wander. My high school creative writing teacher once said I had the most vivid imagination she had come across in her time as an instructor. It was helpful for assignments, but not so much when trying to stop thinking about your best friend's sister.

My mind conjures up scenes of her in my arms, breathless from my kiss. She'd be entirely undone in a new way. A way that has me needing a cold shower. I should go home and do just that, but she's like the sun, pulling me into her orbit.

"Hey, Jones!" I call out, making her drop her other sneaker. It bounces under her black Porsche.

The look on her face is so cold it lowers the temperature outside to negative degrees.

"I can't believe I made you jump. You have to be on your game more than that," I say when I get closer. "Since I scared you, I can get your shoe for you."

She crosses her arms over her chest and sticks her hip out, a look I'm rather familiar with. It's probably supposed to intimidate me, but it just makes me want to kiss her.

She scoffs. "You didn't *scare* me, and I don't need you to get my shoe. I'm not some damsel in distress. I can do it myself."

Sutton has always believed she has to do *everything* herself. I don't know if being a twin made her want to be independent more than ever, but whatever the reason, she holds her autonomy up like a banner for all to see. But while she might be singing *Independent* every morning on the way to work, I know deep down she wants someone who will shoulder some of the burden with her.

"I know you can, but I also know you'll be furious if you get that silk top dirty," I say and I'm rewarded with an eyebrow raise.

"I'm not afraid of a little dirt, Daniels. You should know that by now."

Images of her inserting herself into every game Brock and I played as kids come to mind. There was nothing too muddy or rough for her. But what she doesn't know is that I noticed how every time the game was done she ran to take a shower. And how unless I was playing, she didn't involve herself in anything messy.

"Just let me get the shoe, Jones."

I drop down to my knees and then lay on my stomach to reach under her car for the bright white designer sneaker.

"Now *this* is a view I don't mind," Sutton says and I chuckle as I push back up to my knees.

"It makes sense that you like me on my knees, Jones. It's the only way you could beat me at anything."

"Oh please, I've lost count of how many times I've beaten you."

"So you stopped keeping that cute tally in your diary under your bed? What a shame."

Her mouth pops open and her face tints pink. "How did you know about that?"

"I didn't," I say with a grin.

"I despise you," she says through gritted teeth, only making me laugh.

"Aw, I love you too." I hold her shoe up to her like it's a ring and I'm proposing. "Your slipper, Cinderella."

Sutton's hand lifts like she's going to take it, but then she smirks and lifts her foot up to me. She pulls a sock out of her jacket pocket and holds it out.

"It's the least you can do since you scared me," she says with a too-pretty smile. A woman shouldn't be allowed to look like a model while she's demeaning you. It's disconcerting.

I'm sure she expects me to push her foot away or throw her shoe back under the car, but if there's one thing I love more than teasing Sutton, it's surprising her. I set the shoe down and take the sock from her hand, grabbing her foot before she can pull away.

A little gasp escapes her lips. I bite back a smile and slowly pull the sock over her foot, noticing her red toenail polish as I do. It doesn't surprise me at all that she matched her nails to her shirt. She's a woman who cares about the details.

I let my fingertips brush over the soft skin of her ankle. When I glance up at her, she's watching my hands with intensity. I slide her shoe on next, tying the laces tight. Once I'm done, I push up from my knees and brush the dirt and bits of gravel off of me. She would have hated all of this on her, that's for sure.

"Thank you." Her tone is purely polite, but when I look at her I notice she's flushed and a little dazed. A thrill runs through me knowing she's like this because of me.

"It's nice to see spending four years at Duke didn't erase all of your manners."

"You and Brock aren't ever going to get over me going to Duke instead of UNC, are you?" she asks.

I can't speak for Brock, but I know I won't get over it. For a whole list of reasons she'd never believe if I said out loud.

"Does Brock still mess with you about it?" I ask instead of answering.

She gives me a look. "Don't pretend you two don't talk almost daily. I know he told you he got me a bunch of UNC gear for my graduation."

I smile, remembering him talking about it while we were playing video games. He told me all about the look on her face when she opened the gifts. I hated that I didn't make it there to see her walk across the stage. Not that she would have wanted me in the crowd, but I still wanted to be there.

"He said the look on your face was priceless."

A soft smile replaces her scowl. "He was a jerk for that, but he made up for it by scoring me this job."

My stomach tightens. Lying to Sutton about anything other than my feelings for her isn't a habit of mine, but this lie helped her achieve her dream, so Brock and I made a pact not to tell her that *I* was the one who pushed for her to get the job. They wanted to hire someone with more experience, but I sold them on her. It really didn't take much once I started describing just how brilliant she is.

Sutton's phone starts to ring before I can respond. She answers it right away.

"Hey Mom! No, I'm not busy," she says and starts to walk to her car door. Well, I guess our conversation is over.

"Hey, Mama Jones!" I yell out and Sutton scrunches up her face the way she used to when we were kids.

"Yes, he's here." She sighs and then looks up at me. "Mama says hi and she misses you." Sutton shudders as if just relaying the words makes her want to gag.

I snatch the phone from her, making her glare at me. "Miss you too, Mama Jones!" I say.

"Oh it's so nice to hear from you, Shaw. Are you being good?"

"I'm always good, you know that." I smirk at Sutton, who starts to try to get the phone away from me.

"Mhmm, you just stay out of trouble. And make sure you take care of my girl."

I grab Sutton's wrist and hold it away from me. She tries to pull my hand off with her other one, but she's not strong enough.

"I'll take care of her," I say, then laugh when Sutton hits my chest. "I think Sutton is itching to talk to you."

"Okay, well I want to see you soon. Don't be a stranger."

"Yes, ma'am." I hold the phone high up in the air away from Sutton. "Say please," I command in a quiet voice, meeting her angry brown eyes.

The fire in her gaze sets me ablaze in the best way. If only I could get away with kissing her full lips right now.

"Daniels, if you don't give me back my phone right now, you're going to regret it," she warns.

"Say please, or else I'm going to tell her about the time you snuck out and went to Jeremy Dunmore's party."

She looks like she's at war with herself, her eyes flicking up to her phone and back to my face. Her mom's voice comes through the phone, probably wondering why no one has answered it yet. Sutton has always been an overachieving good girl type, but she had a streak during high school where she tried out the party scene. She gave it up once she got a lower grade than me on a math test, but her mom has always thought she was an angel who did no wrong. I know she wants that perception to stay intact.

"Fine. *Please*," she practically growls.

I hand her the phone with a grin, then shoulder my duffel bag, intent on walking away.

"Yes, Mama, I'm being nice," she says into the phone and my grin widens.

"*Nice*?" I mouth and she swats at me.

I jump back so she misses. With a huff, she turns her back to me and opens up her car door, then tosses her heels inside.

"Today was great, actually. I think people liked me."

My smile softens as I watch her slide into her car. I hate how she still worries about that sort of thing. She doesn't worry about my opinion though, that's for sure. She's just herself. It's like getting my own version of Sutton Jones that no one else gets to see. I know the real her, and even if she wouldn't believe me, I love that version of her the most.

Chapter Three

Sutton Jones

"How is Shaw?" Mama asks me as I drive toward my apartment.

I sigh. "Fine, I guess."

I'd tell her how he actually is, which is annoying and insufferable, but she wouldn't like that answer. Mama *loves* Shaw; it's one of the few subjects in life that we disagree on. She watches all his games–which, okay, I do too, but only to critique his performance–and has given him an open invitation into my family's home. So he's able to come and go as he pleases. I know that he takes her up on the offer too, staying in the guest bedroom during the off-season.

"He sounded good, but I worry about him living there by himself. I hate that you both moved so far away. At least you have each other now, though."

I pull into my parking space and resist the urge to audibly gag. Shaw reminds me of home all right, but not in a good way. When I see him I feel like a kid again, competing and vying for the attention that was always given so easily to him.

"According to the internet, he's rarely alone. So I wouldn't worry about him too much."

I get out and lock my car behind me, smiling to myself as I walk through the courtyard of my apartment building. To my right, the pool and multiple hot tubs shimmer in the morning light, and on the left are an array of picnic tables and grills available to the residents.

An apartment may not seem like much compared to buying a whole house, but it means a lot to me. It shows what saving my money and working hard can do. It shows that I don't need anyone to take care of me because I take care of myself.

"You shouldn't believe everything you see on the internet, dear." My mom thinks Shaw's and my rivalry is more playful than it actually is. I don't know how she's missed the animosity between us all these years.

"Says the woman who bought a swimsuit off one of those weird foreign sites and ended up with a Barbie-sized bikini."

"It was a whole swimsuit for a *dollar*, I had to order it."

I laugh. "Whatever you say."

"If you keep making fun of me I'm going to keep your care package for myself instead of sending it to you."

"Care package?" I ask as I unlock my door. I'm on the bottom level, which I specifically requested. You're not going to catch me lugging my groceries up the stairs, or waiting on a crowded elevator.

"Yes, I purchased some of your favorite things to send to you."

A warm feeling spreads through my chest. I'm so lucky to have good parents. "Mama, you shouldn't have."

"As much as you try to resist it, I do my best to take care of you in any way I can."

I shake my head at her not-so-subtle admonishment. She's always trying to get me to let her pay for spa days or special treats because she thinks I work too hard. And I do give in sometimes—mostly because I can't resist a good massage—but the majority of the time I refuse. I work hard because I like nice things and *I* want to pay for them. At the end of my life, I don't want to look around and think that anything I have was handed to me.

"Well, I appreciate it," I say with a sigh. No use in telling her to keep it, she'll just send more stuff.

I drop my keys into the gold metal bowl on my kitchen island.

"Coming, honey!" Mama yells, sounding like she pulled the phone away from her ear. Then she says into the phone, "Your dad needs me. I'll talk to you later, okay?"

"Okay, I love you."

"Love you too, sweetie."

She hangs up and the silence of my apartment closes in on me. I haven't lived by myself, well, ever. When I went to college, I moved into a dorm, and then I moved into an apartment with Ariel. This is my first time being on my own and the lack of noise is making my skin itch.

When I moved in last week, I had things to do to distract me. Boxes to unpack, photos to frame, and paperwork to do. Now, all of that's done.

I walk into my living room and snatch up the remote, turning on a winter ambiance video using the YouTube app on my TV. The sound of a crackling fire and howling blizzard calms my nerves.

I'm sure I'll get used to it, and maybe even learn to love the quiet. I'll use my new solitary lifestyle to pick up a new hobby, maybe learn a fourth language. I've always wanted to add Italian to the list of romance languages I'm fluent in.

"I can do this," I tell myself. "I don't need anyone but me."

Turns out, repeating Italian words to the app on my phone doesn't kill much time. And after organizing and reorganizing my makeup collection, scrolling through all my social media accounts until my hand went numb, and making a batch of caramel chocolate chip cookies ... I was still bored.

So, exploring my new city, Huntsville, Alabama, became the objective of the evening. I'm buzzing with the need to talk to someone–*anyone*–when I walk through the doors of a bar and grill next to the arena. Normally, if I'm going out to eat I like to choose a nice sushi restaurant or a white tablecloth establishment. But tonight I just needed to get out of the house, and this place was the first to pop up when I typed *best restaurants near me* into the search bar.

It's upon entering that I realize my mistake. The entire restaurant is *covered* in Rockets gear and paraphernalia. Not only that, but most of the seats are taken by Rockets players. I don't have to know them personally to recognize them. I've watched all of their games since the day Shaw got drafted. And it looks like just about the whole roster is here. I wasn't prepared to see all of them tonight. *Is Shaw here?*

A sign near the door tells me to seat myself, and I bite my lip while considering what to do. No one has seen me yet, I could just go home

... I straighten my back. *No.* I can do this. I wanted a night out on the town, and I'm going to get it.

I waltz up to an empty seat at the bar and boost myself up onto it. The seats on either side of me are vacant, which is good because I don't think I'm prepared to insert myself into the fold of players just yet.

The bartender, a curvy woman with pitch-black hair and the sharpest winged eyeliner I've ever seen, comes over to me.

"What can I get you?" she asks and I feel the attention of the men surrounding me turn in my direction.

"Could I get a Moscow Mule, please?" I ask her and she nods.

"Can I see an ID?"

I unzip my black Prada mini bag and pull out my ID. She nods and then reaches under the bar to pull out a slim menu.

"You're new, right?" The dark haired woman asks. I nod. "I'll give you the rundown, then. Here's the menu. It's simple, and never changes, except on game nights when Ricky does half-off wings, and on trivia nights we do buy one get one free margaritas. You can't make any substitutions, so don't even bother asking. Rockets players and staff get a twenty percent discount. My name's Ophelia, if you need anything just shout."

"Thanks," I reply, a little overwhelmed at her spiel.

She turns away from me to start making my drink, and I slide my card back in my purse, holding it in my lap. I glance to my left and notice a line of players staring at me with curious expressions, so I glance to my right only to find the same thing. Do people not understand the art of a glance? You're not supposed to *show* that you're staring at someone.

I turn my attention to the menu, trying to focus on anything but the dozens of eyes on me. This is definitely not my usual place, but I'm sure it's still good food considering the reviews and how packed it is.

When Ophelia slides my drink to me, I order chicken tenders and curly fries. Then I gather my courage and look around the bar. The guys nearest to me immediately turn their attention to the TVs above the bar, and I have to stifle a laugh. It's a good thing they took up hockey and not espionage. There are other patrons here, but I guess me having introduced myself to them earlier makes me more of a target for their attention.

When no one greets me or looks at me again, I shift my focus to my drink, toying with the lime slice that decorates the rim of the cup. Maybe it'll take some time for them to warm up to me. I don't want to be pushy and try to introduce myself to them. I've never been shy, but I have always wanted to make the best first impression. If I tried to insert myself into some sort of team tradition, I could end up tainting my image. It's best to let them come to me.

"Need some company?" a deep voice whispers close to my ear.

Shaw.

I jump a little in surprise, but recover quickly enough to throw back an elbow, hitting him in the stomach. He makes a small *oof* sound but still manages to grin down at me when I swivel around to face him. He's traded his post-practice sweats for dark jeans and a fitted black long sleeve shirt. It's tight enough to show his hard-earned physique, but not so tight that it outlines each muscle. I'm surprised he didn't go a size smaller. He's always been a show-off.

"I'd have to drink a lot more to lower my standards to your level, Daniels," I say, and one of the guys to my right–I think his name is Vinnie–laughs.

"Ouch," Vinnie says. "How does it feel to get shot down, Shaw?"

"You're the expert on it, Vin. Why are you asking me?"

A few of the guys around the bar start to laugh.

"I bet she'd choose me over you, wouldn't you, sweetheart?"

I scrunch my nose up in distaste. Shaw's expression darkens. There's that competitive streak I know. He can't stand someone being chosen over him. I'm almost tempted to say yes to Vinnie. But his weird approach grosses me out too much. "Ew, no," I say, making all of the guys burst into laughter. Vinnie's face turns red.

The shadow of jealousy leaves Shaw's face, proving my point.

"Is all of the team here?" I ask Shaw, and he looks around, then shrugs.

"Just about."

I place one hand on the bar and then push up so that I'm standing on the wooden bar stool. It's not the most stable setup, but it draws the attention of everyone in the grill. There are plenty of non-players here too, but now's as good a time as any to share what I'm about to say. Especially after the comments I heard in the locker room when I was introduced.

A warm, strong hand wraps around my ankle. I look down to see Shaw holding my leg.

"What are you doing?" I ask him.

"What are *you* doing?" he counters.

I huff. "I asked you first."

He rolls his eyes. "Making sure you don't crack your head open. Brock would kill me if he found out."

I roll my eyes back at him and choose to ignore the heat creeping up my leg from the spot he's touching. Then I clear my throat and clap my hands twice. Heads turn and the room quiets.

"This is a message for the Rockets: I don't date hockey players, so please refrain from asking me out. No, you won't be the one to change my mind. I can assure you my mind is very made up on the matter. Thank you." Murmurs break out across the bar. When I glance down at Shaw he looks more amused than anything. Figures. I don't think I've ever been able to intimidate him.

"Are you done?" Ophelia asks, her hands on her hips.

"Yes, I think so."

"Then please get down before you break my bar stool."

"Yes ma'am," I say with an apologetic smile.

Before I can formulate a plan to get down safely, Shaw's hands wrap around my waist and lift me off the stool. He sets me on my feet inches from where he stands. I hit his chest. "Who gave you permission to touch me, you big brute?" I huff and tug down my athletic jacket. My face feels too hot all of a sudden.

"You do know that you just issued a challenge to every player who's single, right?" he asks instead of acknowledging my frustration at him manhandling me.

"I told them not to bother trying."

"That's just going to make them try harder," he replies, and his sharp tone makes me look up to meet his gaze.

His indigo eyes are stormy, catching me off guard.

"They'll get the picture real quick when I turn them down." I cross my arms. "What's your problem, Daniels? Besides your lack of respect for personal space."

He's still too close to me, crowding me against the bar counter with his large stature. He puts a hand on either side of me, effectively caging me in.

"My *problem*, Jones, is that you're going to create chaos on my team by making them compete for you."

"It's not my fault your team doesn't listen. I'm not seeking attention for fun, that's more your speed."

He leans in closer, the sounds of the bar fading away. It's just me and him, facing off against each other.

"Do you really expect me to believe you don't want them to try? That if they pursued you enough you wouldn't give in?"

"I don't expect much of you at all, Daniels," I say to him, earning a dry chuckle. "But I won't be giving in to anyone. There's no hockey player on the planet that could change my mind."

"Oh, I could." His egotistical claim should surprise me, but it doesn't. "If I wanted to, that is."

I roll my eyes. "I'd like to see you try."

"Maybe I will," he replies, his face too close to mine. We're sharing air, his minty breath fanning my face. His eyes are too blue and so intense it's making my heart beat out of my chest.

"You'll have to take a number then, apparently there's going to be a line."

Something unreadable flashes in his expression. I'm not sure if I've ever seen this look in his eyes before. It's disorienting and I don't like it. I push his shoulder and step around him, willing my hand not to shake as I grab my drink and let the icy liquid cool me down.

Ophelia comes by and brings me my food, glancing between Shaw and me before walking over to another patron.

"In all seriousness," Shaw says, sitting down in my spot again, "if any of the guys bother you, let me know, and I'll handle it."

I keep my eyes on my food. "Quit pretending you care. You're not my brother."

I swear I hear him mumble *'you got that right,'* but I can't be sure because someone just scored on TV, making the bar erupt into cheers.

I tell myself not to worry about what he said as he walks around the bar, a few girls in Rockets gear immediately approaching him. My stomach turns when one of them places a hand on his shoulder. His eyes find mine as if he knew I was looking, and I quickly avert my gaze. I don't need him to think I'm watching him. He'll tease me even more. And besides, the last thing I want to see is Shaw flirting with some girl. *Gross.*

But now I'm left with no one to talk to again because Shaw has gotten in my head about the guys on the team wanting to date me. That was probably his goal all along, just to mess with me. I sigh and take a bite of a chicken tender, letting the salty crunch soothe me. At least the food's good.

Maybe all of this will blow over once I officially start working with the players. And maybe Shaw will see one of the other physical therapists so that I don't have to talk to him much at all. I hold on to that hope as I finish my food, praying that this first week with the Rockets won't be a disaster. If anyone could cause one for me, it would be Shaw.

Chapter Four

Shaw Daniels

"If you get killed one more time, I swear I'm going to fly to Alabama and *actually* kill you," Jason says, his agitation clear through my headset.

I'm not doing so hot tonight. After running into Sutton at the grill, my mind is scattered. All I can think about is her sweet scent and the heat of her hips under my palms. I shouldn't have touched her. It was a huge mistake. But as per usual, I just couldn't resist.

So now, I'm bombing in the rare game night with my friends Jason, Miles, and Emmett. We're all incredibly busy, so any time we don't have a game or an appearance to make, we try to get online together and play *Halo*.

"Chill, man. It's just a game," Miles says back. He's probably the most laid-back of all of us, even though he gets pretty intense when he's on the green. You don't win the Masters by being easygoing, that's for sure. Miles was only twenty when he became the youngest golfer to win the Masters. He's now won it twice and is hoping to add a third time at twenty-four years old.

We chase after the players that just stole the flag I was supposed to be guarding, but since I got distracted, they killed me and took it.

"Sorry," Jason says with a sigh. "I got a stupid email from my publicist today and I'm still mad about it. I haven't been out in months, and after going to *one* bar last week, I'm back in the media with that idiotic bad-boy-of-football headline. If another brand distances themselves from me, I'm going to launch a football at the head of the first paparazzi I see."

From college football to now being in the pros, Jason "The King" Kingsley has had a reputation for being fond of parties and late nights. He saw the light recently and realized that the party lifestyle wasn't for him anymore, but he's still dealing with the repercussions of his past choices.

"Don't sweat it," I reply. "I'm sorry I'm killing our numbers tonight. My head just isn't in the game."

"It's fine, you're not much worse than Emmett," Jason replies, making me chuckle.

Emmett is a phenomenal pitcher, the best in the MLB by far, but he's atrocious at video games. All that hand-eye coordination goes out the window when he picks up a controller.

"I'm only playing this because you force me to. Video games are a waste of time," Emmett replies in his usual gruff way. He doesn't speak much in general, but when he does it reminds me of what I imagine a grizzly bear would sound like if it could form words.

"Guys, don't make fun of him, he can't help it. He's too old for this sort of thing," I chime in and laughter fills my headset.

Emmett is the oldest of all of us at thirty-five years old, so we like to tease him. He's also the most established of us, considering he has a daughter. He was married too, but his cheating ex-wife left him to raise his daughter on his own a year ago.

"I'm too mature for this, that's for sure," Emmett grumbles.

"Mature is just another word for old," Miles says, keeping the laughter going.

"I don't know why I hang out with you guys." Emmett's tone says he's done with us.

"Because you *love* us," Miles teases.

"Love is much too strong a word. Tolerate, maybe."

"Tolerate is basically love in your book, ET," I say, knowing the nickname will get on his nerves even more. His middle name is Thomas, and once we found that out we all started calling him ET.

"How many times do I have to tell you not to call me that?"

"Apparently a few more, because I have no plans of stopping."

Something akin to a growl sounds through the headset, but he says nothing more.

We lose our flag to the opposing team and lose the match as a whole.

"Before we start the next one and you make us lose again, maybe you can tell us what's on your mind?" Jason asks and I sigh, tossing the controller beside me on my couch.

I sink back into the expensive cushions and scrub my hands over my face. The thing is, I wouldn't mind talking about my dilemma with Sutton. But they all know who she is because they all know Brock. The four of us connected at Brock's birthday party. He represents all of us as an agent and we all hit it off. Brock tries to keep things business-focused with the other guys and only makes an exception for me since we grew up together, but he's still shared about his family.

So, if I get specific, they'll know before Brock does. But maybe if I'm vague, I can still get advice. They don't know our history, just that I grew up with Brock. It could work.

"There's this girl."

A collection of groans floods my ears.

"Of course there is," Jason says.

"Why am I not surprised?" Miles adds.

Emmett says nothing, but I know his feelings toward relationships aren't very positive after his ex-wife. Actually, all of the guys don't have the best reputations when it comes to commitment. Jason isn't entirely averse to it, but his media persona would lead you to believe otherwise. Miles wouldn't touch marriage with a ten-foot pole, due to his parents' divorce. Then there's me, who only has eyes for a girl who would gouge them out if given a chance.

I stay quiet, now not so sure this is the best group to voice my problem to.

"Just tell us about her," Emmett speaks up.

If Emmett is encouraging someone to talk about *feelings*, I won't turn him down. It's about as rare as a perfect game.

"She's gorgeous, witty, incredibly smart. And she hates me."

"Sounds like she has good taste too," Jason quips.

"Thank you for that. You're so encouraging," I deadpan.

"Why does she hate you?" Miles asks, sounding like he's holding back a laugh.

"We've known each other for a while," I say, trying to keep things vague. "And we're both competitive, which can get out of hand. I guess the friendly competition turned not so friendly over the years for her, but as for me..." I trail off.

"You're down bad for her," Miles supplies, and I nod even though he can't see me.

I'm more than that though, I'm full-on in love with the woman. But I can't explain that to these guys, at least not yet. "Yeah, basically."

"Just tell her. You're Shaw Daniels, she won't turn you down," Jason says.

I roll my eyes. "She doesn't care who I am. Also, please don't tell me that's how you operate in your life."

"They don't call me The King for nothing," Jason replies, and I can envision the smirk on his face right now.

"This is why the media hates you."

"I was *joking*. But I do think you should just be straightforward."

"Nah," Miles interjects. "I say play it cool. Just flirt with her and see where it goes."

The problem is, our flirting looks a whole lot like fighting. So I don't know if that method is the way to go.

"ET, what's your vote? Be straightforward, or play it cool?" I ask.

"I'm not the one to ask. Jason and Miles go on more dates in a week than I have in my whole life."

Most guys would be embarrassed to admit that, but not Emmett. I'm convinced nothing embarrasses him.

"You know her better than us," Emmett adds. "It doesn't matter what we think, it's about her."

"That's a good point," I say, thinking it over.

It doesn't make my mission any easier, but it is clear what I should do. I'll use everything I know about Sutton Rae Jones to win her heart. Because something tells me if I don't do it soon, I'll lose her forever. A woman like her doesn't stay single for long.

· ♥ · ♥ · ♥ · ♥ · ♥ ·

"Good work, guys, I want you to go home and rest up for the game tomorrow," Coach says in the locker room.

I start to rip off my gear, chest heaving from the hard practice. We ended practice with sprints for conditioning and it was intense, to say the least. Everyone is hyped up for the game tomorrow against the Louisiana Gators. There's been plenty of trash talking through the media about the game, and even though they aren't our rivals, they're close enough after all they said.

So all that energy channeled into practice and made for a lot of competition between us, even more than usual. I was determined to keep up, which I'm paying for now.

I take off my shoulder pads, gritting my teeth against the pain in my right wrist. It's been bothering me this season, but I don't want to miss a game just because it's hurting a little more tonight. We're gunning for the Stanley Cup, and I'm going to be on the ice helping get us there every game I can.

"Daniels," Coach calls out, drawing my attention to him. He gestures for me to come over, so I follow him out of the locker room and into the hall. I feel the eyes of a few of the players as I pass. No doubt they're wondering what Coach wants.

"What's up?" I ask, running my hands through my damp hair.

"How's your wrist?"

"It's fine, just a little sore."

"We can sit you out tomorrow–"

"No," I cut him off, he gives me a hard look. "I'll be fine after I rest. Rick said I was good." Rick was one of our previous physical therapists. He left for another team recently, and Sutton replaced him.

"Go see Ms. Jones. I want to hear her report."

I'm sure Sutton would love nothing more than to tell me that I can't play. So while I wouldn't mind getting to see her beautiful face, I'd rather not have her bench me.

"Rick approved me last week, Coach."

"I want a second opinion. You're the one who recommended Ms. Jones for the job. Don't you trust her judgment?"

"Yes," I grit out. "I just think this is unnecessary."

"I disagree. Head over there now." He nods toward the recovery room.

I sigh, but walk past him without another word. Maybe Sutton will be professional and give me the same diagnosis Rick did so that I can be on my way.

When I walk into the recovery center, Sutton and another therapist, Connor, are both working. Maybe Connor will finish up working on Vinnie's knee before Sutton is done bandaging up Lance's wrist and I can just tell Coach *Ms. Jones* was busy.

I watch as Sutton places a piece of tape on Lance's wrist, her brow furrowed in concentration. All of her focus is zeroed in on the task at hand. It's the same look she used to wear while taking a test in school, and when she was figure skating, much to her coach's dismay. I remember sneaking in to watch her practice and hearing her coach tell her she had to relax her face, but she never did until it was performance time.

On performance days, she was effervescent. Her face shone with the kind of joy that always took my breath away. And the way she moved on the ice was a thing to behold. It was as if she was made to wear skates. My mind drifts into memories of tugging a ball cap down low over my face and sitting up atop the bleachers just to get a glimpse of her. If she had seen me, she'd have thought I was there to tease her or throw her off, so I made sure she never knew I was there.

"I want you to ice it ten minutes on, twenty minutes off until you go to sleep tonight. No video games, don't hold your phone or anything, just ice and rest it on a pillow." Sutton's voice breaks through the memories I was lost in.

"Thanks, Sutton," Lance says, flexing his fingers.

"Come by before warm-ups tomorrow so I can look at it, okay?" she asks with a gentle smile on her face.

What I wouldn't give for a smile like that. But I know as soon as she sees me...

"Really, Daniels?" She rolls her eyes. "You couldn't have at least put a shirt on before coming in here?"

I look down, realizing that I hadn't grabbed a shirt from the locker room after taking off my practice jersey and gear. "I thought you deserved some eye candy to celebrate your first day on the job."

Yeah, saying things like that is probably why she doesn't give me soft smiles. But she does give me that sassy look that makes my blood heat. So, you win some, you lose some.

Lance shakes his head at me as he walks out of the room, probably thinking I'm one of the many who are going to try to get Sutton to break her no-hockey-player rule. Well, he's correct, but I've got something none of those guys have: history. I know Sutton better than any of them could hope to.

"What do you need?" she asks while sanitizing her hands. Her voice is taut with annoyance.

"Coach sent me in here for my wrist," I answer.

"Your file mentioned issues with your right wrist mobility, but Rick noted that you were good to play this week. Is it bothering you?"

"Define bothering," I reply and she raises a brow.

"What you do to me every day."

I smile at her. "See, I always thought what we had was more of an adorable back-and-forth, something to look forward to each day."

"Should I check you for a concussion too? Because this level of delusion has to come from hitting your head against the plexiglass one too many times."

Someone snorts, and I glance to my left to find Vinnie and Connor watching us with amused expressions. Sutton notices as well and lets out an exasperated sigh.

"It's always bothering me," I say, trying to steer us back on topic. "But it hasn't hurt more than usual. Coach wants a second opinion, specifically yours."

Sutton glows at this, her smile so unexpected it steals my breath. Even if it has nothing to do with me, just having her smile directed at me is enough to feel warm all over.

"Okay, let's do some mobility exercises then and see where you're at," she says and I nod.

She demonstrates the first exercise and I perform the motion with ease. Maybe this won't be so bad after all. It's not that I thought Rick lied when he said I could play, but my wrist definitely isn't functioning at a hundred percent, so it's a little nerve-wracking to have my abilities on display.

Thankfully, Vinnie leaves the room and Connor starts cleaning up his area, so there aren't any eyes on me. Except for Sutton's ever-critical ones, of course. She stops me as I do the second movement.

"Pull back more," she says and I clench my jaw as I attempt to do as she says. "No, like this."

Her fingertips send a wash of pleasure over my skin before she pushes my hand and sends a wave of pain crashing down. I hiss and drop my arm, rubbing at my wrist. She frowns at me and my stomach drops.

"It's just a little sore after practice," I explain and her eyes flick up to meet mine. I've come to know Sutton's various looks over time, and right now she's in full-on analysis mode. She's hunting for the answer and won't stop until she finds it.

"Try this one," she says and shows me another movement.

Just looking at the position makes my wrist ache, but I attempt it. Judging by the furrow of her brow, I failed that one too.

"Sit down in the chair over there," she says, gesturing to a padded chair to the right.

"I think after a night of rest I'll be fine," I tell her.

She ignores me, walks over to a table, and pumps something into her hand before rubbing her hands together. It's only when she's closer to me that I realize it's lotion.

"The muscles in your wrist and forearm are inflamed. I'm going to use some deep tissue techniques and pressure points to reduce the inflammation."

"Okay." I barely manage to get the word out. My mouth is so dry it feels like I've been gargling sand. *Sutton is about to massage me.*

As soon as her hands make contact with my skin, I suck in a breath.

"Is it too cold? I tried to warm up the lotion," she murmurs.

"No–" I clear my throat. "It's not cold."

Silence settles over us, the tension between us as taut as the muscles she's working on. She gently kneads my muscles and I have to clench my jaw against the urge to pull her into my lap and kiss her right here and now.

Her sweet and spicy scent surrounds me in a delicious haze, and her warm hands are making my whole arm feel better than it has in months. I can't help but close my eyes, trying not to hum in pleasure as her thumb draws a line from my palm to the inside of my elbow.

When she hits a particular sore spot I grunt, gripping the arm of the chair with my free hand.

"Sorry," she whispers.

I blink my eyes open and meet her soft brown ones. Her forehead is wrinkled in concern, her plump bottom lip drawn between her teeth. *Does she ... care?*

"I would have figured you'd like seeing me in pain," I grit out as she continues working the tender spot. She's being gentle, but it still hurts.

"I'm not evil, Daniels. You get on my nerves, but I don't want to hurt you." She pauses. "Most of the time."

I let out a breathy laugh. She pulls her hands away, taking their warmth with them. My wrist feels much better, but my heart is beating out of my chest. I watch Sutton clasp her hands together, drop them to her side, then cross them over her chest. It's as if she doesn't know what to do after touching me.

"How do you feel?" Her voice is low, almost a whisper.

"Good," I rasp out.

"Good–that's good," she says and turns away from me, busying herself with adjusting things on a nearby cart filled with bandages. "You should be okay to play tomorrow so long as you rest tonight and do those mobility stretches during warmups tomorrow."

Relief fills me like helium in a balloon. I'm so happy I could float away.

"Thank you, I'll be sure to do those things."

Sutton nods, her back still to me. Maybe I have more of an effect on her than I thought.

"I'll see you tomorrow," I say, taking a step toward the door.

"See you." Her quiet dismissal burrows beneath my skin as I walk back to the locker room.

It's not like Sutton to be so quiet and without a quip to throw at me. But if she felt even a portion of what I did, that could be the reason for her sudden awkwardness and silence. There has to be something between us, something more than competition and teasing. I just hope that Sutton won't shut me out while I try to find that something.

Chapter Five

Sutton Jones

I think I might throw up. My hands are still shaking as I walk out to my car after work is over.

I *touched* Shaw. Not hit or pushed or brushed by him either. No, I *massaged* him. My hands still tingle from the warmth of his skin. I washed them twice and doused them in sanitizer, but the memory is still there, etched into them like new lines on my palms.

It was hard enough not to stare when he walked into the room with all of those rippling muscles marked by scars and bruises from years of hockey. But now I know what those muscles *feel* like. I thought working with Shaw would be difficult because of his incessant teasing, but whatever this terrible feeling is? It's worse, much worse than just arguing with him.

I slide into my car and turn on the heat, even though I feel hot just thinking about Shaw and his stupid abs. It's not like I haven't seen him without a shirt before, so I don't know why I'm getting so worked up. I've seen him jump into my parents' pool hundreds of times. He's walked around without a shirt while spending the night too, which I called him obnoxious for on several occasions.

But for some reason, seeing him walk into the recovery center with just those hockey pants on ... did something to me. Something terrible. He didn't look like the annoying teenage Shaw who liked to flex his biceps during pool parties. No, he looked like a man with a body built from hard work and dedication to a brutal sport.

"Oh no," I whisper, pressing a hand to my swirling stomach. "I think–I think I find Shaw Daniels *attractive*." I gag on the last word, hating that I said it aloud, even if I'm alone.

I take a few deep breaths, trying to make sense of my jumbled thoughts. I feel like I'm on a tilt-a-whirl ride, spinning round and round with no end in sight.

"It doesn't mean anything," I mutter to myself. "He can be *physically* attractive, but that doesn't mean I *like* him."

I shudder at the thought of feeling anything but disdain for Shaw and begin to pull out of the parking lot. I need to get home before someone sees me talking to myself in my car.

As I drive, I try to steady my nerves. But it's difficult when I can't stop thinking of his incredibly blue eyes staring up at me while he gripped the chair. I remember girls in class sighing over that shade of blue. They'd prop their chins up, a dreamy expression on their faces as they gushed over how one glance from him left them weak in the knees. I just rolled my eyes and focused on studying so that I'd be valedictorian instead of him. And I was, so it paid off.

The sweetness of that past victory boosts my mood as I pull into my apartment parking lot. Maybe Shaw got in my head today, but he won't tomorrow. I've now seen his abs and touched him. I stared into his sapphire eyes and came out just fine, albeit a little shaken up. There won't be any sugary sighs or dreamy far off looks from me. Just a renewed determination to keep things between us as professional as possible.

I unlock my front door and walk inside, greeted by the vanilla pine scent of my air freshener plug-ins. The soothing scent releases some of the tension within me.

Everything is going to be fine, I tell myself. It was just a fleeting emotion. A combination of hormones and forced proximity. Nothing to worry about.

I drop my purse onto my kitchen island as I walk by, then head to my bathroom. What I need is a bubble bath and a comfort movie. I turn the water on, pour in some lavender bubble bath, and then grab my tablet and set it on my bath tray.

Once the air is filled with a soapy floral scent and the tub is full, I slide out of my work clothes and into the tub. I hum in delight at the feeling of the warm water on my skin. Before I sink in completely, I turn on my favorite movie, the one that I keep a secret from most people: *Star Wars Episode II: Attack of the Clones.*

Hopefully, Anakin will help me forget all about my moment with Shaw.

·♥·♥·♥·♥·♥·

It's game day. Pure adrenaline is coursing through my veins, like it has on every game day I've ever attended, or even watched from home. Since I was a little girl, watching Brock and Shaw sprint down the ice has given me a rush like no other. There's just something about it that gets my blood pumping.

I'm practically bouncing in my seat as I breathe in the electric atmosphere of the arena. Everyone is buzzing with excitement for this game against the Louisiana Gators. Most of the fans on both sides have seen the trash talk online. Whatever happens on the ice tonight will set the record straight. It's the kind of thing that gets a crowd going even more than usual. And I'm no different.

It's strange, but I haven't felt this level of excitement since I was able to watch Shaw and Brock on the ice in high school. When my brother decided not to continue on in his hockey career, I kept up with watching Shaw still, but I focused a lot of my attention on my college hockey team and my ex-boyfriend, who was the captain. Maybe the reason I feel all of this excitement is because I'm working with the team now. Whatever the reason, I'm ready.

I've already checked on all of the players that needed it, and watched warmups to make sure they listened to me about stretching. Connor took care of Shaw, whose wrist is thankfully in good enough condition to play. Now, I'm sitting behind the bench, anxiously awaiting player introductions.

Music is blasting at eardrum-bursting levels, lights are flashing like we're at a nightclub, and the air is scented with that classic concession food smell. The arena is *packed*, I'm not sure there's a single seat open. Connor is sitting beside me, and he's tried to make small talk a few times, but I can barely focus because this is the first NHL game I get to watch as a *staff member*.

I've dreamt of this moment for years. It may not be as glamorous as a CEO or brain surgeon–both professions I had people tell me they expected of me in high school–but it's what I'm passionate about. Hockey has always been it for me.

The only reason I never played in a league myself was because I loved the idea of doing something different from Brock. Being a twin, even of a different gender, can sort of lump you together. So there were times I chose activities just because Brock chose a different one, even if it meant losing out on an opportunity to show up Shaw.

The arena goes dark and screams erupt from the audience. The Rockets' pregame introduction begins with a projection on the ice of NASA preparing for a rocket launch. Audio of the preparation plays overhead on speakers. I squeeze my hands into fists, my heart pounding out of my chest.

The classic countdown begins and I shout out with all of the fans.

"*Five ... four ... three ... two ... one! Alabama, we have lift-off!*"

I shoot to my feet, cheering along with the fans. The stadium is a sea of black-and-white Rockets gear, with some purple-and-green Gators fans mixed in. Everyone is screaming and clapping, and I'm convinced this is one of the best feelings in the world.

The players skate around the rink, and I clap for all of them, showing my support as loudly as possible. I'm not a quiet fan, that's for sure. I've always been one to let everyone know how I feel. It has led to some, uh, *passionate* discussions in arenas and at watch parties, but I don't plan on changing any time soon.

Shaw skates by the bench, slowing down to wink at me as he passes. I roll my eyes, trying to ignore the way my stomach flips seeing him.

The other team is introduced to a chorus of boos that I may or may not participate in, then the national anthem plays. After all of the pre-game traditions are done, it's finally time for the game to begin.

Shaw skates to the center of the ice for the faceoff. At the ref's signal, the players swipe for the puck and Shaw manages to secure it first.

I stay standing as I watch, unable to sit with all of this nervous energy pouring through me. I feel like a bottle of Diet Coke someone just dropped Mentos in, ready to explode.

The thing about hockey is that it's so fast-paced, and almost every moment is packed with meaning. It can be difficult to keep up with because if you watch for the puck, you'll miss a player interaction, but if you focus on a player, you might miss a goal.

Tonight I find my focus drawn to Shaw over and over again. But since he's a star center, it doesn't mean I miss a goal. In fact, I get to watch him make a beautiful slapshot as the first goal of the night. The crowd goes wild, and even though it's Shaw, I do too.

A few of the guys slap him on the back and he raises his stick up in celebration. It's unfortunate how great he is. If he keeps it up and takes care of himself, he could make it into the Hall of Fame. It makes it really hard to criticize him.

After the first period is over, I head to the recovery center in case any of the guys need any medical attention during intermission. Tonight we also have a few different doctors here in addition to Connor and me. They stitch up the cuts that happen fairly often and are here for emergency purposes as well. Hockey is a violent sport, so a full medical staff is necessary.

Players are in and out throughout the intermission. I check on a few injuries, but there's thankfully not too much to handle. Shaw doesn't come in, which I'm grateful for. With all this game-time adrenaline, I don't know if I can handle seeing him.

"Hey, Sutton," a rookie named Danny calls out. He just got stitches on his cheek, which is probably the only thing keeping him from wearing a cocky grin as he saunters in my direction.

"Yeah?" I reply, keeping my tone neutral. He's nineteen, and his maturity level is even younger than that. So I'm trying to discourage his advances as much as possible. He's already been fairly forward with me, though not disrespectful, which is good.

"A bunch of the guys are getting together to celebrate after the game at Liam's house. You want to come?"

"How do you know you'll be celebrating?" I ask with raised brows.

"C'mon, have you seen us out there, baby? We're not losing."

I cringe at his term of endearment.

"You are not old enough to be calling anyone baby," I tell him, making the other players in the recovery center laugh. "And if you call *me* that again you're going to need more stitches."

"Aw, why'd you have to be like that? I'm just having fun."

I stare him down, hands on my hips. "Go *have fun* in the locker room, little boy."

The guys laugh again, while a red-faced Danny leaves the room in a huff.

It's almost time for the second period to begin, so the guys start to head out. After cleaning up my station, I walk out beside Connor back to our seats.

"You really should come to the party tonight," he says as we sit down.

"Parties aren't really my thing," I say, though that's not necessarily true. It's just that a party with a bunch of hockey players sounds like a great way to bring up bad memories. Ones where I watched my boyfriend get too drunk and then drove him back to his dorm, trying not to get caught so that he wouldn't get in trouble with his coach. And then of course the party after he got drafted–the one where he told me he needed to "be on his own for a while." If it wasn't for my deep love of hockey, my experience dating Mason could have been enough to make me rethink my career choice.

"It's a good way to get to know the players," Connor says, pulling me from my thoughts, "and it would be nice to have a woman there who *doesn't* want to date a hockey player."

I laugh, knowing what those parties are like. Lots of girls dressed up and hanging all over the players. I don't blame them, though. Who wouldn't want to date a hot, athletic man with an obscene amount of money? I spent a fair share of my girlhood drooling over the players. And until Mason broke my heart, I thought I would marry one.

"I guess it couldn't hurt to show up," I say and look over to find Connor smiling.

It occurs to me why he mentioned my not wanting to date a player. If he's gone to a few of these parties, he probably didn't have a lot of women to talk to since they were only there for the players. Which means he thinks *I'll* be one of the ones he can talk to and potentially date.

I take a moment to study him. He's got dirty blond hair and eyes that are either brown or hazel–I can't tell under the arena lights. He's fit, but not in an obvious way like the players. And he has a nice smile.

Maybe going tonight and flirting with Connor wouldn't be so bad. It could be good for me to put myself out there again.

I smile back at him, my decision made. I'll go to the party, befriend the guys who aren't trying to flirt with me and ignore the ones who do in favor of Connor. It's a foolproof plan.

Chapter Six

Shaw Daniels

When I was in college, and then for the first year or so after I got drafted, I thought post-game parties were the best thing in the world. I'd waltz in and feel like royalty. Girls flocked to me, my teammates patted me on the back and gave me drinks. But now, even though all those things still happen when I walk into a party, I'm over it. If I could go home right now, I would.

Liam's home is a classy place, all modern with clean lines and metallic accents. He's married, but his wife Natalie doesn't mind hosting an afterparty on occasion. I'm sure if they have kids in the future that'll change, but for now his house is definitely the best venue for having the whole team plus their invites over. Whenever anyone else hosts, I try to avoid it because cramming into a penthouse just isn't my idea of a good night.

I'm only twenty-three and I feel like I'm twice that sometimes between the aching muscles and the way my eyes start to droop by midnight after a game. After a really big win, sure, it's fun to chug an energy drink and party the night away. But most nights I just want to go home, take a burning hot shower, and fall asleep on my luxury mattress.

Tonight would be one of those nights, if I wouldn't have heard that Sutton was coming. Beyond the fact that I want to see her outside of the arena, I also want to keep an eye on her. My instinct to protect her has never left, even when we were apart. That's why Mason Walker hates me. Because after I saw a photo of him on my buddy's Snapchat story a little too *close* with a scantily clad woman, I checked him into the glass more times than necessary the last time we played each other in college. And each time I let him know that if he ever even so much as *looked* at another woman while he was dating Sutton, I'd do much worse.

If I thought Sutton would have believed me, I'd have told her back then what I saw. But she'd think I was sabotaging her relationship like it was high school again. Which, for the record, all of those guys were immature idiots as well.

"Lighten up, man. You look like we lost," Sawyer, a right wing player on my line, slaps me on the back. The energy drink I'm pretending is alcohol almost sloshes out of my cup. I don't want to drink tonight, and I need the energy to make it through this party.

"Sorry, I–" My words evaporate when Sutton walks in the room.

Liam's living room is crowded, but it's as if the sea of people parts just for her. She's changed from what she wore to the game into a little black dress that makes my neck hot. It shows off her long legs, made to look even longer by the black heels she's wearing. Her blonde hair is in waves down her back, shimmering golden even in the low lighting of the party.

"You're going to catch flies," Sawyer says on a laugh.

I snap my jaw shut and clear my throat.

"So you're throwing in your hat with the rest of the team, huh?" he asks.

I watch Sutton walk over to where Connor is standing with a few of the equipment managers. She's wearing a timid smile, but is carrying herself with the quiet confidence that comes from years of having eyes on her. Between being incredibly smart and competing in figure skating, I'm sure she's used to the feeling of being watched.

Connor returns her smile with a grin of his own, looking very happy that she's here. My stomach sours at the sight. I'm not worried about the other guys on the team, because I think Sutton meant what she said about not dating hockey players. But someone like Connor could be a problem. I need time to build a good relationship with her, one that leads to romance. I'm going to have to undo years of misunderstandings and wrong impressions. If she starts dating someone else, I won't have a chance to do that.

"Nah, I'm just watching out for her. She's my best friend's sister," I tell Sawyer.

"If she was my sister I'd punch your lights out for looking at her that way."

I laugh and shove Sawyer to the side. "Shut up."

Sutton laughs from across the room, and I clench my jaw. I need to do something to get her to spend time with *me* instead of Connor. He's a nice guy, so I hate to do this to him, but he hasn't been in love with Sutton for close to a decade. *I* have.

A chance for me to steal her attention comes when she steps away from the group and heads in the direction of the kitchen. If there's no one else in there, it'll be a chance for us to be alone since the kitchen is closed off from the rest of the living room. I push off the wall I'm leaning on and follow after her, ignoring Sawyer's snickering.

"I don't think Liam has any kombucha in there," I say to her back as she rummages through the fridge that Natalie stocked with drinks for the night. "But you could just pour some juice into a beer, it'll taste the same."

Sutton's favorite drink is kombucha. I think it's terrible. It's vaguely reminiscent of beer but much, much worse in taste. She closes the fridge, turning to face me.

"I should have known you'd be lurking around here. You never miss a party."

Another assumption on her part that I wish I could correct. I can't say it's not my fault that she thinks this way, though. I wonder if she'd believe me if I said I'd rather be asleep right now.

"And by the way, kombucha is *nothing* like beer. Beer is disgusting."

I smile at her correction, anticipating that it was coming. She'll die on the hill of her opinion, at least when it comes to arguing with me. I've seen her acquiesce to others, but not to me, *never* to me. It's partly why I love teasing her, because it's a dance all our own. Connor may get her timid smiles and good-natured laughs, but I get fiery looks and sassy remarks.

One day, I hope to have all of it. All of *her*. I want all her dreams and fears, her sleepy smiles, her sick days, her uncontrollable laughter and her tears. Because I may know Sutton better than any person at this party, but I know there's so much more to learn. If I'm lucky, I'll get a lifetime of learning every little quirk and trait of hers.

"Do you ever admit you're wrong?" I ask her and she rolls her eyes.

"I could ask you the same question."

Laughter sounds out from the other room, a reminder that we aren't entirely alone like I wish we were.

"Why would I have to admit something that isn't true?"

"Is it exhausting walking around with a head as big as yours?" Her brown eyes shimmer in the fluorescent kitchen lighting.

I shrug. "The muscles make it pretty easy."

Her eyes rove over me, blazing a trail of heat. A smirk pulls at my lips.

"Want me to spin around so you can get the full picture?" I ask her and she blinks as if coming out of a daze, her cheeks tinting pink.

"I'm done talking to you," she says with a huff, spinning back around to look in the fridge. "I'm going to get a drink and go talk to people who don't make me want to bang my head against a wall."

Ouch. If she didn't just check me out ten seconds ago I'd think she was telling the truth.

"Being at a party like this reminds me of high school," I say instead of acknowledging her dig. "Remember Calvin's afterparty on prom night?"

She pulls out a can and shuts the fridge. It looks like sparkling water, which is just as gross as kombucha, if not worse.

"I remember my date not showing up because of you," she says, glaring at me.

"My date didn't show either," I remind her. The blush staining her cheekbones deepens a shade. She's always insisted she had nothing to do with my date bailing on me, but I have reason to believe otherwise. One of them being the not-so-innocent look on her face right now.

"But I wasn't talking about prom. I said the afterparty," I say.

Realization crosses her expression before it twists in anger once more. "Oh yes, I remember that party. That's where you cheated at pool and convinced everyone there that you were the rightful winner."

"I didn't cheat," I defend myself, but she just scowls.

"You did."

I close the distance between us. Her sweet scent wraps around me like a warm cashmere blanket. She smells like honey dripping fresh from the comb. The urge to kiss her is so strong it feels like a gravitational pull. But considering the fact that her cocoa brown eyes are glaring up at me right now, I don't think it would be a good idea.

"How about a rematch, then? Liam has a pool table downstairs."

Her eyes narrow. "You're on, Daniels."

I smirk, mentally celebrating my win. I've successfully captured Sutton's attention. She can't resist a challenge.

"Follow me and prepare to lose *again*, Jones."

"Less talking, more walking." She shoos me toward the kitchen doorway. I chuckle and start to walk out.

We manage to make it through the living room and down the stairs without much interruption. The basement is empty, just as I'd hoped. Liam doesn't care if people come down here, but he usually tries to contain the party to the living room so that he can keep an eye on everyone.

I flick on the lights and walk toward the pool table, where the balls are already racked and ready to go. Liam is kind of a neat freak, and so it doesn't surprise me one bit that it's organized this way.

Sutton and I both grab a cue from the wall nearby.

"Do you want to break them?" I ask her.

"You can do it," she replies, swirling blue chalk on the tip of the cue.

I make the first shot, scattering the balls. A solid sinks into the right corner pocket, making that my pattern for the game. I take another shot, but I miss, making it Sutton's turn.

It's quiet down here, the only sound the clink of the pool balls hitting together after Sutton's shot. She doesn't make one, and her face scrunches up in distaste.

"Not the best start," I say and she sighs.

"Just take your turn."

I sink two before I miss again, turning it over to Sutton.

She misses yet again, her frustration evident on her face.

"When's the last time you played pool, Jones?"

She looks around the room, basically anywhere but at me.

"You haven't played since high school, have you?" I ask, unable to contain my surprise.

She huffs. "Fine, I haven't played since that stupid party. But not because of you," she says, pointing at me. "I just don't care for the game."

"So why accept my challenge?"

Something flashes in her eyes, an unreadable emotion that makes my stomach flip.

"I never turn down a challenge," she answers. "And maybe I thought it would be like riding a bike."

I snort and she hits my bicep.

"Don't laugh!"

"I'm sorry, I tend to laugh at ridiculous notions."

She pushes her lips to the side, clearly trying to hide a smile.

"I guess there's no point in finishing the game. You win." She pulls a face, making me laugh again.

When she walks over to place her cue on the wall, I realize I'm going to lose my chance at spending time with her.

"Wait," I say and she stops, looking over her shoulder. "Let me teach you."

She turns slowly to face me. "You want to teach me how to play pool?"

I shrug, trying to keep my expression neutral. "Why not? Maybe then you'll actually be able to beat me."

"I beat you at that party," she insists. "But fine, you can teach me. Only because Brock got a pool table at his place and he's been trying to convince me to play him whenever I visit."

I'm surprised she agreed. I fully expected her to laugh in my face or ask me what prank I was pulling on her.

"Okay, put your cue on the wall. We'll just use mine for now."

She does, then meets me back at the table.

"Now set up how you usually would," I instruct.

She bends over the table, propping up her cue.

"Your grip is too loose, you have no control." I lean over her, my chest pressed against her back. She takes in a sharp breath, but doesn't say a word. I smirk at her reaction, happy that I'm the cause of it.

I guide her hand into a better position, then reach back with my other hand to shift the cue to aim better. After I have her aiming properly, I rest one hand on her waist. She doesn't move away or question me. My heart is beating wildly in my chest. One wrong move and this perfect bubble will burst.

"Try now," I say in a low voice near her ear. "Don't give it too much power, be gentle."

She slides the cue back, then forward, lightly tapping the ball. A red stripe sinks into the right middle pocket and I smile.

"That was perfect. How did that feel?"

She turns her head and we're practically nose to nose. Our eyes lock, and in the dim light of the basement her irises are dark, like a strong cup of coffee. The air between us is electrified. I can barely breathe. When her eyes flick down to my lips and back up I'm convinced I'm dreaming.

She opens her mouth like she's going to say something when my phone starts to buzz in my pocket. We both jump at the sudden noise breaking the tense silence. I quickly pull it out and silence it. It's just my dad. No doubt he just stumbled out of a bar somewhere after watching the game and wants to call to congratulate me–aka ask me for more money.

"Sorry about that," I say with a nervous laugh.

"No-no it's fine. I should get back upstairs anyway." Her eyes go wide. "I had a friend waiting on me, but I got distracted." She clears her throat and smooths down her dress.

The frustration at losing the moment between us is made marginally better by the fact that I made her forget all about Connor for a little while, at least.

"You sure you don't want to keep playing?" I ask her and she nods, taking a shaky step back.

Her foot slips, making her knees buckle. I reach out to steady her, grasping her forearms and feeling the heat of her skin through the thin fabric of her dress. Her eyes meet mine once more. I watch as fear tramples desire within her gaze. I'm disappointed, but I know I've got a long ways to go before she can trust me. She pulls out of my grip.

"Yeah, I'll beat you some other time. Thanks for the lesson," she blurts out then books it back up the stairs before I can form another word.

That was ... interesting. I've definitely got a lot more to go on than I did before. An almost kiss isn't a real kiss, but it's close enough to determine that there's something between us, something worth chasing after.

Chapter Seven

Sutton Jones

I'm unsteady when I re-enter the living room. After being in the quiet basement with just Shaw, coming in here feels like jumping into a swimming pool of noise. It's overwhelming, and if I didn't feel bad about abandoning Connor, I'd leave right now.

Maybe it's a good thing for me to stay. If I can distract myself by talking to other people, I won't have time to spiral about what just happened downstairs.

"Sutton, there you are," Connor says, looking relieved and a tad confused.

"Hey, sorry I got a little lost," I say with a nervous laugh.

Connor shakes off his confusion, giving me a good-natured smile. "Don't apologize, I get it. It's crowded in here."

It's at this very moment that Shaw comes up the basement stairs, holding my sparkling water. Shaw's eyes flick between Connor and me, and he saunters in our direction. My stomach drops. He's going to hand me the drink and Connor is going to make a lot of assumptions really fast. Some will–unfortunately–be true, but others will not. And the possibility of a date with him will be ruined. But worse than that, everyone will think my 'no hockey players' rule doesn't hold any weight. Rumors like that spread faster than wildfire within a team.

Shaw meets my gaze, his crystal blue eyes sparkling as he lifts my drink up to his lips and takes a sip. The action is too intimate, knowing just moments ago my mouth was touching the same spot. I press my lips together hard, ignoring the heat climbing up my neck.

What is he doing, and why is he doing it?

"Great game tonight, Shaw," Connor says, reminding me that he's right next to me. I look at him, embarrassed that I wasn't giving him my full attention.

"Thanks, man."

"If you keep it up, we'll be in the playoffs for sure."

"I can't take all the credit," Shaw says, gesturing around the room. "It's a team effort."

"Shaw, over here!" a deep voice calls out, and I see Danny waving him over, surrounded by a handful of women.

"Let me go make sure he doesn't get in any trouble," Shaw says. Connor laughs, but I roll my eyes. As if Shaw is one to talk. He's nothing *but* trouble.

Shaw lifts my sparkling water up as if he's toasting us, then walks away wearing a smirk that should make my skin crawl, but makes it tingle instead.

"He's a good guy," Connor comments.

Shaw has always been the favorite and well loved, so it's no surprise that Connor thinks the best of him. It also seems that he reserves his incessant teasing and annoying tendencies for me. I guess I'm special in that way.

"Yeah," I force myself to say as I watch Shaw saunter toward the group of women. "He is."

· ♥ · ♥ · ♥ · ♥ · ♥ ·

I wake up to my phone ringing on my bedside table. I groan and fumble for it, intent on silencing it until I see my brother's name. He'll just keep calling until I answer, or he'll send someone to come make sure I'm alive. And that someone would be Shaw, since he's his best friend and closest in proximity. So I'd rather answer the phone than deal with the man who's the reason I got zero sleep last night.

"What?" I groan and fall back into bed as I answer the call.

"Why do you sound like you just woke up?" Brock asks.

"Oh maybe because I *just woke up.*"

"It's four in the afternoon. Why were you sleeping?"

A memory of tossing and turning last night comes to mind. After the party, I couldn't sleep no matter how hard I tried. Every time I closed my eyes I felt Shaw's strong hand on my waist, his breath on my neck, saw his lips on my drink. But when I tried to think about the situation, logic eluded me. I couldn't figure out why he acted that way, and more than that, why I let him.

This morning I went and helped a few of the players through some rehabilitation exercises. I spent the whole way to work with my stomach in knots about seeing Shaw. Thankfully, Connor took care of Shaw's wrist, so besides feeling his eyes on me, I was able to make it through the day without interacting with him much.

As soon as I was done with work, I came home, took a lavender bubble bath, then climbed into bed. I planned on staying under the covers until I was hungry or woke up to my alarm set for tomorrow morning, whichever came first.

I blink, realizing I'm still on the phone with my brother.

"Because I enjoy sleep and I didn't get enough last night." I pause, and then because I'm feeling sassy, I add, "Also because I can do whatever I want."

"Well it's time to get up."

I scrunch up my face, pulling the covers to my chin and relishing in the warmth of my cozy bed. It's too cold outside of the covers, as always. I found the perfect sheets and comforter to turn my bed into a fluffy pastel blue cloud. Most mornings I spend at least five minutes convincing myself to leave it, which is how I know I made the right purchase.

"Why?" I whine. "We can FaceTime later."

Brock travels a lot for work, and when he's not traveling he lives in North Carolina, down the road from my parents. So he likes to check in often, but he hates texting and prefers the closest thing to face-to-face as possible.

"If I wanted to FaceTime you, I would have called you with my camera on."

"Then what on earth are you calling me for?"

I don't have the energy or patience to interact with anyone right now, not even my own brother.

"Because I'm in town and I want to see you."

"Oh," I say, suddenly feeling bad for my sassy remarks. "I can get ready and meet up with you. What are you in town for?"

"Shaw has a photoshoot with Under Armour on Monday. I wanted to be there in person since it's such a big endorsement deal."

My eyebrows raise. A deal with Under Armour is no small thing. It doesn't surprise me though, considering Shaw's talent.

"Okay, do you want to meet up for dinner? Or do you want to see my new place first?" I don't say anything about the deal, because that would mean complimenting Shaw, which I would never willingly do in front of another person.

"Let's meet at the pub by the arena. I'm craving a burger and Shaw always raves about the place."

I'm about to agree, but his mention of Shaw has me pausing. "Is he going to be there?"

"Who?" Brock asks, sounding too nonchalant. A deep chuckle comes through the phone and I stiffen.

"You're with him right now, aren't you?"

"Hey, Jones, sorry to hear you didn't sleep well last night," Shaw says and I grit my teeth.

"Why am I on speaker, Brock? What if I would have said something personal?" My frustration bleeds into my tone.

"I didn't think it would be a big deal. We're playing video games right now, so I put you on speaker phone."

"Can we go to dinner just us?" I ask, ignoring his explanation. I need to focus my energy on getting out of this terrible arrangement.

"Aw, Jones, you're hurting my feelings," Shaw teases. "We had fun at the party last night, didn't we? Why don't you want to see me again?"

"I'm going to hurt more than just your feelings if you don't stop talking," I say through clenched teeth.

"You went to a party last night?" Brock asks. He sounds surprised. "Who did you talk to? Did you drink? Did you drive or get a ride share?"

Brock is a *little* overprotective. He acts like a big brother even though I was born a minute before him.

"Dude, breathe," Shaw says to my brother with a laugh. "I was there, I kept an eye on her."

"I don't need anyone keeping an eye on me!" I sit up, my anger like a surge of adrenaline forcing me upright. I'm wide awake now. "I'm a grown woman. I can–and do–take care of myself."

"You're my sister and I care about you," Brock says. "I don't want you by yourself at a party full of a bunch of hockey players trying to get you alone."

The line goes silent, no additions from Shaw. I bite my lip, knowing exactly why he's not saying anything. Last night I was only alone with *one* hockey player, and that was him. And not only were we alone, but Shaw *touched* me. I wonder what Brock would think of that...

"I'm always careful, you don't have to worry about me," I reassure him. "But back to what we were talking about. Why does Shaw have to come to dinner?"

"Because I think the feud between the two of you is dumb and the only way to fix it is by spending time with both of you."

"If you want me to like Shaw, you should have me spend *less* time around him, not more."

"Funny," Shaw says drily.

"I thought so," I reply, smiling to myself.

"Meet us at the pub in an hour," Brock says in a matter-of-fact tone. "Or I'm coming to your apartment *with* Shaw and showing him where you live."

"You're the worst."

"Love you too, sis," Brock says, and I have to restrain myself so that I don't chuck my phone across the room. I'll wait until I'm in the same room as Brock to throw things.

"See you s–"

I hang up the phone before Shaw can finish speaking.

It seems as though it's going to be impossible to get through the rest of the day without seeing Shaw's unnecessarily attractive face. The last thing I want to do is see him *again*. But it's looking like I don't have a choice.

I just wish I could know why he acted the way he did last night, then maybe I'd feel like I'm standing on solid ground again. If I had to guess, it was probably to mess with me. But I can't allow myself to overthink this either. One sleepless night is all I'll allow him.

Chapter Eight

Shaw Daniels

"So how is Sutton fitting in with the Rockets' staff?" Brock asks, taking a sip of his beer. His eyes are trained on the TV screen in front of us, but I know better than to think that means he's not paying attention. Brock cares too much about his sister to be nonchalant about her life.

"Why don't you ask her when she gets here?"

He side eyes me.

"Because you and I both know she'll either paint everything in picture-perfect lighting or she'll self-deprecate until I leave it alone."

I nod, knowing he's right. Sutton is the queen of keeping up appearances. She's too focused on keeping up this strong, independent persona so that no one ever sees her vulnerable.

I'm surprised she didn't go into marketing or public relations. "I think she's fitting in just fine," I answer. "She told the team she doesn't date hockey players."

Brock snorts. "Sounds like her. I guess I don't mind that rule, after everything Mason put her through."

I grip my water glass hard. I'm more than ready to meet Mason Walker on the ice again for the first time since college. This is his first year in the NHL, and we've already played his team, the Mississippi Tornadoes, once. But they didn't let him play because of a sprained ankle, so I didn't get a chance to "welcome" him to the pros. The next time we play them, he'll be out there. And I'm itching to show him exactly why he shouldn't have hurt my Sutton.

"I don't think it's stopped any of the players from flirting with her, but I'll make sure they stay respectful."

"Thanks, you're a good friend." Brock slaps me on the back. "It's hard not being able to look out for her myself. But you've always been there when I couldn't be."

"Except when she went to Duke," I remind him, knowing it'll rile him up.

"I can't believe she chose that stupid devil school over UNC," Brock says, his disgust evident on his face.

"Are you ever going to get over that?" Sutton's voice has me looking over my shoulder.

I clench my jaw to keep it from dropping at the mere sight of her. She's wearing leggings and an Alabama Rockets sweatshirt. Her golden curls bounce as she moves, and her lips are shining with some sort of gloss that begs to be kissed off.

"No, I'm going to teach my children and grandchildren about your traitor ways. They'll all go to UNC, by the way." Brock slides off the bar stool and wraps her in a hug.

"What kids?" she says, returning his hug. "You'd have to actually go on more than one date with a woman to accomplish that."

"That's cold, sis," Brock says, but there's laughter in his voice. "But I can't say it's not something I expect from a Duke alum."

Sutton rolls her eyes, then sets her gaze on me.

"I was really hoping you wouldn't show up," she says, plunging a dagger through my chest while wearing a smirk.

I must be delusional, because all I want to do is tangle my hands in her curls and kiss that little smirk right off her lips. I'm not sure what it says about me that her insults don't deter my affection, but rather increase it.

I shrug. "If I didn't show up, who would you direct all of your poorly executed insults at?"

"I couldn't tell you, since my quips are always witty and perfectly aimed."

"You have all the time in the world to fight when I'm not here," Brock chimes in, throwing an arm around Sutton and squeezing her shoulders. "So why don't you both pretend to be friends for the night?"

"Sounds fun," I say at the same time Sutton says, "I'd rather go home."

"I guess I'll have to return your gift then…" Brock trails off and Sutton's eyes light up.

Seeing her brighten makes me smile. She's always loved getting gifts. At Christmastime she practically glows because she's so happy.

I hated missing last Christmas; I know it would have been better spent with the Jones family than my own. But I felt guilty about spending another holiday away from my parents. My mom and dad are divorced, but they both live in Charlotte, North Carolina. So, I attempted to visit each of them. My mom asked if I could buy her boyfriend a new car as a present, and my dad wasn't sober for a single second while I was there. Oh, and he asked if I'd just give him cash after I gave him a jersey signed by his favorite hockey player–which isn't me.

I didn't spend long at either of their houses and ended up eating Christmas dinner alone with my grandmother. I felt like going to the Joneses' house would have been weird after saying that I wasn't coming. Brock knows my family is terrible, but it somehow still felt wrong to show up to his perfect home smelling like cigarettes, alcohol, and sadness.

"You got me a gift?" Sutton boosts herself onto the barstool next to me where Brock was sitting before, nudging his beer to the side with her nose scrunched up.

"What kind of brother would I be if I went to Disney with a client's family and didn't bring home my Star Wars obsessed twin a gift?"

"A dumb one," Sutton says and I chuckle.

Brock grabs a bag from under the barstool and places it in front of Sutton. The bag is blue with a bunch of Chewbacca heads all over it. Sutton's smile grows as she looks at it.

"This bag is amazing," she says with a laugh before pulling the tissue paper out and throwing it in my direction.

I catch the paper, bunching it up and–like the true sap I am for this woman–imagining a world in which I'd get to do this for all holidays with her. Nothing would make me happier than to watch her open presents on Christmas morning while I shoved the paper in a trash bag. And with the way she's smiling, I'd get her a present for every other holiday, even Arbor Day, all for the opportunity to bask in the warmth of her joy.

"Oh. My. Gosh!" She squeals as she pulls out a figurine of Anakin Skywalker, one of her favorite characters.

"I wish I could have taken you with me," Brock says to her as she admires the gift. "But I figured a present would keep me in your good graces."

Sutton hugs him tight. "You're never out of my good graces. You're the best brother a girl could ask for."

I avert my eyes from their hug and take a sip of water. Growing up alongside Brock and Sutton made my childhood more bearable, but it also stung too. They have a loving and supportive family, plus their weird twin bond. So, during moments like this, it's hard not to feel jealous of their relationship. I wish I would have had a sibling, but then again I wouldn't want anyone else to have gone through what I did.

"Even though I brought Shaw?" Brock teases, drawing my attention back to them.

Sutton shrugs, still wearing a smile. "He hasn't been so bad." My heart skips a beat.

"Careful, Jones, that's almost a compliment."

Sutton rolls her eyes. "I only said it because you haven't been talking. Now you've ruined it."

I laugh, shaking my head at her. "Sounds like someone is still mad I beat her at pool again."

Sutton's eyes widen, probably surprised I'd bring up the party. It's hard not to, what with the situation playing over and over again in my mind on repeat. For the record, I didn't sleep either. I spent the entire night wondering what would have happened if my phone wouldn't have rang. Would we have kissed? What was she going to say?

"There is no *again*, Daniels. I beat you at Calvin's and you know it."

"Are you seriously talking about that time you played against each other in *high school*?" Brock asks incredulously. I don't know why he's surprised, given that he's known me since kindergarten and Sutton since, well, the womb.

"Yes," we answer at the same time.

"Do they have a pool table here?" Sutton asks, craning her neck to look around the pub.

"No, but they do have darts. Want to play? Loser admits defeat at Calvin's once and for all?"

"You're on."

"What about me?" Brock asks with a huff. "I'm the one visiting."

"You can keep score so he doesn't cheat," Sutton answers and I shoot her a look.

"Oh, joy," Brock drolls.

We order some appetizers and ask to have them sent over to the high tops by the dartboard. Then we walk over and I hand Sutton three black darts.

"I want the red ones," she says and grabs them from my hand, her fingertips brushing over my palm, sending tingles up my arm. She drops the black darts in my hand then turns away, leaving me wishing for more of her touch.

"Did you take those just because I chose them first?" I ask and she throws her first dart, getting twenty points. Looks like she's better at darts than pool.

"No, I took them because red is my favorite color."

I frown. "Blue is your favorite color. That light shade with the girl's name, what is it?"

"Tiffany blue?" Brock says, but it comes out muffled because he's eating wings.

"Yes." I point at him. "Your favorite color is Tiffany blue, not red."

Sutton eyes me, still holding on to her other two darts. "How do you know my favorite color?"

I swallow, trying to come up with something other than *I've memorized every detail about you because I'm in love with you.*

"Because I had to help paint your room in middle school. I'm pretty sure I still have paint in my hair from when you dumped the paint tray on my head."

She laughs at the memory and I join in. "I'm pretty sure we got more paint on us than the walls."

"Didn't you track blue on the hardwood floors?" Brock asks and Sutton bites back a smile.

"Yes, because *someone* tried to dump an entire gallon on my head." She looks at me and I duck my head to hide my guilty look. "I had to run. There's no way I would have gotten that much paint out of my hair before spring formal. I think you can see a blue mark on my collarbone in the photos my mom took."

You can. I know, because my grandmother has a copy of the photo of us together hanging up on her wall. I saw it on Christmas day and looking at it made me genuinely smile for the first time that day.

"You're lucky she even let you go to the formal," Brock says.

Sutton nods. "I know. I think she felt bad for me when I came home crying about Dennis."

Brock's lip curls. "Ugh, Dennis. He was a piece of work."

"He was twelve!" Sutton laughs.

"So what? Twelve year olds can be jerks. He fits right in with the rest of your terrible boyfriend choices."

Sutton's easy smile falls at Brock's words, and he cringes.

"Sorry, I shouldn't have said that."

"It's fine." She tries for a smile, but it looks melancholy at best. "You're not wrong."

I don't say a word, because the last thing I want to do is actually upset Sutton. Teasing is one thing, but I'd never purposefully hurt her. She turns her attention back to the board and throws her last two darts.

"You're surprisingly decent at this, Jones," I say to her as she takes down the darts. Her lips lift a little at our version of a compliment.

I throw mine in quick succession, purposefully hitting mid-range numbers. Not so low that she'll be suspicious, but not high enough to beat her. I've played here since I first started with the Rockets. I could win this blindfolded, but I know the win will make her happy.

Never in my life did I think I'd throw a game for a woman, but love makes you do crazy things.

Chapter Nine

Sutton Jones

I lace up my skates and pull my leg warmers down over them. It's been too long since I've been on the ice. I grew up figure skating multiple times a week, and I competed from a young age all the way through college. But since starting the moving process to Alabama, I haven't skated at all.

So, I asked if I could come out this morning before the Rockets' practice, and got permission. As I skate to the middle of the rink, all I can hear is the sound of the ice scraping under me. The entire arena is empty, and I couldn't be happier about it. Skating has always cleared my head, and after the past few days, I need clarity.

I warm up by doing a few laps forward and then backward, smiling at the feeling of my hair blowing with each movement. There's just something about skating with my hair down that feels free, like nothing is holding me back.

I speed up and make my first jump, grinning when I stick the landing.

"Not bad, Jones," a familiar voice yells out, and I skid into a stop, spraying ice.

Shaw is standing on the other side of the plexiglass. His hands are tucked into the pockets of his joggers and the easygoing smile he's wearing makes me dizzy like I just did a hundred spins instead of one simple jump.

"What are you doing here?" I ask, staying far away from the glass.

If the past few days have taught me anything, I need distance from Shaw to keep a clear mind. I can't win whatever game he's playing without staying focused.

"My physical therapist says I need to do mobility exercises before practice. I like to get here early to do them alone."

He moves into the bench area, then pushes open the door and skates onto the ice.

"You do wrist exercises with your skates on?" I ask him, gliding backward as he skates toward me.

"No, but when I saw you on the ice I thought I'd join you."

"Why?"

He shrugs, circling me with a teasing smirk on his lips. "For old times' sake. Remember when we used to play tag on the frozen pond at my Grandma's house?"

"I remember beating you *often*, yes." Granted, that was in elementary school, but that's beside the point.

He smiles, looking unbothered by my words. It feels like I've stumbled into a trap, like I'm exactly where he wants me. I spin around, following his movements so he's never behind me.

"Think you could still keep up?" he asks.

"I know I can."

I'm not sure why I'm blatantly lying. We both know that he's going to win, he plays at the professional level. I just can't admit defeat around Shaw. When his grin widens into something wicked, my blood heats.

What is wrong with me?

"Then try and catch me."

He winks and propels himself backward. Without giving it a second thought, I sprint after him. A leisurely skate is one thing, but I didn't prepare for an all out race across the rink. I'm grateful for keeping up with my cardio training all these years, or else I'd be done for right away.

Shaw is fast, there's no doubt about it, but I'm still able to catch up with him. I reach for him and he cuts to the left, laughing.

"You almost got me."

His teasing smirk sends fire through my veins and I force my legs to go faster. He's skating backward now, letting me get closer and closer.

"I'm sure you can reach me if you try hard enough. I believe in you." His faux patronizing tone has me rolling my eyes.

"It's too bad the NHL doesn't give awards to the most *annoying* player on the ice, you'd be a shoo-in," I say and he laughs.

I close the gap between us, him still skating backward. It's annoying how fast he is and how well he knows the rink without even glancing back. He's always been a natural on the ice, though.

Suddenly, I'm colliding into a solid, warm chest. His strong arms wrap around me, and he uses our momentum to spin twice before halting. I slowly lift my head, meeting his strikingly bright blue eyes.

We're both breathing heavily. Our chests are rising and falling, little puffs of air turning white between us.

"Why did you stop?" I breathe out when I can latch on to a thought.

He doesn't answer, his eyes locked on mine. My heartbeat is loud in my ears and heat pools in my abdomen. My mind is spinning as I try to decipher the look he's giving me.

Being this close to him allows me to see just how gorgeous he really is. It's always apparent, but our proximity heightens the effect. His bright blue eyes are framed with dark, full lashes, and his sharp jawline is dotted with the kind of stubble that makes a girl wonder what it would feel like against her skin. Not me though, I've never wondered that. Not even now, when I'm inches away from being able to find out.

His hands slip to my waist, fingertips ever so slightly digging into the dip. My lips part to ask what he's doing and his gaze zeroes in on my mouth, making my words catch in my throat.

The sound of raucous laughter immediately clears the hazy fog around my mind. I push off Shaw's chest, and his hands fall from my waist. The spot where his hands were tingles. I hate that he has any kind of effect on me. It's awful.

My face is hot as I skate in the opposite direction of him, my eyes trained on the group of hockey players coming up the tunnel. I shake out my hands before waving at the players.

"Are you teaching Shaw how to skate? Because based off the last game he needs a little refresher," one of the players, Sawyer, jokes.

I force myself to smile and let out a laugh. A few of the players start to make laps around the ice.

"I tried, but he's a lost cause," I say as I skate over to the bench and walk through the door in the wall.

"Last I checked, I outscore you every game," Shaw says as he hops the wall instead of going through the door.

"It's pretty hard to insult the man when he's probably the best in the league," Sawyer says to me, shaking his head with a *what can you do* look. He sits on the wall dividing the bench area from the ice.

"I don't know, I find it pretty easy myself," I say, grasping for normalcy. Maybe if I pretend nothing happened, Shaw will too.

Shaw smiles as he grabs a duffel bag from beside the bench. "Keep talking, you two, it doesn't bother me; I know I'm the best."

"The best at having an insufferably large ego," I shoot back.

"As much as I enjoy our repartee, Jones, I have to get going. Coach will get upset if his number one draft pick isn't ready for practice."

He hops the wall again and skates through the tunnel. Sawyer skates away while laughing. Other players start trickling in, so I don't reply. I probably shouldn't have spoken that way around Sawyer. It's not professional. But arguing with Shaw is as natural as breathing, and holding back feels like holding my breath.

I sit down on the bench with a sigh. I don't know how I'm supposed to work after what just happened. My fingers are stiff from the cold and I struggle through untying my laces. I should have worn gloves. That's what I get for rushing out onto the ice in excitement.

Once my skates are off, I slide on my sneakers and throw my duffel bag over my shoulder, then walk toward the recovery center. Maybe reorganizing the med cart at my station will help calm my nerves. It's what I used to do when I interned for my college's hockey team. I'd be so nervous about messing up that I'd count each individual roll of medical tape in the supply cabinet.

Shaw is exiting the locker room wearing practice gear when I get to the door. He smirks at me as he passes, his coastal blue eyes gleaming beneath his helmet visor.

I ignore him and walk into the recovery center, not even sparing him an eye roll or glare. Whatever this new feeling is between us needs to go away. I can't comprehend why I'd feel anything other than annoyance and disdain for Shaw. Apparently my body didn't get the memo from my brain that he's a pest. All the tingles down my spine and my rapid heartbeat has me questioning my sanity.

Connor grins at me from his station and I paste on a smile in response. He's who I need to be focusing on. He's sweet and kind, a little shy and most importantly: *not a hockey player.*

· ♥ · ♥ · ♥ · ♥ · ♥ ·

"I'm so excited that I'll get to see you!" Ariel says, beaming at me over video chat.

"I feel the same way. I've missed you so much. I wish I could stay longer.."

I carefully fold my leggings and place them in my Tiffany blue packing cube. Even though I'm only going to be gone for one night, I want to be organized.

"Once the season is over you'll be able to visit more. I'm just grateful I'll get to see your face not on a screen."

The team is headed to North Carolina to face off against the Carolina Bobcats. I was chosen to be one of the medical staff that traveled with them this time. My parents and Ariel bought tickets to the game in order to see me–well, my parents also wanted to see Shaw, but I'm still in denial about that.

I'm going to try to spend time with them, but I told them not to expect much more than a passing hug. I've been told that traveling with the team means we're on the same plane, staying in the same hotel, and eating at the same restaurants. I'm actually excited for it, because it means I'll start to fit in more and maybe earn my place in the Rockets' family. But it does mean that I can't run off and stay at my parents' house for the night, or grab dinner with Ariel.

My smartwatch starts to buzz on my arm, indicating that I need to leave for the airport in thirty minutes. I didn't get much notice ahead of time, but thankfully I'm used to traveling and getting packed quickly from a childhood of skating competitions and hockey games.

"I should probably get going," I say to Ariel. "I don't want to forget anything important."

"I doubt you could, what with your tried-and-true packing system complete with a packing list for each kind of trip you take."

I shoot her a look as she laughs. Over the years, I've developed packing lists for different situations. Going on a three day cruise? There's a list for that. Quick overnight trip? List. Going overseas? There's a whole binder for that, with tabs for each country I've been to. You won't catch me getting anything confiscated at the airport because I didn't know the rules.

It's not something I advertise to many people, because they tend to throw the words *high maintenance* or *neurotic* at me, and even jokingly, it stings. I just like to be prepared. Those same people will ask me if they can borrow a myriad of things because they *can't believe they forgot them.*

"Hey, my *system* saved you from forgetting your passport on spring break," I point out.

"True, true. Okay, I'll let you go. See you at the game tonight!"

We hang up and I check 'leggings' off my list. Then I zip up my packing cubes and place them in my carry-on suitcase. The Rockets have their own jet they take to games, but I still don't want to pack larger than a carry-on. Then I'd really be seen as high-maintenance. It's not like I need more space either. I could be even *more* prepared with some wiggle room ... but I'll stick with what I have this time.

Once everything has been checked and then checked again, I load up my car and head to the airport. Anticipation flutters within me like a whole migration of butterflies. This is truly the life I've dreamt of for years, and I'm living it. I spend the whole drive jamming out to upbeat, happy music.

I'm feeling on top of the world by the time I walk up the steps to the jet. It's only when I step on and spot a certain mischievous grin that it hits me: I'm about to spend the next twenty-four hours with Shaw Daniels. My only break will be for a few hours when I go to sleep late tonight. My stomach drops. After our weird moment on the ice two days ago, he's the *last* person I want to see.

My dream is starting to look more like a nightmare.

Chapter Ten

Shaw Daniels

This is going to be the best plane ride of my life, all because of the woman sitting across from me. I usually put on my noise canceling headphones and try to get myself into a good mindset for the game–which is what pretty much everyone else on the plane is doing–but with Sutton here, I wouldn't dare. This is the perfect chance to get under her skin, and hopefully in a good way.

After our time on the ice Monday, all I can think about is how close I was to kissing her. And I think–emphasis on the word *think*–she would have let me. It's difficult to tell how she feels, even with knowing her so well. Sutton can tend to mask her emotions, and on top of that, she's never looked at me like she wanted to kiss me, so how can I know what expression she'll have?

So that's why I made sure the seat near me would be the only one left, that way she'd be sitting right across from me. The only thing separating us is a small table. It would be better if we were closer, but at least this way I can make conversation with her, if she'll let me.

"I can't believe I'm forced to stare at your face for an hour and a half," Sutton says, shifting in her seat.

Well, we're off to a swell start.

"I know, it must be so difficult to hold yourself back when you're so attracted to me," I quip.

She rolls her eyes, crossing her arms over her chest. "It's a wonder how you're able to find women willing to date you."

I see we're not pulling punches today. If I were a more sensitive man, that might have hurt.

"I find that my charm usually renders them incapable of refusing me."

"Are you sure it's not your money?"

I snort at her implication, and her lip twitches as she tries not to smile.

"I know you're joking, but I have dealt with my fair share of gold diggers," I admit. "It sucks to find out that someone is only dating you because they saw your salary on Google."

She pushes her bottom lip out in a pout. "Aw, poor Daniels, he's got so much money that women throw themselves at him. How sad," she coos in a patronizing voice.

I throw an empty paper cup at her. She bats it away, laughing. Her unbridled laughter trumps every sound I've ever heard. My favorite song, birds on a spring morning, the score from my favorite movie–all of it pales in comparison. I'd give every penny of the money she's teasing me about away if it meant I got to hear this every day.

"You think you're funny, huh?" I try to keep a straight face.

"I know I am," she says, still giggling.

Her whole face is lit up and there's this little mischievous glint in her eye that makes me want to grab her and kiss her smirking mouth until her giggles melt into sighs. *One day.*

The flight attendant walks down the aisle, pausing to pick up the cup off the floor.

"Sorry about that," I say with an apologetic smile. "She pregamed before the flight." I mime drinking and give the attendant a wide eyed look.

Sutton gasps. "I did not! That's your cup." She turns in her seat, facing the flight attendant. "That's his cup."

"It's okay ma'am." The attendant gives me a polite smile. "Your secret is safe with me."

Sutton's mouth drops open and I press my lips together to keep from laughing. The flight attendant walks over to check on the rest of the team.

"You're *evil*!" she says and I burst into laughter. "What if she tells the press? I could lose my job."

"You think she's going to tell the press about a physical therapist whose name she doesn't even know?" I ask her and she narrows her eyes.

"She might." Sutton sniffs and crosses her arms. "But if she does, you better believe I'm taking you down with me, Daniels."

I smile. "I wouldn't expect anything less, Jones."

She rolls her eyes and then picks up her backpack off the floor. She starts to riffle through it, her expression morphing into one of frustration as she does.

"If you're looking for your dignity I think the flight attendant took it with her when she left."

"I'm looking for a *hair tie*," she grumbles, not looking up at me. "It's too hot in here. But I don't know if I packed one."

I don't say that it's probably only warm to her because of her embarrassment, the evidence of which is found on her rosy complexion.

"Was it not on your packing list?" I ask and she looks up, narrowing her eyes at me. "What? Do you not use a list anymore?"

I've traveled with Sutton quite a few times. Her parents always felt bad for me since I had a crummy home life, so they often paid for my ticket and let me join them on family vacations or hockey games. And Sutton could always be found triple checking her list before we left.

"Yes, I do." She huffs. "But I don't want to be made fun of for it. It's good to be prepared."

"Why would I make fun of you? I started using a list because of you, and it's saved me quite a few times."

She blinks, her stormy expression clearing. "Really?"

I pull out my phone and open the app with my game day checklist, then pass it to her. She looks it over, her lips lifting in a faint smile.

"You pack your own pillow?" she asks and I quickly grab my phone back from her. I didn't expect her to *read* the list.

"Hotel pillows are terrible," I defend myself and she laughs.

"I actually like hotel pillows," she says after her laughter subsides. "But I do bring a silk pillowcase to protect my hair."

After she says 'hair', she frowns, looking down at the bag in her lap.

"I *swear* I packed a hair tie. My bag must have eaten it."

I chuckle at her explanation. "I've seen girls wear them on their wrists. That's a thing, right?"

She scrunches up her nose. "I hate doing that. It makes my wrist itch and depending on my outfit, it could throw off the whole look."

I shake my head at her, smiling. "You're very particular about things, Jones."

She drops her backpack beside her feet and crosses one long leg over the other before folding her hands primly in her lap, as if she's a member of the royal family.

"There's nothing wrong with that."

"Never said there was."

She eyes me as if waiting for me to tease her about something, but I say nothing. Because as much as I love to tease her, I'm trying to get her to see something more in me. I haven't been doing the best job of that so far. But maybe if we can have a nice conversation, she'll see that I'm more than her enemy.

Eventually, she relaxes back in her seat. She looks out the window and I use her shift in attention as a moment to openly admire her. She's wearing a white oversized Rockets hoodie, black leggings, and the same white tennis shoes I helped her get from under her car on her first day. Her long blonde hair is a curtain over her side profile, looking feather-soft. What I would give to run my fingers through it.

I have to figure out a way to change the direction we're going. Because right now, it's looking like at best, I'll be her brother's best friend. That guy she sees at Thanksgiving when she's introducing her fiancé to her family. The thought makes me sick. My only hope is that the little moments of closeness we've had recently mean something to her.

She turns her head back toward me.

"What?" she asks and I blink out of my trance.

"What?" I echo her question and she rolls her eyes.

"You were staring at me."

"I was just zoning out," I lie and she eyes me, but doesn't argue.

Yeah, I need to get a grip, or else she's going to find out before she's ready that I'm hopelessly in love with her.

Chapter Eleven

Sutton Jones

I don't think the hotel knew what they were getting into when they booked rooms for the Rockets. We're a tornado of sound as we enter the lobby after the game. After an amazing win–secured by a perfectly executed shot from Shaw–the guys are another level of hype.

A group of them split off upon entering, heading toward the bar to celebrate. The rest head to the elevators, likely to continue the party in their rooms. Or, if they're the rare, quiet type, they'll be going to bed. But I doubt even the most introverted player on the team stays in after the win tonight. It was two to two down to the last minute before Shaw scored. My ears are still ringing from how loud the arena got. Rockets fans tend to travel to support their team, but a lot of the noise was of the angry variety from the opposing team.

I spot my parents and Ariel off to the side. My smile grows. They said they'd meet me here after the game so that I had some time with them. I start to weave around the crowd of players, and by the time I make it to them, Shaw has already beaten me there. He's wrapped up in a hug from my mom.

When they pull apart my mom is smiling like he's her pride and joy. I try not to smile myself. As much as I hate it, Shaw deserves the praise tonight. And I don't know that I've ever seen his family at a game before, so if my mom wants to shower affection on him, so be it.

Growing up there were times I resented Shaw's hovering presence in our home. He seemed to always be there, and my parents were constantly praising him and telling him how great he was. Looking back, I know they weren't choosing him over me, but loving on a kid who needed it. I wish I could have seen that then; maybe things would be different now. But then again, Shaw did a lot all on his own that made our relationship rocky.

"Sutton!" Mom's eyes find mine, her greeting full of a motherly love that makes my eyes sting.

"Mom," I say back with a smile and throw my arms around her.

She squeezes me tight, swaying back and forth.

"Are you ready to move back home yet?" she asks when she finally pulls away.

I smile and shake my head at her. My dad pulls me into a side hug. "I *just* moved."

"It feels like you've been gone a year already," Ariel says and I hug her too. "I miss my roomie."

My throat tightens at the thought of going back to Alabama without her. It's been hard not having any friends yet. I'm hopeful I'll make some, but I think I'll always miss my best friend.

"I know, I feel the same way. I love my job, but I wish I could see y'all more. Tonight doesn't feel like enough," I say with a frown, checking my smart watch. It's already 10:30 at night. They'll have to head back home soon if they don't want to be on the road too late.

"We should get going, actually," my dad says, and my mom sighs.

"Yes, it's been a long day, and driving at night is hard on both of us."

"Thanks for coming to the game," Shaw says, reminding me of his presence. " Are you sure you don't want to stay? Just say the word, and I've got you both covered for tonight."

My mom shakes her head, lovingly patting his arm. I look up at him as he looks at my parents. I can't believe he'd offer to pay for a room for them. That's actually ... *nice*.

"That's sweet of you, but we couldn't stay the night. All of our medications are at home, and Gary's back isn't fond of hotel beds." My mom turns her attention to me, hugging me again. "I'll talk to you soon. You be good and have fun with Ariel."

My brow furrows. "With Ariel?" I look to my best friend and see that beside her feet is a floral print duffle bag. My mouth pops open in surprise as her grin widens.

"I figured we could use a sleepover," she says and I smile. This night just got a whole lot better.

I finish my goodbyes with my parents, trying not to tear up. We exchange promises to talk soon and take care. For some reason, my mom tells *Shaw* to take care of me. I roll my eyes, but he just smiles and says *yes ma'am*.

Once they're gone, I turn to Ariel and bounce on my toes.

"I can't believe you got a room here. I know it wasn't cheap; this place is high end," I say and she gives me a sheepish look.

"Wellll ..." she trails off and glances to Shaw. "I didn't pay for it."

"You did this?" I ask Shaw and he shrugs.

"All I did was sweet talk the team admin into booking you a room with two beds. I figured if you had a night with your best friend you'd be nicer to me on the plane ride home," he says and I hit his arm.

"You're the one who told the flight attendant I was *drunk*," I whisper-yell, but he just grins.

Ariel starts to laugh and I shoot her a look.

"It sounds like you have a lot to tell me," she says after stifling her laughter.

"Oh, I do, so we should get to the room." I loop an arm through hers, then look up at Shaw. "Thanks." The word feels weird in my mouth when directed toward him. It's like trying a new food that I'm not sure if I like or not. I'm sure my gratitude seems weak, but maybe he's known me long enough to know I mean it.

He merely tips his head in response and walks off toward the bar.

"Okay, now that he's gone." Ariel whips her head toward me in a dramatic fashion, her brunette braid hitting her cheek and making me laugh. "What is going on between you and Shaw?"

My brows push together. "What do you mean?"

"Oh don't give me that. He went out of his way to surprise you with this gesture. He called me last week to make sure I'd be free and bought tickets for me and your parents."

"He did?"

Ariel rolls her eyes, looking at me like I'm as dense as I feel. "I always thought he had a thing for you."

My mind flashes to our moment on the ice ... and the one in the basement ... and when I was massaging his arm... Okay, when you stack those little moments together it doesn't look like nothing. But it's also not a *thing* either.

"Daniels? You're joking." I fake a laugh and drag her toward reception to get my room key.

"That was your high-pitched liar laugh," she accuses, then gasps. "Have you *kissed* him?"

"No, I have not *kissed* him. Now be quiet before someone hears you."

She pauses her interrogation while I check in, but as soon as we're alone in the elevators she starts again.

"Something happened between you two, didn't it?"

I sigh, leaning against the elevator wall.

"Maybe? Kind of? I don't know." I cross my arms, hugging my torso.

"Has he asked you out?"

"Yeah, he asked me to go to a movie and get ice cream after," I deadpan, giving her a dry look. "Of course not. I would have told you if he did."

"I'd like to think you would, but apparently there's something going on that you aren't telling me."

The elevator dings, and we step off, walking to our room. I stay silent, trying to gather my thoughts as we make our way down the hall. Once we make it inside our room, I fall back onto one of the beds with a dramatic groan.

"I don't know if anything has actually happened, that's why I didn't tell you," I begin, and she falls back on the bed beside me. "Mainly because it's Shaw. How can there be anything romantic between us?"

"Pretend he's not him," Ariel suggests.

I do as she says, imagining that Shaw isn't my brother's best friend and the bane of my existence, but instead an attractive hockey player with billboard worthy abs and a smile that makes my skin tingle.

"He's still a hockey player," I reason, more with myself than with Ariel. "And I won't date a player ever again."

"Okay, pretend he's not a player either."

"I think we almost kissed," I blurt out instead of trying to play pretend in my head again.

I sit up so fast my head spins. Ariel follows suit and grabs my arm. "*What?*"

"I was skating Monday morning and he came out on the ice before practice. I ran into him and he caught me and our eyes locked."

"That's so romantic." Ariel lets out a dreamy sigh.

"Not helpful."

"Well, it is." She pauses, and the silence is deafening. Being alone with my thoughts right now is not good. "Do you like him?"

"No, definitely not. How could I? He's made my life miserable for years."

"You didn't seem miserable when you were hitting his shoulder and laughing with him earlier."

"I-well-that's–" I sputter and she raises a brow. "That's not the point. There's too much history, and he's a hockey player. Let's not forget that." She opens her mouth to say something, but I continue. "And he's got a nice rotation of women according to the press."

"You stalk him online?" she asks, instead of acknowledging my points.

My face heats. "Only to dig up dirt to use against him."

"*Sure.*"

"Can we talk about something different?" I whine.

"Fine, I'll tell you about the terrible state of dating apps today," she says and I laugh, grateful that she isn't pushing anymore.

I have no idea what's going on between me and Shaw, but hopefully if I ignore it, it'll go away. Because I can't afford for it to go anywhere else.

· ♥ · ♥ · ♥ · ♥ · ♥ ·

My sides are hurting from laughing so hard, and my face is sore from smiling too much. It's the best feeling, and I wish that I didn't have to say goodbye in a few hours. Ariel and I have been up all night. It's three in the morning, and after talking about everything under the sun, we finally started to get too sleepy to talk.

But as per usual, I'm *freezing* and can't sleep with how cold it is in our room. So I'm sneaking out to see if I can get an extra blanket at the reception desk. Ariel just fell asleep, and I don't want to wake her.

I tuck my hands into my Rockets hoodie pocket and pad down the hall. Even after putting on a hoodie, my Star Wars pajama pants, and socks, I'm still shivering as I head to the elevator.

I almost trip over my own feet when Shaw turns down the hallway. He's wearing jeans and a black long sleeve Rockets t-shirt. His curls are mussed and his scruff is dark. When he sees me he grins and my heart skips. He looks like all the morally gray movie villains I end up crushing on.

"Jones, what has you out and about tonight? I hate to break it to you, but the party just ended downstairs." He gives me a once over, and I'm suddenly very aware of my slouchy outfit. "It's too bad too, your fuzzy socks would have made for a great conversation starter."

"Don't talk about my socks, you wish you had socks this comfortable," I say and then mentally facepalm. After staying up so late to talk to Ariel, I'm off my game.

"Is the party really just now ending?" I ask so that he doesn't have a chance to respond to my previous statement. "Have you been drinking this whole time?"

He doesn't look drunk, just a little tired. But Mason always drank too much after a win. And after a loss. I guess he just drank a lot in general.

He gives me a confused look. "I had one beer when I first got to the bar, but nothing after that. I mainly stick around to make sure the guys don't end up on the news for getting too rowdy."

"I'm pretty sure you used to be the one getting all the guys riled up in high school."

He smiles, tucking his hands in his pockets. Why does he have to look so sexy all of the time? He's even better looking than a model because he has this edge to him, probably because of the scars from years of hockey. It's annoying that I'm attracted to him, because he's everything I don't need.

"High school was a long time ago, Jones. I like to think I've grown up a little." He pauses, letting that statement sink in. "What are you doing up?"

"I'm going to see if they have any extra blankets downstairs. If I don't do something I'm going to turn blue from the cold," I say and he chuckles.

"Well I hope they have some for you. If not, you can knock on my door on your way back."

My eyes widen. *What did he just say?*

His eyes get big too and he shakes his head. "That sounded weird. I just meant I could give you one of the blankets in my room. I'm a warm sleeper. I always end up throwing the covers off in the middle of the night."

"Oh, uh, thanks. I'll knock if I need to."

I take a step to the right to move around him. I need to get those blankets and bury myself underneath them before I die of embarrassment.

"My room is 1568."

"Okay. I'll see you tomorrow."

"See you," he says, scratching the back of his neck.

I speed away from him, my face warm even though my body is cold. What was that? Shaw and I have been a lot of things, but awkward has never been one of them.

My stomach swirls as the elevator descends. I press a hand to my abdomen and take a few measured breaths.

This is not good.

Chapter Twelve

Shaw Daniels

I think something is different between Sutton and me. After our late-night encounter–after which she *unfortunately* didn't stop by my room for a blanket–she purposefully sat far away from me at breakfast. Then, on the plane ride she put on her headphones and closed her eyes, mumbling something about not getting enough sleep. I'm used to her throwing sassy remarks my way, not ignoring me.

The absence of her usual snark still has me reeling and I've been home for a few hours now. But after some thought, I can't help but think she wasn't just grumpy from being up all night. That maybe she was thrown off by me booking that room for Ariel and paying for her family's tickets. In a good way. But there's also the possibility that I've disrupted our odd relationship dynamic and now she's never going to speak to me again.

I pull my headset over my ears and log onto my Xbox. The guys mentioned they had time to spare today for a game or two, and I desperately need to think about something other than Sutton. Unfortunately, when I log on, there's another Jones in the chat. I'm glad Brock has time to hang out with us today–he's usually too busy–but he's a reminder of the one person my brain has been revolving around lately ... his sister. It's also a reminder that I haven't told him about my feelings.

"Hey guys, what's up?" I say into the microphone.

"Same old, same old over here," Jason answers first.

"I'm glad I found time for this," Brock says. "I had no less than eight incidents to deal with for clients yesterday."

"Yikes. That's unfortunate," I say and then look at the list of names in the corner. "Where's Miles?"

"We were going to ask you the same–" Jason gets cut off when Miles comes on.

"Sorry I'm late, guys." He sounds out of breath and angry, which is unusual for him.

"Bad day on the course?" I ask and he sighs.

"No, I had to fire another assistant."

"Another one?" Jason asks. "That's like the fifth one in the past two months."

"I know," Miles grumbles. "I feel like it shouldn't be this hard to find someone."

"What did this one do?" Brock asks.

"He mixed up every appointment, meeting, and tee time I had this week. And I caught him smoking in one of my guest bedrooms."

"At least he didn't wait in your bedroom in lingerie like Kira did," I say, and a chorus of laughter rings out.

"Please don't bring her up. I'm scarred for life. My *mother* was the one who walked in on her, in case you forgot."

"Oh, I remember," I say, still laughing.

"None of us could ever forget that story," Jason adds.

"I had to deal with the press when your mom chased her out without letting her change," Brock says.

Emmett doesn't speak–as per usual–but his low chuckle says enough.

"Okay, enough about me, what's going on with y'all?" Miles quickly changes the subject. "What happened between you and that girl, Shaw? Have you convinced her to stop hating you yet?"

I stay silent, because this is exactly what I didn't want to happen.

"There's a girl?" Brock asks, confusion evident in his voice. "You haven't told me about a girl."

"I talked about it with the guys when you weren't on," I reply. "I've been meaning to tell you about her."

"Well tell me about her. Miles said she hates you?"

I sink into the couch cushions, wishing that I could disappear. If I fake a bad connection and log off, will that seem obvious?

"Uh, yeah. She doesn't like me all that much."

"Why are you holding out on us?" Jason asks. "Did something happen?"

"Wait a second," Brock says, and I don't like the realization in his voice. "She *hates* you?"

"Man, way to harp on that detail," Miles says. "Shaw just said they've got a bad history, that's all."

I close my eyes, preparing for Brock to say it out loud. He wasn't supposed to find out this way. I was going to tell him face-to-face, after buying him a nice gift.

"You like Sutton," Brock states and the other guys go quiet.

"I was going to tell you," I say, trying to fix this as best as I can.

I don't want to lose my best friend, and Sutton would definitely stop talking to me if she found out Brock ended our friendship.

"I just wasn't sure how or when," I add.

"How long have you liked her?" he asks and I blink my eyes open, staring at the vaulted ceiling in my living room.

"Well, if we're laying it all out there, I'm in love with her, and have been for years now," I say and it somehow gets even quieter. I have to check and see if the guys are even still logged on. They are. I'm sure they don't want to miss this.

"You love Sutton." He sounds almost robotic, or like he's in shock, which is understandable. "Sutton, as in the woman you can barely be in the same room with because you argue so much?"

"Yeah, I love her. And I know it probably doesn't make sense to you, it barely makes sense to me."

"I'm guessing she doesn't know?"

"No, definitely not. I've been trying to get in her good graces since she started working with the Rockets."

"That's why you bought my parents' and Ariel's tickets," he says, sounding like he's piecing it together. "And why you got her a job there in the first place. Huh. Who would have thought? My best friend is in love with my twin sister."

"Are you mad?" I ask, because I can barely breathe not knowing how he feels.

"No," he says, then laughs a little. "I'm surprised, though looking back it makes sense. You were a little *too* eager to beat up on all her jerk boyfriends. I just thought you had anger issues."

A laugh bursts out of me and relief soothes the ache in my chest. I'm not losing my best friend. As long as I don't screw up with Sutton, that is.

"Yeah, it probably wasn't the most healthy thing, but it was high school." And a little bit in college, but Mason is different. I don't regret the times I went after him on the ice. I would–and will–do it again if I need to.

"So are you two good or do we need to choose sides? Because if so, I'm choosing Brock," Miles interrupts.

"I'm hurt, but since he's your agent, I understand," I say back.

"Thanks, Miles, but we're good. As long as Shaw doesn't hurt her, we'll stay good." Brock's tone is casual, but I know he's serious. I may be like family, but Sutton is his sister. And the whole twin thing takes it to another level.

"I won't hurt her. I can promise you that."

"Good. Because you're like a brother to me, but I'd have to do what we did to all of her other exes if you hurt her."

I swallow, thinking of the fights we got into over the years. Brock didn't take kindly to anyone hurting Sutton. Usually, he'd start off easy, talking to the guy in an eerily calm voice. But once the guy made a degrading comment or threw the first punch, Brock always showed them why you don't mess with a Jones. And if the guy didn't get the memo, I stepped in and made sure he did.

"Understood."

"Now, who wants to shoot some stuff?" Brock asks and all the guys agree.

I feel lighter now that my feelings are out there. If only I could share them with Sutton without fear of her running away or thinking I'm playing some game. I'll just keep doing what I'm doing though, and hope that her avoiding me means it's working rather than not.

Chapter Thirteen

Sutton Jones

There are many ways to ruin a Monday morning. You could wake up late, forget to put gas in your car the day before, or get caught in traffic. Maybe you didn't do laundry over the weekend and all your work clothes are dirty. I'd rather have *every single one* of those things happen to me today than what I woke up to this morning.

Ariel: I wasn't sure if I should send you this ... but I figured it's better to hear it from me.

Attached to Ariel's text is a link to an Instagram post. A carousel of professional photographs greets me. Each one showing off a giant diamond engagement ring on the hand of swimsuit model Sahara Smith. Her new fiancé? Mason Walker.

The man who looked me in the eye and told me he couldn't commit to me because life on the road was too tempting. The man I gave my heart to, only for him to skate over it with freshly sharpened blades. Yes, he's getting married. And not just to a random woman, but a swimsuit model.

My stomach churns. I plug in my curling iron and carefully wrap small sections of my hair around the hot iron. I don't usually curl my hair–or even come in with it down–for work, but I need the confidence boost after seeing Sahara and Mason all smiley and cozy together.

After my hair and makeup are done, I stand in front of the mirror in my bra and underwear, staring at my pale winter skin and the cellulite on my thighs. Sahara looked like she just spent a week in the tropics. For all I know, she did. And she *definitely* doesn't have cellulite, or split ends, or bruised feet from skating.

I force myself to turn away from my mirror, pulling on my favorite black leggings with a sigh. I just need to get to work, so I can put my mind to something productive. I carefully tug my Alabama Rockets quarter zip over my head. It's pointless to compare myself to a literal model, but I can't help it.

Why was she worthy of marriage after a few months when I spent four *years* catering to Mason's every need?

"It's good you didn't stay with him," I say out loud, looking into the mirror once more. "He was a terrible boyfriend and would have made an awful husband." Saying it aloud helps solidify the idea in my brain. It doesn't lessen the ache in my chest, though.

Three more deep breaths, and I'm ready to go to work. It's a short, silent drive to the arena. My steps echo through the halls to the recovery center. I'm early, which I usually love, but today I'd rather have the chaos of the players coming in and out to distract me.

My phone starts to buzz in the pocket of my leggings, so I pull it out, sighing when I see Ariel's name.

"Hey," I answer.

"Just checking in since you didn't text back. I wanted to make sure you aren't wallowing in despair."

"Is there something worse than wallowing?" I ask her while running my fingertips over the gauze pads and medical tape. "Because if so, I'm doing that."

"I checked your location before I called, it showed you at work. That means you didn't stay in bed to cry all day, which is a win!" She tries to infuse cheer into her tone, but it falls flat.

"Why could he marry her and not me?" I ask the question that's been tumbling through my brain like a marble in a pinball machine. Ariel is silent for a moment.

"Why do you care?" She doesn't ask this with a harsh tone; no, her voice is gentle, akin to a hug. But it still steals my breath like a fall on the ice.

"I did *everything* for him, Ariel. I cheered him on at home games, and traveled to the away ones as much as I could. I drove him home from parties and bars while he babbled about how great of a player he was. When he finally got drafted, I *cried*. I shed tears of joy because his dream was my dream. And then he threw it all away because he didn't want to be tied down."

Tears burn my eyes before streaming down my face. "He wanted the bachelor lifestyle. A girl in every city. And now?" I clench the hand not holding my phone. "Now he's engaged to a swimsuit model he probably met on an app. Four years of my life–*wasted*."

Something overcomes me, and I push over the cart by my station. It clatters to the ground, supplies scattering everywhere. My pent-up anger deflates as it hits the ground. Suddenly I just feel stupid and pathetic. I'm not one to let my anger out in general, much less in a physical way like this. I guess keeping it pent up for so long has me on edge.

"What just happened? Are you okay?" Ariel asks, but then another voice comes from behind me.

"What did that cart ever do to you?"

I look over my shoulder to find Shaw walking into the recovery center.

"I'm fine, I have to go. I'll talk to you later," I say in a low voice to Ariel before hanging up. Then I speak louder to Shaw, "What do you need, Daniels?"

The tremor in my voice is unmistakable. I wipe my tears with the sleeves of my jacket, then bend down to start cleaning up my mess. Why did I think flipping this thing over would make me feel better? I'm usually smarter than this.

"I came to have you check on my wrist before practice," Shaw says, squatting down beside me. "But it seems like you're the one who needs to be checked on. Are you okay?"

"I'm fine." I'm sure it's obvious I'm lying, but I don't need Shaw of all people to hear about Mason's rejection. "I just ran into the cart." Another obvious lie.

Wordlessly, he starts to help me pick up the scattered supplies. I sniff as my nose starts to run, avoiding his eyes by keeping mine trained on the task at hand. The last thing I want right now is for Shaw to see me like this. I should have been more controlled, held in my emotions until I was off work and could cry at home alone. But I've been holding things in for so long it felt impossible to keep in.

Every move I make, my hair falls into my face. It's the last irritating straw on my very fragile emotional state. I huff in frustration, sitting back on my knees and aggressively pushing back the strands from my face.

"I think I'm going to shave my head," I grumble and Shaw chuckles, making me realize I spoke out loud.

"Don't do that, Jones. I wouldn't be able to tease you when you have a blonde moment." I try not to smile and look down at the floor again. "Here," he says, his wrist coming into my line of sight. On it is a black silk hair tie.

"Why do you have a hair tie?" I scrunch up my nose. "Is it some weird trophy from a girl? I don't want a *used* hair tie. That's gross."

Shaw sighs. "Jones, it's brand new. I can show you the receipt in my car if you'd like. You said you always forget to bring them with you, so I got some just in case."

I blink in confusion. I look up at him, meeting his crystal blue eyes, then back at the hair tie, then back at him. "Why?"

He rolls his eyes. "Because when you're annoyed you take it out on me. Just use it." He waves his wrist in front of me.

I reach out and pull it off his wrist, my stomach swooping when our skin touches. My eyes meet his again, and my heart picks up speed. I must not be thinking clearly after the emotional turmoil of the morning, because ... I think I want to kiss Shaw Daniels.

He gives me a gentle smile, one that I don't know I've seen on him before. It's the kind of smile reserved for Christmas lights, videos of puppies snuggling, or–and this one can't be right–someone you love.

My skin heats and my breaths shorten in anticipation. He shifts forward as if he might actually want to kiss me too. But that can't be right, can it? We hate each other. My head is shouting at my heart to stop galloping and my stomach to stop swirling. But neither listen.

I bite my lip and his eyes flick down, then back up, heat flaring like a lit match in his irises.

I haven't felt this way since—ice cold water rushes through my veins as the realization hits me. The last time I felt a semblance of this was for Mason, who broke my heart. I can't be so foolish as to make that mistake again, with another hockey playing bachelor. I shake my head, letting out a nervous laugh.

"Uh thanks for the hair tie." I look down at the mess on the floor. "And for trying to help. But I've got it from here." I pull my hair back into a ponytail, making sure not to look at Shaw again.

"Are you sure?" he asks, concern coating his voice. "You seemed pretty upset when I came in."

"I'm fine, Daniels. I'd be even better if you left," I say, then wince.

My hands shake while trying to pick up a box of band-aids. I shouldn't be so rude to him after he helped me, but I need him gone. I can't think like this, not with him so close. He smells like freshly squeezed citrus and looks obnoxiously attractive in his gray sweatpants and fitted black shirt.

If he stays, I might *kiss* him and then what? If he kisses me back, then I'll be tangled up with a guy who lives the lifestyle Mason left me for. And if he doesn't, he'll hold it over my head the rest of our lives. Neither of those can happen. And I won't accept the notion of a third option, either.

"I still need my wrist looked at," he says in a quiet voice. Is that disappointment I hear? It can't be. There's no way that Shaw wants anything to do with me.

I stand right as Connor walks in.

"Connor!" I say, making him jump, but he smiles big when he sees me. "Can you look at Shaw's wrist? I accidentally knocked over the med cart," I say with a forced laugh.

"Sure, I'd be happy to."

"There, Connor can look at your wrist," I say, daring to look at Shaw.

His eyes are filled with questions and his mouth is downturned, but he doesn't protest. He simply walks over to Connor's station and pushes up his sleeves. His muscular forearms combined with the way his shirt forms to his muscles has me feeling all sorts of things I shouldn't.

"Stupid hot," I say under my breath.

Shaw turns around, a smirk replacing his soft smile from earlier. I drop back down to the floor and start grabbing miscellaneous items.

"What was that, Jones?"

"Hm?" I look up–big mistake–and force myself to keep my eyes on his face.

"I thought I heard you say something."

"Me? No." I let out a high-pitched laugh. "Connor, did you say something?"

"No, I didn't," he replies, still wearing his easygoing smile.

"You must be hearing things," I say to Shaw with a shrug.

"Must be." I ignore the way the teasing lilt of his voice sends tingles down my spine, and focus on tidying the cart.

I don't look at Shaw for the rest of the time, even when he leaves for practice. And even though I enjoy watching the guys play, I stay in the recovery center today. I need a hockey player detox, but that's impossible with my job.

I'm suddenly regretting saying yes when the Alabama Rockets offered me this position.

Chapter Fourteen

Shaw Daniels

I clench my jaw as I sprint down the ice and back. We have conditioning today, but I wish we had a game. I need to get out all of this pent-up aggression. Somehow, even miles apart, Mason can still make Sutton cry. I overheard her speech to Ariel on the phone, and it made me sick.

Sutton deserves to be treated like royalty. She's the most amazing woman I've ever met. She's caring and gorgeous and whip-smart. Her only two faults are that she can't see her worth and she has terrible taste in men.

"Are you trying to prove something?" Sawyer asks, his chest heaving after our first drill.

"What?" I ask, grabbing a water bottle from the bench area and squeezing it to pour water into my mouth.

"You were a lap ahead of everyone today. And don't go getting a big head and saying that's every week, because it's not. Something is going on."

I shake my head. "Just wanted to show y'all I've still got it."

"During conditioning?" He gives me a look.

I shrug. Coach yells out to work on passing drills, so Sawyer can't interrogate me anymore.

For the rest of practice, I go as hard as I can. Every time I hit the puck I imagine it's Mason Walker. Which I'm aware isn't healthy, but since I'm not actually hitting him I think it's okay.

By the end of practice, my anger toward him has dissipated, but my heart hurts on Sutton's behalf. I wish I could make her pain disappear. I'd take it on for myself if I could. If only she could see he wasn't worth her time from the start. I knew from the first time I saw a photo of them together that their relationship was off. There was something about the way he looked at her that left me with an uneasy feeling. And then when I saw those photos of him out with other girls, my intuition was confirmed.

I wish the times we fought on the ice would have scared him off, but they didn't. He stuck to her like a parasite, draining the light from her eyes. I tried to get Brock to talk to her, but he said that if he did, she'd probably cling to Mason more just to prove her twin wrong. I'd like to think Sutton would have been more mature, but after years of Brock and I both "sabotaging" her relationships, she tended to overreact when he brought up anything to do with her dating life.

I head straight to the showers after Coach's post-practice speech, intent on turning the water up to scalding levels. I need to burn away these memories. They just serve to make me feel guilty about not telling Sutton how I feel sooner. I've lain awake too many nights wondering what would have happened if I'd told her how I felt in high school. Would she have gone to Duke still? Or come to UNC with Brock and me?

The water burns my back but not my thoughts. I'm stuck in a loop of could've, should've, would've. My mind is a wishing well I've spent almost a decade throwing wishes in. It's overflowing, and I've yet to see one answered. I'm so tired of keeping all of these thoughts inside, but I don't know how to voice them either.

My skin is red and tender when I finally turn the shower off. I dry myself then pull on the sweatpants and t-shirt I wore in, tugging on a Rockets hoodie as well. It's a brisk day, so I'll need the extra layer.

I make my way out of the locker room, avoiding conversation with any of the guys. My feet carry me in the direction of the recovery center. I'll check on Sutton, then leave. She probably won't give me a real answer as to how she's doing, but I know her well enough to be able to read her body language. If she seems like she's doing badly, I'll call Brock or Ariel and see if they can do something to cheer her up.

Maybe I can convince one of them to give me her address so I can send something anonymously, like a box of Nerds Clusters. I know she loves those.

"Wait, uh, can I talk to you for a second, Sutton?" I hear Connor stumble over his words, making me pause. The door to the recovery center is open, but I'm standing to the side where no one inside can see me.

"Yeah, what's up?" Sutton's voice is sweet and gentle, a rare tone in our conversations.

"I-I was wondering," he starts, and I resist the urge to bang my head against the wall. I know what's coming. "Would you maybe want to go out sometime soon? Maybe the day after tomorrow?"

"Oh." Sutton sounds surprised, though I don't know why. The man has been waiting to shoot his shot since the day she started here. "I'd love to."

Hearing her say she'd *love* to hurts a little more than I'd like to admit, but I'm not worried about Connor. He's no heartbreaker, and he's probably not going to steal Sutton's heart either. I've spent enough time around him lately–due to Sutton pawning my recovery off on him all the time–to know that they're not a good match.

"Great! That's great. Can I get your number?"

"Sure."

It's quiet for a moment, but I stay posted by the door. I'll make an entrance soon enough.

"I'll text you to iron out the details soon," Connor says.

"Sounds perfect."

"Good. I'll see you tomorrow."

"See you."

Footsteps head my way so I jog backward some, then start walking toward the center again as if I wasn't standing there. Connor comes out with a giant smile on his face. I nod to him and he nods back, heading toward the arena exit.

I lean against the doorframe, watching Sutton put her phone in her little black bag. Her hair is in a low ponytail, the hair tie I gave her at the nape of her neck. I allow myself a moment to fantasize moving her hair aside to brush my lips against her skin. It's an image that will haunt me tonight, I'm sure, but I can't help it.

"A date with Connor, huh?"

Sutton jumps, turning to face me. Her eyes trail over my figure but snap back up to my eyes. "Why were you eavesdropping on my conversation?"

"I was bored."

"Then read a book." She glares at me as I walk toward her. "We're not repeating high school, Daniels. You aren't going to ruin this."

"Do you want to know how your date with him is going to go?"

She crosses her arms. "If I did, I'd ask *Connor*, not you."

"He's going to text you soon, maybe before I even leave the room. And since he used up all of his courage asking you out, he's going to say *you* should pick out the dinner spot. You're going to choose someplace casual and cheap. Because you'll be too anxious to choose anything nicer, afraid that it will make you look high maintenance–even though you are."

Her mouth pops open. "I am n–"

I cut her off. "Then you're going to meet there, and he's going to laugh too hard at jokes that aren't that funny and agree with everything you say. You'll be bored out of your mind. After dinner, he'll walk you to your car, and if he had some liquid courage, he might be brave enough to try to kiss you, but he probably won't, so he'll give you an awkward hug. You'll tell your Mom and Ariel he was *nice*, but you won't see him again."

She steps closer to me, her brown eyes flashing in anger. "First of all, I am not high maintenance."

"Says the woman who just put her phone in her designer bag."

She shoots me another sharp look. "Second of all, what's wrong with a nice guy? I like nice."

"Do you?" I take a step closer, bringing us inches apart. "Because I think you prefer playing with fire, seeing just how close you can get to the flames without getting burned."

Our eyes lock and the tension between us is stifling. Suddenly my hoodie is much too hot. I'm contemplating grabbing her and kissing her when she speaks again.

"It doesn't matter anyway, because you're wrong about the date."

"If you're so sure I'm wrong, then how about a bet?"

Her expression is wary when she asks, "What kind of bet?"

"If I get every detail right about your date, then you have to give me a back massage every time I ask for a week."

Her cheeks turn the color of ripe raspberries as she stutters, "W-what? No, that's ridiculous."

"Are you scared you're going to lose?"

Something shifts in her gaze. Her brown eyes turn molten, and the dangerous glint in them makes my pulse race. This is the look of a woman who loves a challenge. And this specific look is the reason I'm addicted to competing against Sutton. It's a thrill that never gets old.

We're centimeters apart now, sharing the same air. If either of us moved just a hair we'd be kissing. An ache to do just that swells up within me, but I push it down. I have to wait. The timing needs to be perfect. I won't lose her this time. I can't.

"Fine. You're on. If I win, I get to drive your red Lamborghini for a week."

I smirk down at her. Of course she'd want to drive my favorite car. "Sweetheart, if you win, you can *have* my Lamborghini."

"Start preparing the paperwork, Daniels, because you're losing this time."

A buzzing sound punctures the tension between us.

"Check that for me, won't you, Jones?" I ask her and she scowls at me, but I notice the doubt creeping into her expression.

She pulls out her phone and looks down at it, the color draining from her face. I nod and start to back out of the room, a grin stretching across my lips.

"Cocoa butter," I say to her and she gives me a confused look.

"What?"

"I prefer cocoa butter for my massages."

"You think you're so clever."

"Not clever, just right."

She crosses her arms. "One detail doesn't mean you win."

"True, but it does mean I'm off to a fantastic start. Have a great date." I wink at her and then turn around and leave the recovery center.

I've made my fair share of bets over the course of my life. I've won some and lost others. But this bet? This is one I know is a lock. And *when* I win, I'll use my extra time with Sutton to win an even better prize: her heart.

Chapter Fifteen

Sutton Jones

I have made a terrible mistake. I've made worse ones in my life, sure, but this is by far the worst since moving to Alabama. Nerves are bubbling up inside of me, creating an uncomfortable sensation in my abdomen.

I pace the floor of my apartment living room, pausing occasionally to stare down at my phone screen. There's no reason to keep looking at it. The texts never change.

Connor: Hey Sutton! I'm looking forward to dinner. How about you choose the place?

I should have known better than to make a bet when Shaw was sure enough to put an entire *car* on the line. But all I saw in the moment were his blue eyes, glinting with danger like the edge of a blade. It's a look almost as familiar as my own reflection. Ever since we were kids he'd give me that look and it flipped a switch within me that made nothing but defeating him matter.

Once again, that switch has flipped, but this time, I'm worried I'll lose. Because Shaw was right. And the worst part is he wasn't just right about Connor ... he was right about me.

I've paced my apartment enough to make my calves burn, and I still can't change who I am. I could *never* ask Connor to take me somewhere upscale on a first date. Or any date for that matter. I don't even like choosing what I do with my family or friends. It took *months* of living with Ariel before she realized that I was only going to the restaurants she suggested because I didn't want to seem demanding or snobby.

I groan and flop down on my couch, defeated. This will be the last thing Shaw is right about, though. My date with Connor might be casual, but it'll be fun too. He's a nice guy, and contrary to Shaw's belief, I do like nice. After Mason, I *need* nice.

Sutton: How about Charlie's BBQ?

I let out a sigh after pressing send. Charlie's is a cute little BBQ joint with a courtyard attached that has games like corn hole and ladder ball. We can play some games while we wait on our food and get to know each other. It even has heaters so we shouldn't get too cold.

Connor: Sounds perfect. Do you want to meet there at 6?

My head falls back. I glare at the ceiling, imagining Shaw's gloating face. How did he know we'd meet there? I hate it when he's right.

Sutton: Sure!

Connor: Awesome. See you tomorrow at work :)

Sutton: See you then :)

I throw my phone aside after I send the text and pull a blanket down off the back of my couch. Usually, I take a shower and change right when I get home from work. But this whole scenario has me shaken up. I just need to turn my brain off for a while. I turn on my comfort movie and lay on my side, trying to forget about the day's events.

It doesn't work. Shaw's smirking mouth doesn't leave my brain, and when I finally crawl into bed, he follows me into my dreams, too.

· ♥ · ♥ · ♥ · ♥ · ♥ ·

The adrenaline of game day never gets old. I could do without the added nerves about seeing Shaw again, but besides that, I love the pre-game chaos. I've started to enjoy the last-minute check-ins and retaping bandages for the players. With every player I send out the door, my excitement grows. Soon, I'll be in the stands watching my favorite sport of all time.

Shaw hasn't come in, but his wrist mobility has been better recently, so he should be ready for the ice. Maybe he won't come in here at all, and I can enjoy the game without having a cloud of nerves hanging over me. A girl can dream.

It's close to time for the pregame intro to play when Shaw appears in the doorway. All of the medical staff left to assume their places near the bench and in the tunnel, so we're alone.

"Why are you in here, Daniels?" I ask as I finish wiping down my station. "Did you hurt yourself flexing in the mirror?"

He chuckles and my stomach swoops. I clench my abdomen to dispel the feeling.

"I came to see where we stood in the bet so far."

I throw away the disinfectant wipe I was using to clean my station, using the action as an excuse to face away from him, if only for a moment so I can breathe. Even in full hockey gear the man is a sight to behold. It has nothing to do with his looks either. I've always had a weakness for a man in a hockey uniform. But that doesn't matter, because that weakness led to heartbreak once before.

"Well? Do I need to have paperwork drawn up or have I been right so far?"

"You're going to be late," I reply instead of answering his question.

"Your refusal to respond tells me I'm still winning. Where are you going tomorrow?" His deep voice taunts me. "Maybe I'll show up to see my prediction unfold in person."

I whip around to face him, pinning him with a glare. "You will not."

"Come on Jones, it'll be just like old times. Me, being my hilarious, charming self. You, throwing daggers at me with those pretty brown eyes."

My brain trips over his use of the word *pretty*. Was that him patronizing me, or does he think my eyes are pretty? Why do I care?

"You need to leave. I won't cover for you if Coach Fowler comes looking."

His smirk is unnerving. Actually, everything about him lately has frayed my nerves. I don't know how to win the game we're playing. It's bigger than the bet. There's an undercurrent of *something* I can't figure out.

"I'll go, and I won't show up tomorrow, so don't worry. I know you'll tell the truth of how it goes."

"I will. A bet's a bet." I mean it, too. As much as it would pain me to admit Shaw was right, I'd do that before I lied about winning the bet.

"I trust you," he says, his aquamarine eyes meeting mine with intention.

He holds my gaze for a mere breath, and when he finally leaves the room I'm left reeling. Those three words had weight to them. It felt like a confession.

I walk to my seat beside Connor in a daze. He gives me a smile that I do my best to return. My focus zeroes in on Shaw, quickly finding his black jersey, the number ten easily seen in the bold white print. He's readying to face off at center ice.

How long did it take me to make it up here? I missed all of the pregame festivities.

The game begins with Shaw getting the puck and immediately sprinting down toward the opposing team's goal. He shoots–a bold starting move–and the goalie blocks the shot. The crowd goes wild. The game doesn't let up, and both of the teams are playing rough tonight. I wince when Shaw gets slammed into the glass while going for the puck. My heart is in my throat for the rest of the period, always watching for number ten. He takes a few intense hits and it becomes clear they're gunning for him. They want to hurt Shaw, get him off the ice.

When the first period is over, I assess various players during intermission and watch the door for Shaw. He doesn't come, and I don't know why it concerns me. All of the players know they have to listen to their bodies and get help if they need it. If he was hurt, he'd come in here. I think.

Memories of Shaw pushing himself in various competitions and games flash through my mind. He's always been one to go further than most. Would he push too hard just to stay in? I shake off the thought and go back out to watch the second period. I don't need to worry about Shaw, he can worry about himself.

· ♥ · ♥ · ♥ · ♥ · ♥ ·

"Wasn't the game last night amazing?" Connor asks as he tosses a beanbag toward the corn hole board. It comes up short, leaning against the bottom of the board but not quite on it. One of mine has already landed in the hole, so I'm winning.

I look at him, expecting an argument on whether his point counts or not, but no such comment comes. He just smiles and waits for me to go. Shaw would have tried to argue. So would my brother. So would I ...

I shake my head and throw my bean bag. It lands on the board and sticks. "It was a good game. Our defense needs a little work. If we go to the playoffs, we can't make the mistakes we did last night and expect to win."

Shaw had a great game, even with the other team going after him the way they did. He scored twice, and Sawyer scored the final time. The other team managed to get two in, but it should have been less than that. The opponent wasn't good enough to have warranted that level of competition. Our defense simply wasn't at the top of their game.

Connor nods as I speak, throwing his next beanbag to the left of the board. He doesn't react when he misses. And when my next beanbag goes in the hole, he congratulates me with a smile.

"Yeah, I agree with you," he says as he picks up his last bean bag. "Our defense could use some work."

Another throw, another near miss. There's no groaning or jokes about the wind affecting his aim. I shouldn't be disappointed that he's not a sore loser, but it makes me feel like any celebration on *my* part is excessive.

I grew up in a house where everyone had a signature celebration dance when they won. And if they lost, they didn't lose quietly. My mind drifts to Shaw again, and I reprimand my brain. There is no reason for him to be in my thoughts right now.

We walk to the other side, and I don't even gloat about my score as we collect our bags, which feels like a crime. He throws a bean bag right away, and I bite my tongue. I'm supposed to go first since I have the winning score. I've never played a game where I didn't care about the outcome, but that seems to be Connor's style.

We make small talk as we play until the number for our food gets called. Connor goes and gets the tray while I take a seat inside. I sip my water, recalling how when we ordered Connor switched his drink to water when I said I thought soda tasted like chemicals. I told him he didn't need to switch, but he said I was right and he's been wanting to drink less anyway.

"This looks amazing," Connor says, setting the tray of food down on our table.

"It does," I agree and take my plate of pulled pork, mac n cheese, and broccoli salad off the tray.

Conversation stalls as we eat, but I don't mind it. Trying to talk earlier was a bit of a struggle. Connor doesn't know much about hockey outside of the Rockets, and even then his knowledge was lacking. I tried to ask him about his personal life, but all of his answers were short and to the point. I felt like I was conducting a job interview and quickly discovered most of what we have in common is work, but I don't enjoy talking about hip flexors and bandage techniques in my off time.

"I'm having a great time," Connor announces, drawing my eyes up to meet his. He has kind eyes. They're a dark indigo color, and they don't possess even an ounce of mischievousness. I can't comprehend why, but that disappoints me.

"Me too." I fake a smile.

He grins big in return. "You have such beautiful eyes."

My face heats at his out-of-the-blue compliment.

"Thank you." I take a sip of my water to cool off. Maybe we just needed time to settle in, and now the date will pick up.

"They remind me of the old bricks on my grandmother's house."

I choke on my water a little and cough into a napkin to recover. *Old bricks?* How is that a compliment?

"Are you okay?" Connor stands and comes beside me, patting me on the back. I wave him off, my face scorching with embarrassment.

"I'm all right," I rasp out, then clear my throat and repeat, "I'm all right."

"Good, you had me worried for a second."

He gives me another sweet smile and rubs my back. I don't feel a thing beyond the mild warmth of his hand over my sweater. No tingles, or butterflies, nothing at all.

Eventually, he sits back down and we resume our meal. He doesn't elaborate on his brick compliment, and I don't ask him to. I don't even want to know the reason for his comparison. Even if his grandmother was his favorite person in the whole world, I still wouldn't want my eyes to remind someone of building materials. It just brings back memories of kids in elementary school telling me my eyes looked like dirt.

Our date can't end soon enough. When Connor finally walks me to my car, I hold my breath waiting to see what he's going to do. A part of me hopes Shaw is right because I really don't want Connor to try to kiss me. He didn't have any 'liquid courage' as Shaw put it, so I should be safe...

"This was fun," Connor says, and I nod.

"It was," I lie. I hate lying, but I can't very well tell the man I spent the whole time wishing I was home watching *Star Wars* with a facemask on.

"I'll text you and maybe we can get together again sometime."

I nod, so as to not verbally commit to anything. He opens his arms up for an incredibly awkward and not at all comforting hug, cementing Shaw's win. I slide into my car and wave before driving away, wishing that the entire date could have gone differently.

I hate that it went how Shaw said it would, but not even because I lost the bet. My track record when it comes to dating has been poor to say the least. Shaw and Brock ruined many of my relationships when I was younger, but they probably would have ended eventually. They weren't perfect matches, that's for sure. And then I spent four years of college dedicating my life to a man who dropped me as soon as he got a taste of fame.

All I want is a nice guy who won't embarrass me when I bring him home to my parents. I guess Connor fits that bill, but it would be nice if he *also* made my stomach flip and my pulse race. I've never been the overly romantic type, but I've dreamt of my future husband just like any other girl.

The problem is, my groom always wore a helmet and skates in my fantasies. But I can't bear to have my heart broken by a player again. Maybe I'll find a hockey-loving guy, instead. There's always a chance that I meet someone during a game. I just have to hold out hope. I'm still young. Twenty-three isn't old by any means.

I sigh as I walk into my apartment after the short drive back. A bubble bath, that's what I need. A long, hot bath and then a full night of sleep should wash away my stress. I turn on the water, then grab my jar of epsom salts. After sprinkling a healthy amount of lavender salt in, I pour the matching bubble bath. Lavender steam fills the air, the scent reminiscent of a spa. It makes me long for a spa day with my mom. She'd know what to do about all of these issues. Then again, I don't know how I'd tell her Shaw is mixed up in all of this. She's always loved him like her own, and has even hinted at us marrying to make him officially part of the family. I've always gone into a fit of hysterical laughter during those conversations, because I can't see Shaw and I being civil enough to hold hands much less get married.

I strip down once the bath is full and sink into the water, setting my phone on the side of the tub on a hand towel. The calming scent and warm water eases my nerves a little. Hopefully a good long soak will help me forget my problems for a while.

After only a few minutes, my phone starts to buzz. I blink open my eyes and glance at the screen. Shaw.

I bite my lip, then before I can think better of it, answer the call, putting it on speaker.

"I'm surprised you don't have me blocked," Shaw says. His deep, luscious voice echoes through my bathroom.

"I would if Brock didn't have us in that group text together." Brock occasionally sends us memes in a group chat. I think it's his way of trying to get us to bond. I could still receive the texts with Shaw blocked, but I like to see what he responds with.

"How was your date?" No small talk here. He's just calling to claim his win.

"You won," I say on a sigh. I can't keep the dejection out of my voice.

Shaw is quiet for a moment. "I'm sorry, Jones. I can't say I didn't want to be right, but I hate that you had a bad time."

My brow furrows. Why does he sound genuine?

"Thanks, I guess."

"Did anything good happen?" he asks.

I don't know why, but I want to tell him about it. Maybe it's because I know he'll understand. We grew up together, after all.

"We played corn hole, and he barely tried. He didn't even keep score!"

"What's the point of playing if you don't keep score?"

"Exactly! And he didn't even argue when one of his bags hit the bottom of the board."

"I remember Brock arguing for twenty minutes that his should count because of the angle of the bag."

I smile, remembering that time in our backyard. We played games for hours as teenagers. Every summer night, when Shaw and Brock weren't at a party, we'd stay up late playing games. Whoever won the most games got to choose the movie we ended the night with. We'd all fall asleep in the living room and wake up to my mom making breakfast.

"Who ended up winning? I know you kept score," Shaw says, bringing me back to the present.

"I did."

"Atta girl." Shaw's encouragement makes my stomach swoop. "What else happened besides a terrible game of corn hole?"

"He told me my eyes looked like old bricks."

"*He what?*" Shaw's laughter bounces off the walls and coaxes me into a fit of giggles. "You're lying right now, Jones. He did not say that."

"He did! He said they look like the bricks on his grandmother's house." I can barely breathe because of how hard I'm laughing.

"I think there are actual tears in my eyes," Shaw pants once his laughter subsides. "That's terrible."

"It really was."

I start to adjust myself in the tub, but I slip a little, making the water slosh loudly.

"What are you doing right now?" Shaw asks, voice tight, and my whole body tenses.

"Washing dishes," I blurt out.

"And the truth, this time?"

"That is the truth," I breathe out.

"I don't believe you for a second," he says and I can hear the smirk in his voice.

"Well you can't see me to know if I'm telling the truth or not, so–" I cut myself off, cringing at my choice of words.

"You're right, I can't see you." There's a raspy quality to his voice that sends goosebumps down my arms.

"I-I should finish up these dishes," I stutter, unsure of what's going on right now.

"Enjoy your dishes, Jones. I'll see you tomorrow and we can discuss the fulfillment of our bet."

Why does that sound like some kind of sultry promise? I should be scrunching up my nose at the idea of massaging him, but instead my pulse is fluttering, and I can't quite catch my breath.

"Okay," I reply in a quiet voice. "See you tomorrow."

We hang up and I set my phone down, then sink my shaking hands into the lukewarm tub water.

What have I gotten myself into?

Chapter Sixteen

Shaw Daniels

The sound of skates scraping ice greets me as I make my way up the tunnel. I figured Sutton would be here early, but I still thought I'd beat her here. I push out onto the ice right as she lands a double axel. She spots me after, but doesn't break her stride, continuing to skate around the rink. The graceful, confident way she moves makes it look like she's floating rather than skating.

I catch up with her and she turns so she's skating backward. Her hair is in a ponytail today, with a few strands framing her face. There's a sheen covering her forehead and rosy cheeks that make it look as if she's glowing.

"How long have you been out here?" I ask her as we skate in tandem. Neither of us is going at full speed, just moving enough to keep our momentum going.

It isn't lost on me how easy this feels. It's as if we were made to skate together–made to *be* together. Even with all of our banter and bickering, there's always been this undercurrent of ease when it comes to Sutton. We know each other, and there's comfort in that.

She checks the smart watch on her wrist. "An hour and a half."

I raise my eyebrows. "That's a long time. You've got to be freezing."

I look her over, taking in her fitted black jacket and pants. Even though I want to, I don't let my eyes linger at the curve of her waist, or her long, toned legs. Okay, maybe I pause for a *second*. I'm only a man.

"I've been moving, I'm fine," she says, and it's then that I notice she seems closed off.

My first instinct is to grab her and pull her to me. To try and comfort her with a hug or … something more. But I don't think that would go well, so I do what I know will get her out of her head.

"You call that little jump from earlier *moving*?" I ask, and she narrows her eyes. "That was nothing. You should try playing hockey, that will really warm you up."

My prodding is weak, but it serves its purpose. Sutton's beautiful mouth sets into a scowl.

"You couldn't land a jump if your life depended on it, Daniels."

"If you can do it, anyone can," I say, and she rolls her eyes.

"Then let's see you do an axel jump." She stretches her arms out in a go ahead motion.

This is the part where I regret my taunting. I did not think this through. Do I think I could beat Sutton at speed skating? Yes. At any hockey skill? Of course. But I have zero idea how to do an axel jump. I only know how to recognize one from watching her compete.

"Okay, fine, I will."

I skate around the rink, picturing the move in my head as I go.

"Are you going to jump any time soon? I don't have all day," Sutton taunts.

"I'm warming up," I say.

"Just admit that you don't know how." She smirks as I pass her during my second lap around the ice.

"I know how," I lie and keep going.

After a deep breath, I propel myself into the air and attempt to spin, but I don't land correctly. I slip and my hip takes the brunt of the fall. I wince at the pain, not getting up right away so I can catch my breath.

"Shaw!" Sutton yells out, skating over to me. She gets down on her knees beside me, concern furrowing her brow. "Are you all right?"

"I'm fine," I grunt. "Just might need a hip replacement, but that's okay. I'll be ahead of the game when I turn eighty."

She shakes her head, a smile touching her lips. "You're an idiot. I can't believe you actually jumped. If you're hurt, Coach Fowler is going to kill you."

"I'm not hurt," I assure her. "I'll definitely have a nasty bruise, but I've been through much worse."

"Let's get you to the recovery center anyway," she says, watching carefully as I push to my feet. Her forehead is crinkled in concern, and she's biting her bottom lip.

"If you keep looking at me like that, Jones, I'm going to think you care about me."

Her worried look flattens. "Shut up and get off the ice before you fall again," she orders.

I smile through the throbbing in my hip and skate by her toward the tunnel, tipping my head and saying, "Yes ma'am."

I hobble into the recovery center, slipping off my skates and hopping up on the exam table near Sutton's station. Sutton comes in behind me, sitting down to trade her skates for UGG boots that were in her duffel bag. After that, she slips off her gloves and pumps sanitizer onto her hands.

"Lay back and let me see your hip," she says on a sigh.

I lay back and pull the bottom of my crewneck up. Sutton grasps at the waistband of my sweatpants, making me tense up. Wordlessly, she pulls the left side down slightly. It's not like she's undressing me, but the action feels intimate nonetheless.

I hold my breath as her cool fingertips brush over the tender skin. She presses in slightly, and I let out a hiss.

"I want you to add a few hip exercises into your warm up," she murmurs, her head down as her fingers continue moving over my side. I wish I could see her face without making it obvious that I'm trying to.

"Okay," I say in a low voice.

"It looks like it's going to be just a nasty bruise. Does anything else hurt?"

An ache blooms in my abdomen, reminding me of just how badly I want her. That's not the kind of pain I can talk about, though.

"No."

"Good," she whispers, letting my waistband slide back into place.

Her fingertips trail over my skin, like the brush of a feather, before she grabs the hem of my sweatshirt to pull it down. I grasp her hand, halting her movement. Her head lifts and she meets my gaze.

"Your hands are freezing," I rasp out.

"Oh, I-I'm sorry."

"Don't be." I sit up on the table and hold her hand in between both of mine, attempting to warm it up.

Her hand is so soft. Tingles spread through my hands and arms, my stomach swirling in anticipation. The silence between us is heavy with tension. Unspoken confessions fight their way up my throat, but I clench my jaw against them.

There's so much I want to say, but I can't bring myself to. I've spent most of my life with Brock and Sutton by my side. What will happen if this all goes wrong? I need to be sure of how she feels before I reveal anything. I can't lose the only family apart from my grandmother that's ever cared about me. I love them too much. I love *her* too much.

"What are you doing?" Her whispered question breaks the silence.

I let go of her hand, lifting my head and pulling my lips into a forced smirk. "Can't have your hands cold when you're massaging my back."

Her face twists up, and she shoves at my shoulder. "Of course you're thinking of the bet."

I meet her eyes. "What did you think was on my mind?" She clenches her jaw and looks away. "What did you *want* me to say?" I prod her again, the closest I'll let myself come to admitting the thoughts tearing through my mind.

She turns back toward me. "Nothing. I didn't want you to say anything." She rubs her hands up and down her arms over the thin athletic jacket she's wearing. "I was hoping you'd forgotten about the bet."

"We talked about it last night while you were *washing dishes*." I give her a pointed look and watch with satisfaction as her cheeks flame red. "How could I forget?"

I tug my crewneck over my head and then my shirt, throwing them in the nearby chair.

"You want to do this now? *Here*?" Her eyes widen. I can tell she's concentrating on not letting her eyes dip below my chin.

"You're welcome to come over to my place if you want," I offer with a smirk and she glowers at me.

"Lay down," she grumbles.

I do as she says, shifting to lay on my stomach.

"I'm surprised you haven't backed out," I say, because I'm intent on torturing myself. Some part of me has to know that she wants to do this. That this flame of desire burning within is at least flickering to life within her too.

"A bet's a bet. You of all people should know that."

Her hands start to work on the muscles in my upper back. I squeeze my eyes shut and grit my teeth against the groan threatening to escape my lips. She shouldn't be allowed to be so good at this part of her job.

"What's that supposed to mean?" I ask, trying to focus on something other than the pleasure radiating through me.

"You and Brock have been betting on things since the day you met. Remember freshman year when you bet how long you could stay outside in the snow?"

I laugh, but it comes out half-laugh, half-moan when her hand finds a sore spot in between my shoulder blades. Hopefully she ignores that. "Mama Jones wasn't happy with us."

"But she still made homemade hot chocolate for all of us to warm you two up."

My mind takes me back to warm blankets fresh out of the dryer and hot cocoa topped with a mountain of marshmallows and a sprinkle of cinnamon. Just enough to tickle my nose with the scent every time I take a sip.

Sutton is sitting on the floor, her back against the couch. Her head tips back as she laughs at her mom wrapping another scarf around Brock's neck. She laughs even harder when Mama Jones does the same to me. I don't even care that I look ridiculous because if it makes Sutton laugh like that, it's worth it. Her eyes are warm and happy, the color of the swirling hot cocoa in my mug. I force myself to commit the moment to memory, so that I have something to think about when times are hard. When I have to go back to my mom's house.

I break out of my reverie. "That was a good night."

Sutton hums in agreement.

Conversation stalls, but her hands don't. I have to grip the table when she digs into some of the knots in my back.

"You can stop now." My voice comes out gravelly.

"Hmm, I don't think I will. I think working out these knots is important for your recovery." Her tone is teasing, only serving to pour gasoline on the inferno of passion within me.

"Jones," I warn in a low voice. She presses into another tender spot.

I push up off my stomach and swing my legs around so they're hanging off the side of the table. Thanks to years of hockey conditioning and strength training, I'm too fast for Sutton to react. I snag her arm and tug her in between my legs. She falls into my bare chest, her palms searing my skin when she catches herself.

She tries to move away, but I grasp her wrists, then hook my ankles around her legs. She jerks against my grasp, meeting my eyes with her molten chocolate ones.

"I warned you," I breathe out.

Her pupils dilate and her lips part. I take in how absolutely breathtaking she is. I've known her since we were kids on the playground, and yet each time I see her I'm blown away by her beauty. She's like the first snowfall. I know it's coming, but each year I'm surprised by just how *perfect* it is.

My thumb caresses her wrist, then settles against her pulse point. I note how fast her heart is beating. Her lashes flutter as her gaze falls to my mouth, then skips back up to my eyes.

"Your heart is racing," I murmur.

"I'm scared."

I shake my head slowly. "No, you're not."

"No," she agrees in a quiet voice. "But I should be."

"Hey Sutton, are you in here? I–" Connor's voice makes me let go of Sutton.

She stumbles back a little while scrambling away from me. I reach out to steady her, but she pushes my hand away.

"Hey, Connor," she says to him with a forced smile as he walks through the door. She tucks her shaking hands into the pockets of her jacket. "Did you need something?"

Connor eyes the both of us for a moment. A terrible, *terrible* part of me hopes that he thinks something is going on between us. And that the rumor spreads so that no one on the team or staff will flirt with or ask out Sutton again.

"Coach Fowler wants to review the away game dates with us so that we can set our travel schedules," he says.

"Okay, I'll be right there." Her voice is off, unnaturally high.

Connor smiles at her, then turns his attention to me. "You're here early, Shaw. Something wrong?"

"Just making sure my wrist is in good condition."

"That's good, we can't have one of our best players at less than a hundred percent." His comment is well-intended, but I can tell by his expression that he's trying to dissect what he walked in on.

"Make sure to keep up your mobility exercises," Sutton says, and I know she's really telling me to take care of my hip after the fall.

I meet her eyes. "I will." She looks down at the floor, and I resist the urge to sigh. Just when we were getting somewhere. I need to see her outside of work, preferably alone, but I don't know how to accomplish that. Especially when she seems to take three steps back every time I take one forward.

Connor leads Sutton out, wrapping an arm around her shoulder. I ball my hands into fists. He's trying to lay a claim on her. Suddenly, last night's phone call comes back to mind, and I relax. A laugh bursts out of me. I have nothing to worry about. Because while Connor might be throwing his arm around her, she was laughing about their date with *me* while taking a bubble bath.

Chapter Seventeen

Sutton Jones

Am I breathing? I don't think I'm breathing.

I rush out of the recovery center right as practice is ending and book it toward the parking lot. I think I hear Connor call my name, but I can't hold a conversation with him right now. It's a miracle I even made it this long. Seeing Shaw again is *not* an option, I have to get out of here.

My whole body is on fire. With each person I pass on my way out, I wonder if they can see what happened written all over me. Are there marks from Shaw's searing touch? Do my hands look different after being all over him? What about my lips? Can anyone tell how close I came to kissing Shaw with them?

I burst through the door into the icy morning. My lungs ache as I gulp the frigid air. I pull my phone out and immediately call Ariel, hoping she has time to talk.

As soon as the line clicks I blurt out, "I almost kissed Shaw. And I-I touched him when he wasn't wearing a shirt. Oh, and I answered his call while taking a bath." The words tumble out, jumbling together as if I tipped a box of Scrabble letters upside down.

"Okay," Ariel says. "I'm going to need a second to process all of this."

I nod, pacing in front of the building.

"Let's start with this almost kiss. What happened there?"

My mind throws several memories at me all at once, making me realize how many times I've come close to kissing Shaw since moving here. I decide to go with the most recent one, since that's the cause of my hyperventilation. I'll dissect this awful pattern when I can't sleep tonight.

"I was massaging him because I lost a bet, and then I teased him and he–" I cut myself off, pressing a hand to my stomach as butterflies erupt within me.

The way he grabbed me ... it makes my mouth dry just thinking about it.

"Then he what?" Ariel sounds on the edge of her seat.

"He pulled me to him, and I swear we were about to kiss before Connor walked in."

Ariel gasps. "Your life is so much more exciting than mine."

"You can have my life. I do not want all of this drama. I just want a nice guy that my parents and Brock will approve of."

"Then date Connor," Ariel says, like it's easy.

"Connor compared my eyes to old bricks," I deadpan, and her laughter trickles through the phone.

"He did not."

"Yes, yes he did. I didn't think it got worse than being called dirt eyes in the third grade, but here we are."

"That's terrible. So he's definitely a no."

"And so is Shaw," I tell her before she can bring him up. "He's not nice." Even though he paid for Ariel and my family's tickets to that game in North Carolina. And there's the whole hair tie thing I'm still not sure about...

"Your family loves him, though. And you clearly are attracted to him."

I want to deny the attraction part of things, but I can't. It's like every nerve ending in my body tingles whenever he's near. Sometimes even when he's not close by. I felt more for Shaw over the phone than I did with Connor on a date.

"Neither of those things matter, though. He's a hockey player."

Ariel sighs. "As much as I hate what Mason did to you, Shaw isn't him. I've met them both, and I can personally attest that Shaw is nothing like Mason."

I chew on the inside of my cheek as I continue to pace the sidewalk. "He may not be Mason, but he *is* Shaw Daniels. He's never been without a modelesque date on his arm for an event, not to mention the girls that fawn over him after games."

"You're going to fault the man for dating? And for having fans?"

"We always argue," I add.

"Now that much is true, but maybe you would argue less if you made out more."

My mouth drops open. "Ariel!"

"What?" She laughs. "I'm just saying it's harder to argue with someone if your lips are attached to theirs."

I think of Shaw's hands around my wrists, and his low, raspy voice growling *I warned you*. Somehow, I think we'd manage to argue even while kissing. And it would be fun. I start to fan my face, because even in this frigid February air, I'm heating up.

"Dating Shaw just isn't an option. We're too... combatant. He treats my nerves like a trampoline. I don't think kissing would solve that."

"Only one way to find out," Ariel says in a singsong voice. I stay silent to let her know my distaste. "Okay, fine. Don't kiss him. Just think about kissing him like you are right now."

"If you were here I would hit you."

"I thought you only talked to me that way, Jones. I'm hurt that I'm just one of many," Shaw says, making me whirl around.

His hair is wet from a post-practice shower, falling in tendrils over his forehead that are begging to be pushed back. He's standing a few feet away by the door, but my heart is pounding the same way it was when I was trapped against his chest.

"Is that him?" Ariel whispers through the phone.

"I have to go." I hang up without another word. I shove my hands in my pockets and take a step back. The more distance from Shaw, the better. He disagrees, apparently, because he closes the distance between us quickly with his long strides.

"You weren't in the recovery center after practice," he states, looking down at me.

"I needed some air."

His eyes rove over my face, and I feel as though he sees more than I want him too. It's always been that way with him, though. In school I'd catch him watching me during class. He'd smirk, and I'd roll my eyes. But right before he smirked, there would be this split second of a moment where I'd feel utterly and completely on display. I've never felt that with anyone but him. It's been the thing that's driven me up the wall the most, because why should *he* be the one to see me?

Mason never looked at me like this, and we were dating for almost *four years*. Shaw looks at me as if I'm a test he already has the answer key too. There's this confident gleam in his eyes that unnerves me if I think about it too long. Especially when I consider what he does with the knowledge. He taunts and teases, pokes and prods until I give in and retaliate. Our relationship is a game we both play to win.

Maybe that's why I can't allow myself to feel anything of substance for him, because I'd never know if it was real. Our whole lives have been spent as rivals. Even when he grabbed me earlier, it was in response to me messing with him, not because he really *wanted* to touch me. We can't change the dynamic we have. If we could, we would have already. It seems as though we're destined to be in opposition, even if there have been a few friendly moments lately.

"Are you all right?" Shaw's gentle tone surprises me. I expected a quip about me needing air because he's too hot to be around or something.

"I'm fine, why wouldn't I be?"

"I worried I went too far in the recovery room." He scratches the back of his neck, looking a tad sheepish. It's–unfortunately–a cute expression on him.

I shake my head. "You didn't. We've probably done something like that as kids before." I don't know why I'm trying to explain away what happened. It would be better to act mad at him and tell him not to do it again. But for some reason, I want to reassure him.

"Yeah, but we're not kids anymore."

The heat pooling in my stomach affirms his statement. We need to move away from this topic *fast*.

"I'm trying to give you an out here, Daniels. Are you going to take it?"

He smiles. "I'll take it."

"Do they need me back inside?" I ask him, and he shakes his head.

"Nah, your man has it covered."

I glare at him. "Don't."

"What? He put his arm around you when you were leaving the recovery center. I figured that meant you decided to overlook his inability to excite you."

"What makes you think you know what excites me?"

He smirks and I feel as though I've taken the bait he set out. I can hear the door of the trap shutting behind me. He presses closer, the heat of his body covering my skin in goosebumps. I'm grateful I'm wearing a jacket so he can't see them.

"How's your heart right now, Jones?" The low rasp of his voice sends a tingle down my spine. "I'd be willing to bet it's racing. And that you can barely catch your breath."

"So? That happens when people fight."

"Is that what's happening? We're fighting?"

It feels like I've fallen while on the ice and can't get back on my feet. I don't know what's going on between us and I'm disoriented because of it. Why is he looking at me like he wants to kiss me? What sort of game is he playing?

"We're always fighting," I reply, desperate to keep my composure. "That's what we do."

His smirk falls into a sad sort of smile. "Yeah, but may–"

The sound of my phone ringing cuts off his sentence. I quickly pull it out–glad for the diversion–and see that Brock is calling me.

"It's Brock," I say and Shaw immediately takes a big step back, his expression wary and almost conflicted.

I press the answer button, "Hey, what's up?" Shaw's shift in demeanor is confusing to say the least. I wonder if something happened between him and Brock.

"Hey, I don't have much time to talk, but I'll be in town in a few days for a charity event. Do you want to come? You can get dressed up and eat fancy food, your two favorite things."

I laugh at his accurate assessment. I do love those things, and maybe I can meet a handsome man in a suit who will help me forget all about the attractive hockey player in front of me.

"Sure, that sounds fun."

"Cool. I'll get Marie to send you the details." I'm used to Brock's assistant, Marie, sending me event details, or even Brock's travel schedule. Brock's a busy guy, but he always makes time for family. So him calling out of the blue to invite me to an event is on par for him.

"Thanks."

"Talk to you later, love you!" He hangs up before I can reply. Right after he hangs up, Shaw's phone rings and my blood runs cold.

"Hey, man," Shaw answers, laughing a little, likely at the fact that Brock doesn't know we're standing across from each other. "That sounds like a good time. I'd love to go."

No, no, *no*. I just wanted one night without him around. If only my brother could have chosen a mild-mannered best friend, someone like Connor. But no, he had to choose an arrogant ego-maniac who pushes my buttons like they're a video game controller. Now my chances at meeting a guy are ruined. Shaw and Brock will scare them off like the unwanted bodyguards they've been since middle school.

"Looks like I'll be seeing you another night this week," Shaw says after he hangs up with my brother.

"Does torturing me ever get old?"

He tilts his head side to side. "No, not really. I'd say it gets better the older we get, like a fine wine."

"You're insufferable."

"And yet you answer my calls while washing dishes." He tucks his hands into his pockets with a grin. My face heats. I wish he would forget that. "It makes me wonder what you'd do if you liked me."

A few ideas come to mind faster than I'd like to admit. Most of them involve a repeat of the recovery center incident, but with a different ending.

"I guess we'll never know."

His smile tightens, and a sharp pain flares in my chest. That was a little harsh. But maybe harsh is good. Animosity is better than whatever this is between us, or at least more comfortable.

Some of the guys come out of the arena, walking between me and Shaw. I use the opportunity to slip away and go to my car. All the while ignoring the ache blooming in my chest at the thought of hurting Shaw.

Once I'm in the safe confines of my car, I close my eyes and lean my head back. I've said I despised him before, but something about this time felt different. Hopefully he didn't take it as hard as I think. I'm sure we'll be back to our normal by tomorrow.

Chapter Eighteen

Shaw Daniels

I've wasted two days' worth of opportunities in my week of massages from Sutton. After the intensity of the first, I started to second guess whether my idea was a good one. It might have been too much for her. At the same time, it revealed a lot. I got to confirm that Sutton *does* feel something other than disdain for me. She wanted to kiss me. I felt it in the heat between us, in her rapid pulse beneath my fingertips, in her eyes brimming with desire. That confirmation has me excited for tonight, even though I've missed out on massages.

Usually, I hate charity events. I'd much rather volunteer with the charity itself and donate money anonymously instead of dressing up and faking a smile every time some old guy in a too-tight coat asks me if I think we'll win the cup this year. I only ever go because Brock invites me, and sometimes it's the only time I get to see him. He also says it's good for my career to network, but I think what's best for my career is to be a great hockey player. I guess that's why I'm not an agent.

Tonight, however, I'm overcome with anticipation for this event. I plan on spending the entire evening with Sutton. I doubt that she'll even spare me a dance. But I'm still excited to see her. Since she's moved here, the only time I've seen her outside of work is at the pub. On top of that, I'm wearing a suit. Which, again, usually I'd hate, but I have been told quite a few times that this is my best look. And I know Sutton is all for a classy affair like this one, along with all the fashion that comes with it. I've heard her gush over celebrity red carpet looks several times. So maybe this will help my case with her.

I slide out of the town car I booked to take me to the event, buttoning my coat as I stand. Cameras begin to flash, a few reporters calling out my name. I smile and tip my head to them, even bothering to pause in the middle of the walkway for a shot or two. Might as well milk it since I'm here. It'll make Brock and my publicist, Sherry, happy.

Once inside the venue, I'm greeted by a sea of people in suits and gowns. A large chandelier that could likely fund the charity we're having this whole party for, hangs above. The wall to my left has a series of tables with chefs preparing and serving food. Filet mignon seared right in front of you, a seafood tower taller than me, and even a crepe station featuring a chef with a mustache that makes him look like a French cartoon character. To my right looks to be a silent auction, and in the center is a small dance floor and lots of tables.

I scan the room for Sutton, since she's the main reason I'm here. I spot her talking to Brock and someone I don't recognize near a table. She's gorgeous, as always. The black silk dress she's wearing caresses her curves in a way that makes my mouth dry, and when she turns around to grab her drink off a nearby table, I freeze in place. Her dress is backless, exposing way too much of her perfect, smooth skin.

She turns back around, champagne flute in hand, and her eyes catch mine. People walk back and forth between us, but our shared gaze doesn't break. All I see is her. Our surroundings blur and fade into grayscale, while Sutton stays in blazing color. Everything about her is captivating. From the tendrils of hair framing her angelic face, to the delicate curve of her hip, to her long legs–one of which is peeking out of a slit in her dress. She's a study in perfection, an example of beauty in its most magnificent form.

"Shaw, you made it!" Brock's voice takes a pair of scissors to the invisible string between Sutton and I.

I smile at him and force myself back into motion. The other person who was talking with them walks away, leaving us three alone. Brock draws me in for a hug once I reach their table and pats me on the back.

"It's good to see you again. I was surprised you said yes. You hate these things."

I shrug. "I figured a night out with my best friend was better than being at home. Even if all these rich people make my skin crawl."

Brock laughs, shaking his head at me. "Don't be so judgmental, everyone here is doing this for a good cause."

"We could give more money if we all stayed home instead of spending it on a venue and food and clothes."

Someone says Brock's name, and he looks over his shoulder for a second before turning back to me.

"You'll have to continue your rant to Sutton, because I need to talk to some prospective clients. I'll try to catch up later." He walks off in the direction of a group of suit-clad men.

"You're right, you know," Sutton says before taking a sip of her champagne. "As much as I love dressing up, these things are a waste of money."

"Did you just say I'm right about something? How much champagne have you had, Jones?"

She rolls her eyes, a faint smile hidden behind the rim of her glass. "You know, I'd be much nicer to you if you didn't say things like that."

"Mmm, but that would get boring quick, don't you think?"

Her smile grows, and my chest warms like I'm the one drinking bubbly. But just as suddenly as it appeared, it falls. Her eyes take on a haunted look, staring over my shoulder.

"What's wrong?" I ask, but she doesn't utter a word. I turn in the direction she's staring and clench my jaw. Mason Walker is a few feet away, a dark-haired woman with smudged lipstick draped over his arm. A matching smudge is found on the edge of his infuriating smirk. He's looking right at Sutton.

"I didn't know he was coming. I wouldn't have come." At the sound of panic in her voice, I turn back to face Sutton. "I-I need to get out of here."

I grab her forearms and squeeze lightly. "Or, you have another option."

"What other option? Watch him stick his tongue down the throat of a model all night and pretend I'm unaffected?"

I remove the glass from her shaking hands and set it on a nearby table. "No, you make him jealous."

"How am I supposed to do that?" I draw her to me, settling my hand on her waist. "*Oh*," she whispers.

"Dance with me," I say in a low voice. She merely nods, letting me lead her out to the dance floor.

A slow, sultry song featuring a saxophone plays, making it feel as though we're in a hazy dream. Sutton gently places her hand on my shoulder, and I respond by sliding my hand from her waist to her back. She sucks in a breath as I splay my fingers along the curve of her spine, her skin soft and warm under my palm. I grasp her other hand in my own, holding it against my shoulder as I lead her in a simple slow dance.

Her eyes are trained behind me, and I can feel her body tense.

"Jones," I say and she looks at me with wide brown eyes. "Relax." I rub my thumb in circles on her back. "I promise I won't bite unless you ask me to."

A smile breaks through her nervous expression, and she lets out a soft laugh. "I don't know what to do with you sometimes."

I can think of a few things...

She looks over my shoulder again.

"He's watching, isn't he?" I ask, and she nods. "Then how about we give him a show?"

I dip my head down toward her, my nose brushing hers. Our eyes lock, and I feel as though I've opened the door into her mind. I can see the trepidation in her gaze, but a flicker of something more as well. Could it be–is that *anticipation*?

"Are you going to kiss me?" Her whispered question almost breaks my resolve. But if I kissed her now, she'd think it was to make Mason jealous.

"No, Jones, not here, not in front of everyone." I brush my nose against hers once more, reveling in the intimacy of the act. "We're going to be subtle, but the message will be clear."

She nods, but confusion threads her brows together. I hope Brock is too busy schmoozing future clients to see this next part.

I turn and place my cheek against hers, my lips by her ear. Her breath hitches when I trail my fingertips up her back, then back down. I close my eyes when she relaxes against me, our bodies melting together. Nothing has ever felt so *right*.

"Everyone who looks at us right now is imagining what I could be whispering in your ear," I tell her. "They're wondering if I'm telling you how beautiful you look. How when I laid eyes on you in this dress, the world stopped spinning and I couldn't breathe. And all I could think about was holding you, touching you."

I let my nose brush the shell of her ear. She shivers in my arms.

"They might even speculate on how long we've been together. Some will say the way I'm holding you is intimate, like I've known you for a long time." I pause, breathing in her intoxicating scent. "Others will think we're in a honeymoon phase."

"They might think we just met tonight," she whispers. Her fingertips are mindlessly playing with the hair at the nape of my neck. "That we saw each other across the room and fell hopelessly in love."

I smile even as my chest aches with longing. I've always cherished the history I have with Sutton, but her words are tempting enough to make me wish that was our story.

"Hopeless, huh? That's pretty intense."

"That's the only way to fall in love."

I don't know if it's the only way, but it's definitely what I've done.

"Sutton–" I start to pull back, but the song gets cut off.

"Esteemed and charitable guests, if you could please make your way to your tables, the presentation is about to begin," a man announces into a microphone. A projector screen lowers in front of the stage the band was playing on.

We don't move right away. One of Sutton's hands is still threaded in my hair, the other held in my own hand. She stares up at me, and it feels like neither of us wants this moment to end. I know I don't. I'm living out my dream. The only thing I would change is the color of her dress to white and her last name.

People begin to make their way to their seats, brushing by us and popping our blissful bubble. Sutton blinks a few times as if coming to her senses, then takes a step back. I reluctantly let go of her.

"I guess we should head back to our seats," she says with a shy smile. "Thanks for your help, I think I can make it through dinner now at least."

"You're welcome," I reply, trying not to sigh. It's not her fault she doesn't know how I feel. It's mine. I've been scared for too long.

My phone starts to buzz in my pocket while we're walking back to our table. I pull it out and see my mom's name on the screen. It's fitting that she's calling, since she's a part of the reason I'm scared to make a move. Both my parents abandoned me in different ways, making me reliant on Sutton's family for the love and support I craved as a child. Just the thought of losing the Jones family makes panic rise like bile within me.

Unfortunately, I can't ignore the call and continue my night with Sutton. Most of the time my parents are calling for money, but whenever I don't answer I feel guilty and worry that one day something will be wrong.

"I have to take a call," I say to Sutton as she's lowering herself into a chair. "I'll be back soon."

She nods and gives me a soft smile that makes me hate the fact that I'm leaving even more. The past few weeks around Sutton have shown me that whenever I make headway with her, it's important to capitalize on it, or else she might pull away again.

With a heavy sigh, I walk to the exit and answer my phone.

"Hey, Mom."

Chapter Nineteen

Sutton Jones

"Do you know where Shaw is?" I ask Brock when he sits down beside me at our table.

"No, the last time I saw him was when you two were canoodling on the dance floor."

My face heats at his words. I glare at him to cover up my embarrassment. "Who says canoodling? What are you, seventy?"

"You can make fun of my word choice all you want, but I know what I saw. And you should be thankful that I'm such a great brother, because if I wasn't, I'd have cut his hand off for how low on your back it went."

I gape at him, unable to form words. Were we really that obvious? I guess that was the point of the dance, but I didn't think Shaw was right about everyone watching us. A weight drops into my stomach. That moment with Shaw was … overwhelming. I felt as though I was walking on a tightrope over the Grand Canyon. Every movement was monumental. One wrong step, one wrong *breath*, and I'd be sent tumbling with no net to catch me. But that fall never came. Shaw held me up, and made me feel graceful and beautiful and sexy.

I spent an entire song in the arms of my forever-rival, and I *liked* it. That's the scariest part of all. Not that my brother saw us and made assumptions, but that his assumptions might be *true*. There's no doubt that Shaw gets on my nerves and makes me want to pull my hair out at times, but he also leaves me breathless in a good way. He makes me feel seen. It's ironic that the man I've spent most of my life coming in second to makes me feel like I've just won an Olympic gold medal.

"Hello? Earth to Sutton." Brock's voice pulls me out of my mind and into reality. "Are you going to go find your boyfriend?"

"He's not my boyfriend," I say, standing up and dropping my linen napkin on my plate. "But I will go find him, to make sure he's not causing trouble."

And also because there's this gut feeling I have that something is wrong. But I'm not voicing *that* out loud.

"Have fun, but not so much fun that I have to see my twin sister and best friend plastered all over gossip sites because of public indecency!" Brock sings out, running his words together at the end.

I don't respond, but instead head toward the door that I watched Shaw walk out of earlier. Not that I was watching him in an I-like-to-watch-him-walk-away sort of way, but just out of curiosity. And if I noticed how well his suit fit him ... well sue me for having an eye for good tailoring.

The door leads into an empty hallway. It takes a moment for my eyes to adjust, as the lighting out here is dim compared to the bright ballroom. Once they adjust, I see Shaw a few feet away with his back against a wall, his knees up and head hanging down. The feeling of wrongness rises within me, making my throat tight.

"Was the party so boring that you decided to start your own in the hallway?" I ask as I walk toward him.

His head lifts and my heart breaks. Worry lines are etched into his forehead, and his eyes are red. Has he been crying?

"Something like that," he replies, scrubbing his face with his hands. "I can come back in though. Is Mason bothering you?"

"No, he hasn't been within ten feet of me. Thanks for that, by the way."

I slide down the wall next to him, choosing to ignore the fact that this carpet looks like it hasn't been cleaned in a few decades and the dress I'm wearing is from one of those "rent the runway" services. If it gets ruined, it'll cost half a paycheck to buy it, but I get the feeling that Shaw needs someone by his side right now.

"I was happy to. That guy is a jerk and a pig."

And yet I dated him for four years. I wonder what that makes me? Sad, probably. But since I came over here for Shaw and not for me, I don't voice my insecurities. Even if the lack of lighting makes me feel bold enough to. There's something about a dark room that brings courage to the surface. As if the fact that the person can't see you physically makes you feel safe enough to be seen emotionally.

"Is that why you were out here? So you weren't tempted to punch him like you've done to all my other exes?" I joke, and he chuckles.

"No, I got a call from my mom." He leans his head back against the wall. "I think she's using drugs again."

I look down at my hands, toying with the charm bracelet on my wrist. Shaw's parents have both had issues with addiction in the past.

I remember hearing that his mom got clean while we were in high school, but his dad—as far as I know—never stopped drinking.

That's why even when I used to get annoyed about him being at our house all the time, I was never *really* annoyed. I knew he needed a home, some place besides his grandmother's to feel safe.

"I'm sorry, that's awful." I wish I had better words for him. Mine feel feeble in comparison to the massive weight that must be on his shoulders.

I don't know if it's darkness hiding his potential reaction that makes me do it, or the fact that my heart is breaking for Shaw, but I lay my head on his shoulder. He wraps an arm around me, and I feel completely and utterly safe. It doesn't make sense, but I do.

"Thanks." It's a simple expression of gratitude, but I can sense the weight it holds.

"If you want to talk about it, I'll listen."

He sighs. "Mom's been asking for more and more money lately. I thought she was just getting greedy. Which is terrible, I know, but I couldn't help but think that." His fingertips absentmindedly stroke my shoulder, sending chills down my arm. "But this last time, she sounded panicked. As if she needed the money. When I questioned her, she started trying to guilt me into giving her the money. Said she'd spent more money raising me than I could ever repay her, that it was the least I could do for her."

Tears sting my eyes. I wrap an arm around his midsection in a hug. The action is instinctual, almost involuntary.

"She used to get mean like that while she was on cocaine. So, I called her out, asked if she relapsed, and she went into defensive mode right away. Then her boyfriend grabbed the phone and yelled at me for being a terrible son. I hung up after that."

"You shouldn't have to go through this, Shaw," I whisper. "I-I wish I could do something for you."

"Don't you worry that pretty little head of yours, Jones. I'm all right." He pulls me closer and kisses the crown of my head. My breath catches in surprise at his gesture. "I've got Brock, and your parents, and my grandmother. Not to mention a blonde spitfire who keeps me on my toes." I let out a laugh at his description of me. "I've got all I need."

"Are you sure you're okay?"

He's silent for a moment. "Maybe I'm not okay, but I will be. I'll figure out how to deal with it."

"You don't have to figure it out alone, you know?" I say, voice soft. "All those people you listed would be happy to help you."

"Even the blonde spitfire?"

My lips tip up in a small smile. "Especially her."

"I don't know what to say. I'm not used to you being nice to me."

I smack his stomach over his dress shirt and he laughs. "Say *thank you, Sutton, I'll let you know if I need anything.*"

He shifts some, making me pull back. Our eyes meet in the shadowy darkness, the lack of light intensifying the moment. "Thank you, Sutton, I'll let you know if I need anything." His words come out low and raspy.

"Good," I whisper. And then, when the tension between us becomes so thick it feels as though I can't breathe, fear sweeps in like a thief in the night, stealing all my bravery in one fell swoop. "We should probably get back inside, before Brock starts to worry."

After an agonizing pause, Shaw responds. "Yeah, we should."

Shaw gets up, extending a hand to help me. His hand covers mine in warmth and strength as he pulls me to my feet. I wobble slightly, gaining balance on my stilettos. He keeps a hold of my hand until I'm steady. Then, he opens the door to the ballroom for me.

"Thank you," I say to him and he just dips his head, a smile playing on his lips.

After our dance, coming in from the hallway makes me feel as though I'm on display. My skin itches with the feeling of curious, judgmental, and jealous eyes on me. I rush to our table to try and put some distance between Shaw and me. I'm betting anyone who saw us come in from the hallway is having *a lot* of thoughts right now.

I sit down at the table, and Brock raises his eyebrows. "Not a word."

He just smirks, miming zipping his lips as Shaw takes a seat next to me.

I spend the rest of the night avoiding both Shaw and Brock's gazes. They both see things I don't want them to.

·♥·♥·♥·♥·♥·

I fidget with the hem of my Rockets sweatshirt, glancing over at Connor. He's sitting a few feet away, intently watching the guys practice. Before work this morning, I told him that I didn't think it was going to work out between us. He was kind and took it well, but there's been this awkward tension between us ever since.

I turn my attention back to practice with a sigh. The guys are scrimmaging, which is more exciting than drills, but it's still hard to focus on them. I keep replaying last night over and over in my mind. So much happened that there's still plenty to mentally dissect even after a sleepless night.

Shaw skates up to the bench and grabs a water bottle, tilting his head back to pour it into his mouth. He's so hot he makes drinking water attractive. It's utterly foolish for me to think this way about him, but it's as if his whispered words and strong hands altered my brain chemistry. Now when I see him, I still want to hit him, but I also wouldn't mind jumping in his arms and kissing his gorgeous mouth.

He catches me staring at him and my face heats. He tips the water bottle in my direction, as if he's toasting to me, then skates back out into the action. I bite the inside of my cheek to keep from smiling. He shouldn't do things like that in front of everyone, what will they think? Maybe no one noticed. I look over once more at Connor. He's looking at me, and judging by his expression, he saw Shaw's little gesture. *Great.* Can't wait to have my coworker tell everyone I ditched him for a hockey player after saying *I don't date players.*

I force myself to focus on the guys, watching as they weave around each other. Shaw gets the puck and is clearly going for the goal when one of his teammates knocks him into the glass wall and he falls to the ice. Even after years of watching this violent game, I still wince whenever a hard hit happens. Usually, the hits happen so fast that you barely have time to react anyway before the players are off again.

Shaw doesn't move, and my stomach drops. I immediately stand, watching him use his left arm to get up.

"Shaw, you good?" Coach Fowler calls out from the bench. My chest tightens when Shaw shakes his head. I rush toward the bench area and make it right as he walks through the door.

"Your wrist?" I ask him. He uses his left arm to take off his helmet and throw it to the side.

"Yeah," he grits out.

"Go with Sutton to the recovery center," Coach Fowler says.

Shaw's responding nod is weak. We make our way to the room in silence.

"It must be really bad if you're not making jokes," I say as he sits down on the exam table.

"It's not good."

I help him get off his practice jersey. His jaw is tight the entire time.

I'm gentle as I examine his wrist, coaching him through some movements in a soft voice. He can't manage any of them, and winces at any sort of pressure on the area. I press my lips into a tight line. He's not going to like what I have to say.

"What's the diagnosis?" Coach Fowler asks, coming into the room.

I avoid looking at Shaw. "He can't move it, and is clearly in a lot of pain. It's likely a muscle tear. I'd suggest an X-ray to confirm, but I'm pretty confident that's what it is."

"What does recovery look like? Can he play this week?"

I shake my head. "He needs to rest, keep it in a sling and iced. No playing this week for sure, maybe next depending on the extent of the damage."

"You're kidding, right?" Shaw asks, his tone hard. "I took a hit, so what? I'll rest it and be ready for the game, same as always."

I meet his eyes. "We've been fighting this injury all season. You took a hard hit and now you have to rest or else it's only going to get worse."

"Apparently, everything you told me to do is worthless," he says. "Because if it wasn't, this wouldn't have happened."

I take a step back, shocked by his lashing out.

"Easy there, Shaw," Coach Fowler says, a warning in his voice. "She's just doing her job. This is a common injury."

"Exactly! It's so common it shouldn't be an issue for me to play."

"Go to the locker room and change. I'll take you to get an X-ray and then we'll go from there."

Shaw jumps off the table then storms out of the room, leaving me and the coach behind in silence.

"Sorry about him," Coach Fowler says. "He's not upset with you, just at the situation."

I nod, but I don't know if I entirely believe him. Shaw seemed quite mad at me, enough to take a shot at me in front of the coach. Whatever affection was growing between Shaw and me appears to have died as soon as it sprouted.

Chapter Twenty

Sutton Jones

"No." I groan and pull my pillow over my head. My phone buzzes on my nightstand. It's too early for phone calls. Especially since I barely slept last night on account of my throat feeling like it was full of razor blades every time I swallowed.

I ignore my phone and grab the blue water bottle I keep by my bed and take a sip. Yep, still painful. This feeling, combined with my headache and stuffy nose, is what made me email the Rockets admin yesterday evening to let them know I couldn't work the game tonight. I'd never forgive myself if I got someone sick and caused them not to play.

My phone pauses its buzzing, but only for a second before it starts again. I glare at it, swiping it off my nightstand. Ariel's name is on the screen, making me frown. She knows I didn't sleep last night because I sent her an Anakin compilation video at 3 AM.

"Hello?" I rasp.

"You sound terrible."

"Thanks, I appreciate that," I deadpan.

"Are you sick?" I can hear the concern in her voice. Ariel has always been a caretaker type. If I ever got sick in college, she forced me to rest and brought me whatever I needed. I hated when she did it, because I hate relying on other people. But she told me I had no choice and did it anyway. I always appreciated it though. It's nice to know I have someone to count on at the end of the day.

"Just a cold," I reply. "I'm sure I'll be over it after I get some rest."

"Okay, then it's probably not a good time to share why I called."

I massage my forehead, hoping to soothe my pounding head. "Just tell me, or else I'll spend the day wondering."

"Have you looked at any Rockets fan accounts lately?" she asks hesitantly.

"Why would I do that?"

"You might want to." She pauses. "You're on quite a few."

"Me?" I sit up too fast, causing my head to spin. "Why am I on there?" I grip my sheets as I wait for the vertigo to subside.

"Look at the screenshots I sent you." The wariness in her voice has me feeling even more nauseous than it has since last night.

I put my phone on speaker, then open up my text messages. There's a few from my mom and from Brock, which I ignore and go straight to Ariel's text thread.

"Oh no," I say as I swipe through the photos.

Every single photo shows me on the dance floor with Shaw. His hand on my bare lower back, our faces close together, our bodies even closer. Each one showcases a different angle, but they're all incriminating. The captions are almost as bad as the photos.

@alabamarocketsforever: Looks like Shaw won't be alone for Valentine's Day this year.

@alabamarocketsbiggestfan: BRB, I'm going to cry into a box of chocolates because Shaw is TAKEN!

@nhlgossip: Notorious bachelor Shaw Daniels from the Alabama Rockets was spotted at a charity event getting cozy with this mysterious blonde. Anyone know who she is? DM your suspicions!

@alabamarocketsfanclub: Our beloved #10 is officially off the market. Dear person who sent in the photos: Couldn't you have waited until after Valentine's Day to drop this bomb?

Yes, on top of me being sick and these photos coming out, today is Valentine's Day.

"This is terrible."

"At least they don't know who you are yet," Ariel offers, trying to sound optimistic.

"The key word there is *yet*. What happens when they do?"

"I'm sure they'll move on to other drama before someone figures it out. I only knew it was you because I know you and you sent me a photo of your dress before the event."

"I hope you're right."

"I hope so too." She pauses, and I know her question before she asks. "Is there something you aren't telling me? These photos look like a couple in love, not enemies."

I fall back onto my pillows with a sigh. "He was helping me because Mason was there. It wasn't romantic, just a favor." But even as I say the words, it's hard to fully believe them. Sure, it started out as a way to make Mason jealous, but Shaw didn't have to whisper in my ear the way he did. Or hold me with a tender strength that turned my bones into jelly.

"Okay, I'm going to choose to believe you, even if I think these photos look like something more."

"Thank you," I say and then pinch the bridge of my nose. "And thanks for calling to let me know."

"Of course. What are best friends for?" I smile at her words. "I'll let you get some rest. I hope you feel better soon."

We say our goodbyes, then hang up. I decide to brave the rest of my messages, opening up my mom's first. There's a screenshot from a fan account waiting for me, along with a few other links.

Mom: What's this about you and Shaw? Why didn't you tell me you were dating?!?

Mom: Check out this cute hockey-themed wedding cake!

Mom: If you two get married during the off season, you should have a destination wedding! Remember that trip we all took to the beach that year? Shaw loved it.

I gape at my phone. One of the links is a *wedding board* on Pinterest. What's scary is that the board isn't new. How long has she been adding to this?

Sutton: Mom, we aren't dating. The photos make it look like more than it was. We were just dancing. Please stop planning my wedding.

I press send on the text and switch over to Brock's messages. All he's sent is a screenshot of one of the photos, a GIF of someone wagging their eyebrows, and then the word *canoodling* in all caps. Rolling my eyes, I type out a response.

Sutton: You are not, and never have been, funny.

With that taken care of, I take a few more sips of water, mute my phone, and curl up under the covers, intent on sleeping off whatever is ailing me.

· ♥ · ♥ · ♥ · ♥ · ♥ ·

I did not sleep it off. My whole body is aching, and my throat seems worse than before. I drag myself out of bed, holding onto my nightstand while I wait for the nausea to subside. It does not, so I soldier on toward the bathroom. My body screams in protest at every movement, and when I turn on the lights my head joins in.

It's not long before I give in to the nausea and spend the next few minutes with my head over the toilet. Once I'm finally done, I groan and wipe at my face with a hand towel. I pull myself up off the floor and lean on the counter and walls as I walk back to bed.

Tears sting my eyes when my water is gone. The kitchen feels very far away right now. My throat burns and a bitter taste clings to my tongue.

"Okay," I whisper, trying to gather my strength. "You can do this. Just go to the kitchen, get some water, then lay on the couch."

My self-coaching doesn't soothe my aching muscles, though. If I had to guess, I have the flu, and I'm likely dehydrated. I force myself to stand, but my calves immediately start to cramp up. I fall back down on the bed and wilt into a fetal position.

It's clear that I'm not going to get very far on my own. As much as I hate it, I need help. I grab my phone and call the one person in Alabama that I trust to help me right now.

Chapter Twenty-One

Shaw Daniels

I stare at Sutton's contact in my phone, trying to come up with the words to say to her. *I'm sorry* doesn't feel good enough. The way I spoke and acted was just terrible. Maybe I should buy her a present and bring it to her tonight before the game instead of calling–

My phone starts to ring in my hand. Sutton's name and a picture of her from her graduation that Brock sent me pop up on my screen. I squeeze my eyes shut for a second, then open them again, sure that I'm imagining things. Why would she be the one calling me? Maybe she's finally ready to chew me out for what I did. I wouldn't blame her.

I answer the phone and start talking immediately. "Hey, Jones, I'm sorry about what I said–"

She cuts me off. "Shaw."

"Please let me finish before you go on your well-deserved rant. I was a complete jerk and I already told Coach that you've been a great physical therapist. I even told him to give you a raise. I don't know if he'll listen, but–"

She cuts me off again. "*Shaw, please.*" It's then I notice how weak her voice sounds, and that she's using my first name.

My hand tightens around my phone. "What's wrong?"

"I-I'm really sick. I think I might have the flu? Everything hurts. I can't move," she whispers.

I immediately grab my keys and wallet off my nightstand. Sutton hates asking for help. If she's calling, she must be really sick. "I'm on my way. Can you tell me your address?"

She gives it to me and tells me where she has a key hidden.

"I think I could be dehydrated," she tells me as I'm about to walk out my door. "I haven't eaten either. I don't know if I can keep anything down."

I turn around and head to my kitchen. "I've got some electrolyte packets I can bring, and crackers too." I keep my voice low, in case she has a headache. "Do you need anything else?"

"No, that's perfect. Thank you. I'm sorry, I know it's Valentine's Day. I didn't know who else to call." Her voice cracks, and my chest aches at the sound.

"Don't be sorry, sweetheart. I'll be there soon. Do you want me to stay on the phone?"

"Yes, please."

I throw electrolyte packets, crackers, and Tylenol into a gym bag then rush out the door, all while narrating my actions to Sutton.

"My GPS says I'll be there in less than ten minutes," I say as I pull out of my driveway.

Sutton doesn't say anything in response. I take the curve out of my neighborhood at a speed my grandmother would not be happy about, but getting to Sutton fast is too important to waste time. After another beat of silence, I start to worry.

"I'm going to need you to say something so I know you're all right."

"I'm here," she rasps.

"Good girl. Just hang tight, I'll be there soon."

"Okay."

"I'm going through the intersection next to Walmart," I narrate so she knows how close I am. "Do you remember when we tried to see how long we could stay in Walmart without getting kicked out?" Maybe talking about the past will keep her mind off the pain.

"Yeah," she says in a low voice. "You and Brock got caught, so I won."

"My grandma grounded me for two weeks because of that." I pull into her apartment complex parking lot. "I just parked."

"Okay, I'm in my bedroom when you get inside," she whispers.

I find her door fast, still talking her through each step I take.

"I'm looking for the key now," I say, dropping the bag so I can find the faux succulent she told me about. After finding it, I type in the code and get the key, then unlock the door.

In my frantic search for her room, I open a bathroom door by accident, but open the one to her bedroom after. Sutton is curled up in her bed, shivering beneath the covers. She's pale and a sheen of sweat covers her face. I rush over to her, brushing her hair back from her warm forehead with the hand that doesn't have a brace on it. I'm sure velcro sticking to her hair wouldn't be pleasant.

"I'm here," I whisper. "I'm going to get you some water, okay?"

She nods in response.

I head to her kitchen and mix the electrolytes into a glass of water, then find a straw to put in it.

She raises her hand to take the cup from me, but I place the straw to her lips and murmur, "Just drink, I'll hold it for you,"

She takes a sip with her eyes closed, her face twisted up in pain. Eventually, she pulls away, letting out a heavy sigh.

"Thank you."

"Sutton, you're pretty sick. I think you should try to eat soon and take some Tylenol." Her expression morphs into one that shows her distaste for that idea. "I know, I know, but you need to. We'll give it a minute to make sure this sits in your stomach."

She shivers again, only increasing my worry for her. I don't know if I should take her to the hospital. She'd probably refuse to go, the stubborn woman that she is.

"So cold," she says through chattering teeth.

"You definitely have a fever." I comb my fingers through her hair, looking around the room for another blanket.

"That feels good," she hums, and I smile down at her, happy to help her feel even minutely better. I let my eyes wander around her room as she rests, chuckling to myself when I see just how much blue she's decorated with. Her comforter is blue, and while she has a lot of creams and whites, there are touches of her favorite color everywhere.

"I knew your favorite color hadn't changed."

She hums, mumbling something under her breath that I can't make out. I can tell she's close to falling back asleep, but I can't let her do that just yet, not without eating.

"Are you up to eating something?" I ask in a gentle tone. She scrunches up her nose, but gives me a reluctant nod. "Do you want me to bring you food in here, or do you want to go to the living room?"

"I'm not sure if I can walk yet."

I take that as her wanting to be in the living room, so I carefully scoop her up bridal style. My wrist throbs with the weight, but I ignore it. Sutton is more important.

She wraps her arms tight around my neck. "What are you doing?" Her voice is shaky, so I meet her eyes and give her what I hope is a reassuring look.

"You said you didn't think you could walk, so I'm carrying you. Is that okay?" Probably should have asked that *before* I picked her up, but knowing her she'd refuse since she hates being babied.

She merely bobs her head in response, before relaxing in my arms, her face pressed against my neck. There's another unforgettable feeling to add to the list of moments that will haunt me when I'm lying in bed alone.

I slowly walk to the living room, doing my best not to jostle her too much, then set her down on the couch. After that, I make her some more electrolyte water and grab the package of butter crackers I brought with me, along with a large bowl in case she gets sick again.

"Here you go, beautiful," I say and inwardly reprimand myself. I should be more careful with my words. But it's hard to hold back when she's vulnerable like this. All I want to do is wrap her up in my arms until she feels better.

"Thank you."

I sit down on the other end of the couch as she begins to eat. "How about I put on *Star Wars*?"

"*Episode II*?" she suggests, and I smile.

"I wouldn't choose anything else for you."

Her smile is weak, but I can tell she appreciates my words. I find the movie and turn it on. While she eats, I try to make myself useful instead of staring at her to make sure she's all right.

I remember seeing a few dishes in the sink, so I head to the kitchen and work on unloading and loading the dishwasher. Since her apartment living area is open concept, I can keep a more subtle eye on her while she eats and still be productive. I open the dishwasher and remember her calling me while *washing dishes* with a smile.

I don't think I'll ever let go of that detail. There's a lot of things I'm going to hold on to that have happened over the past few weeks. Sutton staked her claim in my heart and mind years ago, but being around her so much lately has only increased her territory. I'm so wrapped up in her that if it's not me and Sutton in the end–a thought I try not to dwell on–I don't know how I'll be able to unravel myself enough to think of anyone else.

She's in everything. I see her everywhere. When I'm in the grocery store and I see kombucha, she's there. If I turn on the radio and they play an old One Direction song, I think of how she used to listen to their music on repeat in middle school. When I see snow, I see her in each flake that falls, the dreamy look she always gets on the first snow day. And if I walk into the ice cream aisle, I recall how after her bad breakups she'd turn on *A Walk to Remember* and cry into a pint of brownie batter ice cream once she thought everyone was asleep. Every childhood memory, every teenage mishap, she was there in some way.

And even if I managed to forget all of those details, I'd have to give up hockey to get rid of her. Every time I step out on the ice, I think of her. Of her furrowed brow as she competed in figure skating, of the way she cheered Brock and me on in high school. How adorable she looks in her oversized Rockets hoodie. Not to mention the fact that I can't look at my own wrist without thinking of her gentle touch.

All of these memories are why I have to be patient and careful. Mason did a number on her. I grip the plate I'm putting into the dishwasher, resisting the urge to break it. He hurt her badly, and now I have to bide my time while she heals and show her what she deserves. That's okay though, because I'd wait forever for Sutton.

After I start the dishwasher and wipe down her counters with some disinfectant spray I found under her sink–which was meticulously organized in true Sutton fashion–I head back to the living room to check on the woman who's been occupying my thoughts.

I sit down on the couch, leaving a cushion between us so she doesn't feel crowded. I watch as she takes two Tylenol, then looks over at me with red-rimmed eyes.

"Are you staying here?" she asks.

"If that's okay with you," I reply.

She nods, then surprises me by lying down, her head in my lap. My eyes widen, but neither of us say a word. Me, because I don't want to ruin this. And Sutton because, who knows? The fever must be affecting her decision making. I'd sooner believe that over her consciously choosing to lie on me.

I brush her hair out of her face, and she looks up at me. I worry that I've gone too far, but she doesn't look upset.

"You have pretty eyes," she says.

I let out a surprised laugh. "Thank you, so do you."

"Connor said my eyes are like bricks."

I frown. "No, your eyes are like chocolate truffles or hot coffee. They're beautiful." The eyes I'm describing start to fall shut.

"Your eyes are like the ocean." She blinks a few times, trying to stay awake. "They're my favorite color. Blue is my favorite color, remember?"

I tug her blanket up to her chin to make sure she keeps warm.

"I remember; I'd never forget anything about you," I whisper as she falls asleep.

I am so in love with her it hurts.

Once she's drifted off, I stare down at her and find myself in an emotional tug-of-war. I'm torn between wishing that she'll forget all of this when she gets better, and hoping that she remembers every word.

I decide to enjoy the time I do have with her, and resolve to face whatever comes after this head on. Who knows? Maybe this could all lead to the woman of my dreams cuddling with me every night.

Chapter Twenty-Two

Sutton Jones

I blink open my eyes. They immediately start to water, feeling as though someone poured sand into them. I rub them with a groan, pushing up off the pillow I was sleeping on. I take in my surroundings, frowning when I realize I'm in my living room. How did I get here?

My front door clicks, and I whip my head over, heart in my throat until none other than Shaw Daniels walks in with a series of grocery bags.

Am I hallucinating?

"Oh, you're awake," Shaw says as he drops the grocery bags in my kitchen. "How are you feeling?"

He walks toward me wearing a small smile, and that's when my memories decide to push through the haze surrounding my mind. I called him, and he came and took care of me. I reach up and touch my forehead, then my hair, as if the evidence of his gentle touch would be tangible. There are a few memories still covered in shadows, but there's enough there for me to be thoroughly confused.

"Jones?" Shaw's voice breaks through my reverie. I look up at him. "Are you okay?"

"I'm fine, I feel a lot better."

"Good," he breathes out, sounding relieved. He lifts his hand toward my forehead, but I lean away.

"What are you doing?" It could be the low light in my living room, but I swear his cheeks tint pink.

"I was going to check if you're still warm, is that all right?"

"Oh, uh, sure." The back of his hand is cool against my skin, and I have to resist the urge to close my eyes and lean into his touch.

"I think your fever has gone down, but just to be safe, I bought a thermometer. After I wash it, we can see what it says."

"You didn't need to do that. I have one in my bathroom."

"You've been pretty out of it, and I didn't want to go through your stuff any more than I had to." He shoots me another smile before heading back into the kitchen. I watch as he unloads the bags. Vegetables, pasta, chicken, medicines, and a thermometer get placed on the counter.

"What's all of that for?" I ask him.

"I went to the store to get soup, but then I remembered how you hate canned soup, so I called your mom and got the recipe she made when we were kids. Don't worry though, I told her it was for me. I know how she gets when you or Brock are sick."

I'm back to my hallucination theory from earlier, because there is no way Shaw did all of this on top of everything he's already done.

"You're going to make me soup?" I can't keep the shock out of my voice.

"Yes, Jones, I am."

"Why?"

He looks up from the bags he's unloading. "What do you mean, why?"

"Why did you come? Why are you still here? Just why?"

Shaw's eyes meet mine, an emotion I can't discern hidden in their tropical blue depths. "Why did you call?"

His question is a challenge, one that I'm not ready to answer. I tug my blanket up to my chin, suddenly feeling the brunt of the vulnerable position I put myself in. I hate being sick, or needing anyone for anything. If I could have taken care of myself, I would have, simply to avoid having anyone see me like this. But I couldn't take care of myself, so I called Shaw. And ... he came.

Shaw, the guy who could have any girl he wants, is spending his Valentine's Day making soup for me. He starts to chop vegetables, not pushing me to answer his question. We're both dancing around something, but what? Sure, we've had moments of tension and closeness, but is that all?

Maybe the proximity of working together has intensified the attraction to him that's always been there. Of course I ignored that attraction because he's *Shaw*. But lately it's been harder to ignore. Especially when he's rolling up the sleeves of his henley to cook for me. I've seen him shirtless before, but something about his forearms is making me feel like my fever is back.

"I know what you're thinking, I'd make a sexy chef," he teases and I roll my eyes, trying to cover up the fact that I was checking him out.

"I was just in shock that the man who put foil in the microwave knew how to cook."

"I was in sixth grade!" He shakes his head while I laugh. "You're never going to let me live that down, are you?"

"Setting the microwave on fire is too good of a memory to let go."

"And what about you?" He raises a brow, and I sit up straighter.

"I'm a fantastic cook, thank you."

"Don't think I forgot about when you burned your brownies so bad they turned into charcoal. And that was in high school."

"I never said I was a baker," I reply.

The deep sound of his laughter fills up my apartment with a warmth it hasn't seen since I moved in. I wouldn't have thought Shaw would be the first person I had over, but here we are.

"That's fair, but I don't think you need to be a baker to make boxed brownies."

I cringe at the memory of that burnt smell. It permeated the house for weeks, as did the stench of my sadness when the boyfriend I was making them for broke up with me for his ex. My recollection of that time makes me look at Shaw in a new light.

"You brought brownies to school the next day," I say as I remember how dejected I felt going to school on Valentine's Day with nothing but a lame card for my boyfriend. Shaw bought brownies from the grocery store and handed them to me before first period.

"Oh yeah, I forgot about that," he says as he drops chopped onion into a pot.

"I asked you if you'd poisoned them, and made you eat one to be sure. You took a bite, then held it out to me to take one too."

He smiles. "Sounds like us."

"I never thanked you," I realize aloud.

I look over at him, and he shrugs. "It was just a box of brownies."

But it wasn't. It was a sweet gesture that I brushed off because Shaw was the one who did it. How many times have I done that? My head swims and my heart starts to pick up speed. I start to feel sick, but not from the flu. No, I'm sick with the thought that there's a chance I've misunderstood my relationship with Shaw for years.

"Jones, are you okay?"

"I'm fine," I blurt and stand up. "I'm going to take a shower. I feel gross." I'm fully aware that while my reasoning is sound, my delivery is far from eloquent. The look on Shaw's face confirms that as I stumble over my blankets toward my bedroom. I slam the door shut, muffling any response from him.

After going into my master bathroom, I turn the shower on as hot as I can stand it. I can't remember if hot showers are good or bad when you're sick, but I need to burn and scrub away the ick that's stuck to me. The water stings my skin upon entering the shower, but I push through, putting my head under the stream to ensure that every inch of me–including my scalp–will be bright red by the time I'm done.

My mind is racing. I feel as though I've been strapped into a roller coaster of memories against my will, barreling at hypersonic speed through my childhood and teenage years. It's harder to find a memory without Shaw than it is to find one with him. He's been in my life since kindergarten. From pulling on my pigtails on the playground, to punching my boyfriend in middle school, to getting my prom date to bail on me. He was–and is–a menace.

But my brain doesn't allow me to sit in my comfortable perception of Shaw. Suddenly, I recall moments where Shaw has been kind and caring. Like in seventh grade when I twisted my ankle skating on his grandmother's pond and he carried me off the ice, then wrapped my ankle. Or when my boyfriend broke up with me—the one Shaw brought the brownies for—he convinced the lunch ladies to give us ice cream so we could make our own brownie batter ice cream. And now, he's standing in my kitchen making my mom's chicken noodle soup for me, on Valentine's Day, after I told him he couldn't play the sport he loves more than anything.

Emotion lodges in my throat as I realize how often Shaw has taken care of me with little gratitude on my side. There's no doubt that he's been annoying and mischievous and wild all of our lives, but he's not just those things. It's like I've been wearing the same pair of glasses all my life, only to be given a new prescription at twenty-three years old.

I turn off the shower and reach for my towel, only to find there's not one on the shelf I usually put it on. I rip open the shower curtain and my eyes bounce around the steam-filled room, trying to find anything helpful. There's not even a clean hand towel, because I used the one in here to clean myself up when I got sick. And all my clean towels are in a hall closet.

No big deal, I'll just go into my bedroom and dry off with a blanket or something. Only ... I can't remember if I shut my bedroom door. I squeeze my eyes shut, desperately trying to recall whether I shut both my bedroom and bathroom doors, but I can't remember.

"No, no, no," I whisper, shivering as the cold starts to set in. The water droplets going down my body are turning into ice the longer I stand here. While I don't know if my hot shower was bad for me, I do know standing here with a wet head in the cool air can't be good for me. At least, that's what Shaw's grandma always said.

Resigned to my fate, I pull the curtain closed, peek my head around it, and call out, "Shaw!"

I hear one door open and I grip the curtain in a mixture of agitation and embarrassment. I *did* close my bedroom door.

"Jones, did you call for me?"

"Yeah," I say on a sigh. He cracks open the door and my heart skips even though I can't see him.

"Is everything okay?" he asks.

"Everything is fine, I just forgot to grab a towel."

The door opens the rest of the way to reveal a smirk that makes me remember why he's been my enemy all these years. He leans against the doorway, crossing his arms over his chest, those muscular forearms of his still on display. His blue eyes sparkle with mischief, then flick down and for a split second I panic that I'm uncovered, but then I realize he's looking at my bathtub, not me.

"That looks like a great place to wash dishes," he teases. I shut the curtain the rest of the way to hide my now flaming face. "Aw, come on, it's not as fun to tease you if I can't see your reactions."

"Are you going to get me a towel or not, Daniels?" I ask in a tight voice, crossing my arms over my chest, which only serves to remind me of just how *naked* I am. "I'm cold."

"Where are your towels?"

"In the hall closet next to my bathroom."

I listen as he leaves the room, then comes back again.

"Here you go," he says and I peek out to see him extending the towel toward me. Surprisingly, his eyes are averted, as if he doesn't want to accidentally see me.

I go to grab the towel, and it's then that I notice the black silk hair tie on his wrist. I freeze, staring at it. Does he wear that all the time? My chest warms with an unfamiliar feeling, or at least unfamiliar when it comes to Shaw.

"Uh, Jones, are you going to grab the towel any time soon? I'm trying to be respectful, but the longer I stand here the longer my curiosity might get the better of me." There's laughter in his tone, but I snatch the towel away as if his words are a threat and quickly wrap it around my freezing body.

"You can go now."

"Are you sure?" He pauses. "In all seriousness, I want to make sure you're okay. I can find you a robe if you need one to keep warm, or bring your clothes in here so you don't have to go far."

"No, I'm fine."

He starts to leave and I scrunch my face up, realizing what I haven't done.

"Wait," I call out. His footsteps stop. "Thank you," I say in a quiet voice. "For taking care of me while I'm sick, and bringing the towel and buying those brownies in high school."

"You're welcome," he says and I can hear the smile in his voice.

After he leaves, I brush my teeth and do my skincare routine at a slow pace. I'm not ready to see him with my emotions so raw. There's too much I'm still unsure about, but I can't hide away when he's in my kitchen.

So, I decide to face my fears. I get dressed in sweatpants and the UNC hoodie Brock gave me. I don't wear it often; I prefer my Duke one, but I know it will make Shaw smile. It'll be my way of showing my gratitude better after all he's done today. Even if I don't know what to do with our changing relationship, I don't want to give him a reason to think I'm ungrateful ever again.

After I'm dressed, I take a deep breath and open my door, not ready to face all of this change, but willing to try anyway.

Chapter Twenty-Three

Shaw Daniels

"Oh come on, get it together, Michaelson!" I yell at the TV then look at Sutton. "Do you see this?"

"It's pathetic," she says, and I nod emphatically.

We're watching the Rockets game together after eating the soup I made. It wasn't as good as I remember Mama Jones making it, but Sutton seemed to enjoy it. She also seems to be doing a lot better, but I can tell her energy is still low since she's not yelling at the team with me.

The first period ends, and I groan. "We shouldn't be this bad."

"They're thrown off by you being gone. They'll get better once they get used to the feeling of not having you there." She's probably right, but it is hard not being there. Usually, I'd at least be on the bench, but I called Coach earlier saying I had a family emergency. Since I'm hurt anyway, he didn't put up much of a fight about me not coming.

I look over at Sutton. She's tugging the sleeves of her UNC hoodie down over her palms. Even though I'm a Rockets man, and my UNC days are behind me, it still made me grin when she came out in that beautiful baby blue top. Seeing it makes me think that maybe she wore it as a gesture of sorts. It could just be that she had nothing else to wear, but I have a feeling there's something more behind her decision.

"You know it's not your fault I'm not there, right? I was a jerk in the recovery center. Nothing I said was true."

She gives me a weak smile. "I know, but I'll still feel guilty if they lose."

"You shouldn't," I say, holding my wrist with the brace up. "You're helping me recover, not hurting me or the team."

"I'm glad you see it that way. Hopefully the rest of the team does too."

"I'm sure they do." And if they don't, I'll make sure they come to the correct understanding.

Sutton's phone buzzes and she checks it, letting out a weighted sigh.

"What's wrong?" I ask her, and she pulls her bottom lip in between her teeth. She doesn't say anything at first, glancing up at me for a second then back at the phone.

"Have you looked at any of the Rockets' fan pages?" she asks, catching me off guard.

"Not lately, no. I didn't want to check them after I got hurt. Those accounts blow everything out of proportion."

"You can say that again," Sutton mumbles.

I raise a brow. "Did they say something bad about you as a physical therapist?"

She gives her phone screen one last wary look before dropping it onto the cushion between us. I pick it up and my eyes widen in surprise. A collage of photos of Sutton and me from the charity event fills the screen. Some of the photos are cropped and zoomed in on my hand placement. The caption is even more intense than the carefully edited collage.

@alabamarocketslover: Do you see how low his hand is on her back?! And how he's leaning in to whisper in her ear??? Everyone else can mourn Shaw being off the market, but I'll be busy shipping these two. Shaw and his mystery girl are CLEARLY in love. I'm betting they're married by the end of the season.

"The caption says 'everyone else'. Does that mean there are more posts?" I hand Sutton her phone.

"So many more," she says with a pained expression. "Ariel showed them to me this morning, and there are already triple the posts from then. I don't even want to know if it's spread beyond Instagram."

"I guess my plan of making everyone think we were together worked."

"Yeah, a little too well," she says and I chuckle, which earns me a look.

"What? It's some harmless fan chatter. They don't even know who you are. If it makes you feel any better, tomorrow I'll talk to Brock about making a post denouncing the rumors."

"That would help, actually." She meets my eyes, vulnerability shining in her own. "I really don't want anyone making false allegations about my integrity as a physical therapist. There aren't any rules against dating players that I know of, but the media and fans can be vicious."

I reach out and squeeze her hand. "I'll get it straightened out, don't worry."

"Thank you." She flips her hand over and squeezes mine back. "I promise it has nothing to do with you. It's just that I want to be known for the work I do, not who I'm dating."

She's never touched me like this before. The feeling is so rare it feels like I won the Stanley Cup and an Olympic Gold medal in the same year. Her gaze is fixed on me and if she was feeling better, I'd risk it all and kiss her right now. But I can tell by the dark circles under her beautiful brown eyes that she needs more rest. There's a good chance this vulnerability was brought on by a need for sleep.

"I understand. You do great work, Sutton. No one in their right mind would question that."

"Even a player I benched because of a wrist injury?" she asks, and I smile.

"I wasn't in my right mind then, but since I am now, yeah, even me."

She smiles back at me, pulling her hand away. I miss her touch immediately. Man, I'm a sap for this woman. She tucks her hair behind her ear, and I look down to hide the lovestruck grin I'd bet is occupying my face. I might be a sap, but it's worth it. Sutton Jones is one of a kind, and I don't mind being a fool in love with her.

·♥·♥·♥·♥·♥·

I close my front door behind me with a sigh. After watching the game with Sutton, I left so she could get some rest. She could barely keep her eyes open and since she was feeling better, I had no excuse to stay with her. It's probably for the best anyway, I don't want to push her too much too soon. And my wrist is killing me.

I shouldn't have used my wrist so much, but I needed to in order to take care of her. Now I'm paying for all of the movement I did, but I don't even care because each ache and pain is a reminder of how much time I got to spend with her. On Valentine's Day, of all days. I chuckle to myself at the irony while pulling out an ice pack.

For the remainder of the night, I'll be icing my wrist and watching all the hockey games I usually miss because I'm too busy playing my own game. While I wish I was with the guys, it's not so bad having a night off after years of going nonstop.

Before I go to sit on the couch, I grab a packet of immunity-boosting powder and dump it in a shaker bottle, then fill it with water. I can't afford to be hurt *and* sick. After chugging the orange-flavored vitamin drink, I flop down on the couch and place the ice pack on my wrist. The cold stings, but I know soon enough it'll numb the ache.

I'm in the middle of a Mississippi Monsters game–that I'm only watching in order to scrutinize Mason–when my phone starts to buzz. I flip it over with my hand that doesn't have ice on it, and see the group chat with Miles, Emmett, and Jason going off.

Jason: Shaw, why am I finding out that you and Sutton are dating on TMZ?

Miles: The real question is why are you looking at TMZ?

Jason: To make sure I'm not on it. Which, thanks to Shaw, I'm not. Thanks, man!

Miles: I just checked. I forgot how hot Sutton is. I haven't seen her in a while.

Jason: Shaw is going to make sure you never hit a golf ball again if you keep talking about his girl.

Emmett: I'm going to make sure all of you can't compete in your respective sports if you don't quit texting me this late at night.

Miles: Aw, come on ET, this is important!

Jason: Who uses the word 'respective' in a text?

I sigh, questioning my taste in friends.

Shaw: Sutton and I aren't dating. We just danced at an event. I'm going to make a statement tomorrow about it.

Jason: Uh ... it's a little late for that. Everyone knows who she is now and I don't think they're going to let this story go.

My phone starts to buzz again, this time with a call from Brock. This can't be good.

"Hello?" I answer, my heart jumping up into my throat.

"I told Sutton not to end up on gossip sites with you, yet here we are."

"You told–what?" I stammer and he sighs, but he doesn't seem that upset.

"Are you and Sutton dating?"

"No, I would have told you if we were."

"Okay, well everyone online seems to think differently, which means we either need to tell everyone they're wrong or you need to hurry up and convince my sister to date you."

I let my head fall back against the couch. "I told her I'd make a statement, but that was before everyone found out who she was. I didn't think they'd find her so fast."

"These fan accounts are practically FBI agents with the way they dig stuff up. One of them made a video dissecting the photos and it went viral, which helped them find her faster."

"What do I do? Sutton told me very clearly that she didn't want people to think we were dating."

"I'll have Sherry write up a statement and create some posts for your social media accounts. It would help if you were back to your bachelor ways–"

"No, not an option."

"I figured you'd say that. I appreciate that you don't want to date anyone else while trying to win her over, but it's not going to help distance you from Sutton in the media."

"How bad will it be for her to be associated with me?"

"Well, your reputation isn't bad, so that helps. But the fact that she works for the Rockets makes this whole thing more scandalous than it would be if she was just a random woman you met. So far, the fans' response seems to be positive, but it could turn at any point."

I close my eyes, my head starting to pound from the stress of this situation. The last thing I need is another reason for Sutton to be frustrated with me. The dance at the event was my idea. And instead of being a nice memory, it's been turned into ammo aimed her way.

"Have you talked to her?" I ask.

"No, I wanted to talk to you first and come up with a plan."

"Call her and let her know. Tell her I'm sorry."

"You don't want to call her?"

"I think it'll be better coming from you if she hasn't already seen it. She was the one who showed me the accounts."

"When did she show you those? Aren't you at home?"

"I, uh ... went to her apartment. She's got the flu so I took her some stuff she needed."

"Uh-huh. Out of everyone she could have called, she called *you*, yet you're not dating." He sounds skeptical.

"Unfortunately, we're not. And I have a feeling this whole tabloid business isn't going to help my case."

"I'm sorry man, but this is a hazard of the job." He sighs. "I'll do my best to make this go away fast."

"Thanks. Let me know if there's anything else I can do."

"Will do. Talk to you later."

I hang up, throwing my phone down beside me with a sigh. Today I felt like I was getting somewhere with Sutton. But now? Now all my progress could be ruined by a few photos on the internet.

Chapter Twenty-Four

Sutton Jones

I press my ice roller under one eye, then the other, praying that the puffy red skin calms down. Today is my first day back at work since having the flu, and since having my identity plastered all over dozens of gossip sites and hundreds of social media accounts. I spent most of last night crying into a pint of brownie batter ice cream because when the accounts discovered me, they also uncovered my relationship with Mason.

Now everyone thinks my connection to Mason got me the internship for the team at Duke and that Shaw got me my job with the Rockets. Brock assured me that my job is safe. He handled contacting the Rockets' publicist, which was a blessing. And he told me Shaw would be releasing statements saying that we were just friends, nothing more.

I don't know if anyone will believe those statements though, which has me worried for what work will be like. The only thing keeping me from curling up in bed and not going is the encouraging messages from friends and family that keep rolling in. Oh, and the Shaw and Sutton fans. While I don't want people to think we're in a relationship, the people who are 'shipping' us seem to be passionate about defending my integrity as a physical therapist.

I turn on a confidence boosting playlist and try to feign a bravado that I don't have as I get ready for the day. Thankfully, makeup manages to cover up the signs of my breakdown. Once my makeup is done and my hair is in a ponytail, I throw on my favorite oversized Rockets hoodie and walk out the door.

I leave the radio off as I drive to work, soaking in the silence before what I'm sure is going to be a chaotic day. If I make it through the day without crying, it'll be a miracle worthy of celebration.

The arena is quiet when I arrive, and I'm glad I pushed myself to come in early even though I barely slept last night. It will be good to have some time alone before everyone gets here. I can organize the med cart again to give my brain something to focus on other than the awfulness that is my life right now.

I flip on the lights to the recovery center and gasp when I see a figure in the center of the room. But when the figure doesn't move, the terror fades some.

"Is that..." I trail off, letting out a disbelieving laugh. Propped up next to a gift bag is a lifesize cutout of Anakin Skywalker. There's a t-shirt pulled over him that says *I love Sutton Jones*.

I walk closer, my heart still pounding from the shock of seeing what I thought was a person waiting for me.

Stuck to his forehead is a blue sticky note that reads:

I thought you could use a laugh and someone to point to whenever people ask who you're dating.

I know right away that this gift is from Shaw. I'd know his handwriting anywhere. I smile and stick the note in my hoodie pocket. Then I pick up the bag off the ground and set it on my exam table, looking inside. There's a bottle of strawberry kombucha, a t-shirt that matches the one on the cutout, except this one says *I love Anakin Skywalker*, and a box with a sticker that says it's from a local bakery.

I open the box and I have to swallow down the emotion that rises like a tsunami. Inside is a brownie with Happy Valentine's Day written on top in Tiffany blue icing.

I pull out my phone and press call on Shaw's contact.

"Hey, Jones," he greets and my stomach swoops at the sound of his voice, though I'm not sure why. I've heard his voice a million times.

"Thank you for my gifts," I say, pressing my lips together as tears sting my eyes. "This was pretty sweet of you, Daniels."

"Nah, it's not sweet. It's just standard I'm-sorry-that-everyone-thinks-you're-my-girlfriend treatment."

I laugh. "Still, I appreciate it. Though I think if someone got in here before me and saw this brownie it would be hard to convince them I'm not dating anyone."

"Yeah, that's why I got here early, and I've been watching to make sure no one went in before you."

I turn around, looking about the room as if he's going to pop out of a supply closet. "Where are you?"

"About to walk into the locker room. I wanted to give you everything myself, but I figured if someone saw us together that would be counterproductive."

I raise a brow. "So you just watched me from afar like a stalker."

"Not just a stalker, a really *good* stalker, because you didn't even know I was there."

I laugh at his words, shaking my head. "Good stalkers probably don't tell the person they're watching that they're watching them."

"That sounds like the quality of a *great* stalker. I'm sure with practice I'll reach that point."

It's then I realize I haven't stopped smiling since I got on the phone with him. He made all the worries about today disappear for a few moments. Footsteps sound behind me, and I shove the brownie box in the bag, my blissful moment gone. I put the bag behind my med cart.

"Hey Sutton, who's your friend?" Connor asks with a laugh as he walks in.

"Is that Connor?" Shaw asks.

I smile at Connor and point at my phone to let Connor know I'm on it. He nods in response.

"Yeah," I reply. "I should go."

"Same here. Let me know if anyone gives you a hard time today. I'll make sure it doesn't happen more than once." His serious tone sends a chill down my spine. Looking back, I guess Shaw has always been protective over me. But it was annoying then. Now ... well now I might need to walk outside to cool off.

"I will."

"Good girl. I'll see you later, Jones." His words sound more like a thrilling promise than a casual goodbye.

"See you," I whisper then hang up.

I feel lightheaded and too warm after the end of that call. Butterflies are occupying my stomach, and I don't know what to do with them. Butterflies and Shaw Daniels shouldn't mix.

"How are you feeling?" Connor asks, and I slowly look up, still in a daze.

"Much better," I reply, trying to gather my bearings. I look at the Anakin cutout and realize I don't have an explanation for him. "A friend sent me this as a prank," I blurt out.

"That's pretty funny," Connor says, but I can tell he doesn't get it. But that's because it's meant for me, and Shaw knew me well enough to know this would make me smile every time I saw it today.

I move the cutout to the corner of the room and start to prep my station for the day. While I'm spraying disinfectant on the exam table, Connor speaks again.

"I heard congratulations are in order."

My brows furrow. "What do you mean?"

"I heard you and Shaw are together, that it's pretty serious."

I shake my head, my ponytail whipping side to side with the frantic movement.

"That's just a rumor. We're not together."

Connor smiles. "It's okay, you don't have to spare my feelings. I've seen the way he looks at you."

"No, really, there's nothing between us," I try to tell him, but it's clear he's not listening. Before I can formulate an explanation, two players–Sawyer and Danny–walk in. Their attention is immediately on the cutout, laughing when I tell them it was a prank from a friend.

I let out a sigh of relief when neither of them ask about Shaw. Maybe today will go better than I thought.

· ♥ · ♥ · ♥ · ♥ · ♥ ·

I'm smiling as I disinfect my station for the last time today. *Smiling.* I thought I'd be fighting tears, but it's been a surprisingly normal work day. Not a single person asked me about Shaw, or even hinted at the photos online. After Connor's congrats, he didn't bring it up again, and none of the players said anything when I saw them. I couldn't have asked for a better first day back.

There are probably a bunch more posts and rumors online, but so long as this isn't affecting my everyday life, I don't care. Let the fans have their fun and the gossips tear me down from afar.

The sound of someone knocking draws my eyes to the recovery center door. Shaw walks in, and I smile big at him. His eyes light up, and he smiles back.

"What's got you in such a good mood?" he asks.

"I thought today was going to be terrible, but it wasn't," I announce.

"That's good to hear. I was worried about you today." My chest warms at his words. "Coach asked me to come in and get my wrist checked out. I figured after hours would be best so that we didn't have so many eyes on us. Do you have time?"

"Of course, I was just cleaning up." I pat the table. He hops up on it and starts to take off his brace.

"So no one bothered you today?" he asks as I sanitize my hands.

"Not a single person. It was amazing. I mean, Connor asked me about it at the beginning of the day, but none of the players said a word. I was pleasantly surprised."

He rubs his hand over his mouth, hiding a smile. "Good, that's good."

I narrow my eyes at him. "What aren't you telling me?"

"What do you mean?" He gives me a faux innocent look.

"You have that look that says you know something I don't. It's the same look you had when you rigged the homecoming election so that you'd be homecoming king instead of Ricky." Ricky was the captain of the football team and my boyfriend at the time. We were going to be king and queen and get to ride on the float together. Everyone told us we were a shoo in, but come announcement day, Shaw was the one being crowned, wearing the same smirk he is right now.

"I didn't rig the election. I just convinced everyone to vote for me instead." I roll my eyes, not believing him for a second. "But if you insist on knowing, I threatened all of the guys so they wouldn't talk to you about the photos."

My mouth drops open. "You did not."

"Sure did. I told them if any of them said a word to you about it that I wouldn't be the only player on the bench with an injury."

"*Shaw!*" I hit his shoulder, but he just laughs. "Why would you say that to them?"

"Because I knew they'd all mess with you about it if I didn't, and you don't deserve to deal with that." He runs a hand through his hair. "I'm sure they'll interpret my words as being protective over you as my girlfriend, but I'd rather them think that and not say it than tease you."

"You didn't need to do that," I tell him as I start to examine his wrist. I huff. "I'm a grown woman, I can take care of myself."

"I know that," he says, taking one of my hands in his. "But you don't have to do it all alone."

I look up at him, those dreadful butterflies swarming to life once again. "I feel like you've done too much for me already. I don't know how to repay you."

"You don't owe me anything." He pauses, his blue eyes boring into mine. "Ever. Okay?"

"Okay," I whisper. As if it has a mind of its own, my thumb traces a circle on Shaw's hand. "I still feel like I should thank you in some way."

Sapphire eyes, burning with something that looks a whole lot like desire, glance at my lips. I draw in a deep breath, feeling as though everything is about to change. Shaw leans in ever so slightly. It feels like he's inviting me to step into something more, but as I try to gather the courage to do it, I come up short.

I step back, pulling my hand from his. I can't do this. The past few days in the public eye have given me another reason to stay away from hockey players. Not to mention the fact that a kiss would start something between us that, if it ended badly, would result in a rift between Brock and Shaw. I can't do that, not when Shaw has so little family of his own.

It's all too much, too fast. Kissing him would be acting on impulse. I don't do impulsive. I do carefully thought out, meticulously planned.

"Your wrist looks good," I say to him, clearing my throat. "Keep doing what you're doing, and you should be back on the ice soon."

He smiles, but there's something about it that looks a little sad. "Thanks."

"No problem."

He puts the brace back on and heads out, throwing a *drive safe* over his shoulder that makes my chest ache, though I can't figure out why. And when I collect my gift from him on my way out of the recovery center, I find myself wondering what would have happened if I'd taken the chance and kissed him. I guess I'll never know.

Chapter Twenty-Five

Sutton Jones

"I'm never going on another date again," Ariel says when she answers my FaceTime call.

"You said that last week," I point out.

"This time I mean it. I had the worst time today, and I thought this guy was the one!"

I snort. "You said that last time too. You need to stop saying every guy you meet is the one." I tap my nail polish bottle against the palm of my hand to mix it up.

"All of them *might* be the one," she says, and I shake my head at her. "What color are you doing this time?"

When we were roommates, Ariel and I would sit down every two weeks and paint each other's nails. Now, we get on FaceTime to chat while we do them, using phone stands so that our hands are free. There are times when I'd rather go to the salon for the ease of it, but I'd never give up this tradition with my best friend.

"Black, for the big game this week. What about you?"

"I was going to do purple, but I'll do black as well to show my support." She gives me a look of concern. "How are you feeling about seeing Mason again?"

This week we play Mason's team, which is also a notorious rivalry game. I'm confident the Rockets will win–we're the better team–but I know this game has a tendency to get violent. Hockey is already a bloody sport, but rivalry games can be vicious.

"I saw him at the charity event not that long ago. If I can make it through him making out with a swimsuit model in front of me, I can make it through watching him play. It should be fun to watch Shaw wipe the floor with him."

I start to paint my thumb with the glossy black shade.

"Interesting that you called Shaw by name, but not anyone else on the team."

"He's our star player, Ari."

"Mhmm, I'm sure that's why you said it."

I give her a look. "It was. Don't make this into a thing." I point the nail polish brush at her, before moving on to my next nail.

"It is a thing. You blush every time he gets brought up, and when we talk somehow he always comes up."

"That is not true, you're exaggerating."

"I am not. You *like* Shaw," she says in the way an elementary school girl would.

"No, I don't." I focus on painting my nails, keeping my head down.

"Sutton Rae Jones, look at me," she demands. I reluctantly look at my phone. "Now tell me you don't like him."

"What do you want me to say?" I ask, twisting shut the nail polish bottle. "Do you want me to say that I feel like I can't breathe when he looks at me? Or that I look forward to arguing with him more than I've looked forward to any date ever? Or how about the fact that we almost kissed the other day, again?"

"Any of those work," Ariel says with a Cheshire cat grin.

"No, no smiling! This isn't good." I cover my face with my hands. "He's a hockey player!"

"He's nothing like Mason, we've been over this. You're hiding behind that because you're afraid of getting hurt."

"Ouch," I mumble, letting my hands fall away from my face. "Be nicer."

She sighs. "I know Mason hurt you, but that doesn't mean every hockey player will. I supported your ban at the beginning, but Shaw isn't a random player. You've known him for years."

"That's the problem," I say and she gives me a confused look. "Shaw grew up with us. He's like family. What if this goes badly? My family is the only family he has outside of his grandmother."

"That is difficult to navigate," Ariel admits. "But do you really think your family would excommunicate Shaw just because you broke up?"

"If it got messy enough, maybe."

She nods as if she's realizing something. "And now we're back to your fears. You're operating under the assumption that Shaw is going to break your heart."

"I'm being realistic," I try to defend myself.

"I think the word you were looking for is pessimistic."

"Thanks for your help," I droll, and she laughs.

"If I didn't tell you the truth I wouldn't be a good best friend."

"I know, we've always been up front with each other." I toy with my nail polish bottle, twisting the top open, then shut. "I *am* scared of getting heartbroken again, but I don't know what to do about that."

"You find someone worth facing the fear for," Ariel says in a gentle voice. "Someone you can see loving with all that you have."

"And you think that's Shaw?"

She shrugs. "Doesn't matter what I think. What do *you* think?"

I lean back against my headboard. After all the time I've spent with Shaw over the course of my life, this should be an easy question to answer. But our history makes this harder in a way. There are so many emotions and memories tangled up in my mind that it's hard to dissect how I really feel about him.

I've started to have feelings for him, sure. But can I risk heartbreak for him? I don't know.

"I don't know," I repeat the tail end of my train of thought out loud. "I have no idea what to think right now."

"There's no rush. Just take your time. And if you decide he's the one, then jump."

"Okay, I'll think it over," I say, then change the subject to get the spotlight off me. "Now, tell me about your bad date."

Chapter Twenty-Six

Shaw Daniels

Today is the day I've been waiting for since Mason Walker got drafted into the NHL. The opportunity to play him and beat him is one I don't plan on squandering. Mason's always been an egotistical tool who thinks he's better than everyone else. In college, he'd trash talk every game, even though we beat his team over and over.

Even if he hadn't broken Sutton's heart and treated her terribly over the course of their relationship, I'd still find joy in showing him up tonight. But since he's also done those things, it will make my victory that much sweeter.

I clench my jaw as I stretch my wrist. I've been cleared to play tonight, but I want to make sure I'm in perfect condition before touching the ice. So, I'm sitting on a bench in the training gym, thoroughly stretching all of my muscles and working out any tightness I come across.

"How's your wrist doing?" Sawyer asks as he finishes a set of bicep curls.

"It's a little tight," I say, "but it'll be good by the game tonight."

"Good, we're going to need you."

"We'd win with blindfolds on. You don't need me, but I'm glad I'll be there."

He racks the weights he was using, then wipes his face on his t-shirt. "You know they tend to play dirty."

"Yeah, and run their mouths. But we're the better team."

Sawyer cringes.

"What? Do you disagree?"

"No, we are the better team." He scratches his neck. "And they do like to run their mouths, especially your favorite player."

Sawyer knows about my disdain for Mason. He only had to watch one press interview to agree with my assessment of him. "What did he say?"

Sawyer sighs, taking out his phone and clicking a few times before handing it to me. An Instagram post with a photo of Mason and his new fiancée is what I see first, but it's the caption that makes my blood boil.

@nhlgossip: Our sources say Mason Walker has been posting plenty of trash talk to his private story on Snapchat. Quotes like "The Rockets are amateurs" and "I'll show Shaw Daniels what real hockey looks like" have been sent in to us. But the real heavy hitters involve Sutton Jones, Rockets' physical therapist and Shaw's alleged girlfriend: "I'm not surprised Sutton and Shaw are dating. Sutton always had a thing for men in uniform," says Mason while smoking a cigar in his new corvette. "Shaw can enjoy my leftovers. And when he gets tired

of putting up with her, I'm sure she'll find another player to latch on to."

I hand Sawyer his phone back so that I don't throw it across the room.

"I'm going to destroy him," I grind out.

"I thought that would be your reaction." Sawyer gives me a look that makes me feel like a kid being warned by his dad. "Just don't let your emotions get the best of you. If you get too caught up in enacting revenge on Mason, you could cost us the game."

"Oh believe me, I'm going to be laser-focused. We're going to win, and Mason is going to learn to keep Sutton's name out of his mouth."

Sawyer's expression turns wary. "This is going to make for an interesting game."

·♥·♥·♥·♥·♥·

I can hear my blood rushing in my ears as the pregame sequence plays. The fans are already rowdy tonight, chanting 'Rockets' over and over. My heart is pounding in my chest and my limbs are filled with a restless anticipation for what's to come. Soon enough, we'll be out on the ice and I'll make sure Mason regrets everything he said.

"Daniels!" Sutton's voice echoes through the tunnel, and I whip my head around to see her running up the tunnel toward me.

"What are you doing in here? As great as your skating is, I don't think they'll let you play with us."

We both laugh.

"I didn't get to talk to you earlier because I was busy working on the other guys," she yells over the music. "I just wanted to wish you good luck."

I smile down at her. "You don't need luck when you're the best," I say and she rolls her eyes, a smile pulling at her lips. "But thank you, I appreciate it."

She looks behind me as if she's checking if anyone is looking at us, then she wraps her arms around my waist in a hug. I wish I wasn't in all my gear right now so that I could fully appreciate this moment. Even so, it's a taste of everything I've ever wanted with Sutton. For her to be mine, and for me to be hers.

"I better not see you after the first period," she says when she pulls away, completely unaware that she just flipped my existence upside down. "No injuries, okay, Daniels?"

"I'll do my best," I reply, earning a smile from her.

"Okay, I have to go before someone catches me. See you later!" She smiles over her shoulder and jogs back down the tunnel, disappearing from sight right as it's time for the team to head out onto the rink.

I force myself to focus on the task at hand. As wonderful as it is to daydream about a life with Sutton, I've got something important to do *for* her in this arena.

The national anthem plays, and a few more ceremonies and announcements are completed before it's finally time to start. I skid to a stop at center ice, glaring at Mason who's preparing to face off against me. He's not as tall as me, likely right at six feet, but he does have a muscular build from years of hockey. I know I can best him though. And I will.

His smug grin has me ready to take off my gloves and fight, but I suck in a deep breath and focus. The ref drops the puck in between us and we both slap at it, trying to secure it. I get it first and immediately take it down toward the Monsters' goal.

Mason catches me and knocks me into the glass, but his hit isn't strong enough to slow me down. In fact it only makes me more determined. I keep possession of the puck, passing it over to Sawyer. He shoots and misses, and I watch Mason go after the puck as it slides behind the goal. I barrel toward him at full speed and make sure his face gets to know the glass real well.

He curses at me, but I don't bother responding because I have the puck again. I take a shot and make it. The arena erupts in cheers. I slap the hands of my teammates waiting on the bench, and even wave at Sutton who's cheering two rows behind the team.

After my brief celebration, the game is in full swing again. I knock Mason to the ice as I pass him. With each hit, Mason gets more and more aggressive, so I do the same.

Mason snags the puck and manages to score. His team cheers, but he doesn't go to celebrate with them, instead choosing to circle around me wearing a smug grin. I grit my teeth. No need to get a penalty *yet*. I do, however, slam him into the glass as soon as he's next to me again.

The first period ends, and the score is 1-1.

"What is wrong with you?" Sutton asks when I walk into the recovery center. Connor averts his eyes as she drags me over to her station. "Are you trying to get hurt?"

"I need you to re-tape my wrist," I say instead of answering her question.

Sutton glares at me and rips off the tape that's gotten too loose over the course of the period. I'm pretty sure she usually cuts the tape off, so her ripping it is a testament to how angry she is.

"Why are you antagonizing Mason so much? It's unnecessary," she scolds as she aggressively tapes my wrist. I clench my jaw against the pain.

"I'm playing the game, that's all."

"I've been watching hockey since I was born, Daniels. I know when a player is gunning for another player. Is your old college rivalry that important to you?"

I have to resist laughing in her face. For such an incredibly intelligent woman, she really is oblivious to the fact that all of this—really everything I do—is for her. A part of me just wants to admit it to her right here and now. To watch her pretty mouth drop open in shock when I tell her I'm in love with her and fighting Mason on her behalf. But there's not enough time to properly do that, not in the middle of a game.

"It's about something deeper than that," I tell her. Her brow furrows. She'll have to deal with vague answers for now though.

"Just take your foot off the gas a little. Don't wind up hurt or suspended because of whatever this is between you two."

I don't commit to anything, rushing out of the room and yelling out *thanks* as I leave. There's no way I'm hitting the brakes now, not when things are starting to get good.

Chapter Twenty-Seven

Sutton Jones

Shaw—as per usual—did not listen to me after the first intermission. He's back out on the ice with as much intensity as before, if not more. My heart is in my throat and my whole body is buzzing with adrenaline. Shaw is an amazing player. He's strong and fast and smart. But right now he's only two of those things, because he must have left his brain in the locker room and traded it for a healthy dose of male ego.

It's foolish to blatantly go after Mason like this. I know as well as anyone that Mason is a jerk who talks a big game, but since he doesn't actually play at the level he talks, he's not worth the extra energy. The rivalry between the Rockets and Monsters is intense enough without all of this.

My stomach sloshes uncomfortably within me. I watch as Shaw gets hit by two players at the same time, falling on the ice. He gets right back up, but I'm still holding my breath until he speed skates off toward the puck again. I can't believe he's risking injury like this, after all that he went through with his wrist. There are bigger games than this one, and he's practically begging to be benched during them.

Shaw and Mason collide against the glass a few feet away from me. I can see Mason talking, and Shaw's face screws up in anger. Shaw pushes Mason and I groan. Everyone in the arena starts chanting *fight, fight, fight.*

"He's not worth it!" I yell out, but it's no use. Even if Shaw heard me over the crowd, I'm sure he wouldn't listen.

Mason and Shaw drop their gloves at the same time. They start in on each other and the ref watches from nearby, waiting to blow the whistle on the fight.

Shaw is the better fighter, but Mason manages to land a couple shots as well. I'm not even worried about Shaw getting unbelievably hurt at this point. Mason isn't much of a heavy hitter. I'm more worried about the five minutes he's about to spend in the penalty box.

Blood is quickly drawn on both players, but the referee doesn't blow the whistle until Mason hits the ground. Sawyer pulls Shaw back, and Shaw doesn't fight him. It occurs to me how in control Shaw seems right now. He knows exactly what he's doing. That only makes me more angry.

Both of the players are put in a penalty box and for the next five minutes, they're off the ice. I scowl at Shaw, but he's focused on watching the game, likely readying himself to jump back in as soon as he can.

Once he's back in the game, he doesn't fight Mason again, but he doesn't let up on him either. I'm grateful for every line change that takes Shaw off the ice at this point, worried that he's going to get another penalty or start playing sloppily and get injured. Miraculously, neither occurs before the end of the second period. The Rockets are up 3-1 and I am burning up with frustration toward Shaw. The team managed to score while he was in the penalty box, and then he scored again after he was out, but I couldn't care less at this point.

As soon as he enters the recovery center I ensure I'm the one taking care of him. We have other medical staff on hand for things like cuts and scrapes, but I tell them I've got it covered just so I can be the one to talk to him.

Shaw slumps into a chair, his chest heaving from playing hard. There's a cut on his cheekbone and dried blood down his face. There's another cut above his eyebrow. His hair is mussed and he's wearing a smirk that makes me want to throttle him.

"You are ridiculous," I hiss as I grab an alcohol pad and start wiping at the dried blood on his face. "I ask again: Why are you doing this? You don't have anything to prove to anyone. You were a number one draft pick taken out of college to play pro. Mason was chosen after he graduated and didn't even go in the first round. Everyone knows who's better."

"You forgot to mention my scoring record, that's pretty impressive too." One of the guys nearby, Killian, laughs and Shaw joins in.

I grab his chin and force him to look at me. "Whatever ego-driven nonsense this is, *quit it*."

His eyes darken and my blood heats with something very different from anger. A large hand envelopes my wrist, holding just firmly enough to let me know how strong he is.

"Careful, Jones," he says in a low voice, just loud enough for me to hear. "If you keep grabbing me like this, it might tempt me to do the same to you."

"You don't scare me, Daniels," I say and he chuckles, not even wincing when I use my other hand to press an alcohol pad to one of his cuts.

"I wasn't trying to scare you." His thumb caresses my pulse point, his gaze telling me *exactly* what he was trying to do.

I jerk my wrist out of his grasp, feeling flushed all over. Someone calls his name from behind, so he gets up, still a little bloody but not seeming to care.

"Don't make things worse than they are," I tell him, but he doesn't say anything. "Shaw, I'm serious."

He smiles down at me. "I know you are. Don't worry about me, Jones. Even though you look cute when you're concerned." He winks before leaving the recovery center.

Insufferable, infuriating, terrible–

"Uh, is everything okay?" Connor asks. I look up, realizing I must have been saying my thoughts out loud.

I fake a smile. "Peachy. Everything is just peachy." I walk out of the recovery center feeling more emotions than I know what to do with. All I know is that little conversation with Shaw is not the last he will be hearing from me about this.

·♥·♥·♥·♥·♥·

The Rockets won, which isn't surprising. It's frustrating because besides some time in the penalty box, Shaw experienced no consequences for his actions. He got to celebrate a big win and personally beat Mason in not one, but *two* fights. Mason left the ice during the third period with a bloody nose. I can't say I was devoid of satisfaction at seeing that, but it was unnecessary for Shaw to do that to him.

Mason wasn't the only one with blood all over him. My exam table has an inordinate amount of dried blood on it. Games between the Monsters and Rockets are infamous for being intense, but this is ridiculous. The paper I kept on the table didn't help much, neither did cleaning between periods. But that's okay, because it gives me something to take my anger out on while I wait for Shaw to meet me.

I texted him after the game to come to the recovery center after the press conference. He could avoid me and head to Sawyer's for the celebration party, but I know he won't. I'm sure he's dying to gloat about winning. He might think he's right, but he won't by the time I'm done with him.

All this time waiting has given me time to sit in my anger. The more I thought about everything, the angrier I got. He's supposed to be better than Mason, to be the bigger man. But instead, he sunk to Mason's level for no good reason.

Maybe it shouldn't bother me. It's not like it matters who Shaw fights during a game. But for a reason I can't discern, it irritates me that Shaw might be seen the same as someone like Mason.

"You're going to break the table if you keep scrubbing so hard." I glower at Shaw as he walks in the door. "I take it you didn't use your time alone to calm down."

I throw the rag I was using down on the table, crossing my arms over my chest. "No, I did not."

"Well, go ahead." He gestures to me. "Let me have it."

I despise how calm he is right now. How relaxed his stance is. Besides the red cuts on his face, he looks unaffected by what just occurred out on the ice.

"First of all, I don't need your permission to tell you how dumb you were." He smiles, but I stay scowling. "Second of all, I can't believe you would stoop to Mason's level. I told you over and over not to, and you still went after him. No rivalry or trash talk is worth that."

"It wasn't about the rivalry, it was about you."

My brow furrows, but then I realize what he's saying. "Did Brock put you up to this? I can't believe he'd put your health and reputation at stake over a stupid breakup."

"This has been going on long before you two broke up."

"What are you talking about?"

He rakes a hand through his hair, his gaze bouncing around the room before settling back on me.

"Sutton, I've been out to get Mason since the day I found out you two were dating."

"What? Why?" I take a step toward him, my anger bursting within me like a flare gun going off. "I thought we were done with high school games."

"You don't understand–" He cuts off. I can see he's warring with himself. "Just seeing you in his jersey made me sick."

"He was my *boyfriend*, whose jersey was I supposed to wear?"

"MINE!" He places a hand on his chest. "It should have been *my* name on your back. You were supposed to go to UNC with me and Brock. We'd have gone through college just like everything else: together. I would have gotten you to see me differently and we would have dated. And when I got drafted I would have asked you to come with me instead of leaving you behind like that cheating low-life did."

I open my mouth to respond, but I don't know what to say. This can't be right. Shaw wanted to date me? I can wrap my head around him wanting me now, but before college?

"I-I don't get it. What are you saying? You had a crush on me?"

He looks up at the ceiling and lets out a soft laugh. "Sutton, I am in love with you." He meets my eyes. "There, I finally said it. Doesn't get any clearer than that."

I search his expression for any hidden emotion or motives. A part of me expects him to smirk and say he was just kidding, but that doesn't happen.

"You're not in love with me. How could you be? That's impossible," I say, my chest rising and falling as my breathing becomes rapid. This is too much.

He closes the distance between us with quick strides, grasping my upper arms. "Well, I must be redefining the word impossible, because I love everything about you, Sutton Rae Jones. I love your *Star Wars* obsession and how you hate the new movies but cried when Kylo Ren died. I love how you open presents like you're trying not to ruin the wrapping paper even though it's going to be thrown away. I love that you have a list for everything and that you have expensive taste but don't want anyone to know it. I love seeing your face light up while you're ice skating and the furrow in between your brows when you're working on something. I love your witty remarks, your smile, and your brown eyes that look like rich hot cocoa. *I love you.*" He pauses, staring into my eyes with such hope that it steals my breath. "And it's okay if you don't know how to feel about that, but I know exactly how I feel and I can't pretend you aren't everything to me any longer."

His hands brush over my shoulders and up my neck until he's holding my face. My heart is racing and my head is spinning. His forehead presses against mine, and my eyes flutter shut. Here I am again, standing on the brink of a decision that could change everything. Except this time, I'm not going to watch him walk out the door with regret in my heart.

"Shaw," I whisper, placing my hands on his chest. "You sound so sure of everything, but I-I'm a mess of emotions right now. The only thing I know is that I want to kiss you–"

His lips crash into mine before I can finish my sentence. My hands clench his t-shirt and his hands push into my hair. There's no slow buildup in this kiss. We're lit matches tossed into an ocean of gasoline. His kiss is nothing short of devouring. Every brush of his lips feels desperate, like he can't get enough of me. He starts guiding me backwards, then lifts me by my waist until I'm sitting on the exam table.

I rake my hands through his hair, the damp strands sifting through my fingertips. I can't count how many times I've thought of doing that over the years, but ignored the impulse. The satisfaction that rolls through me is like nothing I've ever experienced.

Shaw growls against my lips, then deepens the kiss. He tastes like mint and something undeniably him. It's immediately addicting, and all I can think of is *more*. I wrap my legs around his waist and pull him closer. Nothing seems close enough and by the way he's gripping my hips, he agrees.

I've heard people describe getting lost in a kiss but that's not what this is. Kissing Shaw is like being found. Like being rescued after wandering in the desert or floating in the middle of the ocean for days. He knows me, all of my quirks and tendencies, and he wants me.

Shaw breaks the kiss, tracing his lips down my jaw, pausing right below my ear. "Is this–"

I cut off his question. "*Yes.*" He kisses the delicate skin he was hovering over, and I melt against him, one of my hands still tangled in his hair. I tilt my head to the side further, and his lips blaze a trail of heat down my neck. When he tastes the spot above my collarbone I tug him back to my lips, undone by the tender kiss.

He brushes his lips against mine, not letting me pull him into a full kiss again, but teasing me by kissing the corner of my mouth.

"Do you always have to be in control?" I ask.

He smiles against my lips. "Do you want to be?"

"I don't know if anyone has ever let me try," I breathe out the quiet confession. "Though I've never kissed anyone quite like this either." Another admission I'd usually never say aloud. But Shaw makes me feel safe. I think he always has, even when I saw him as my rival.

Shaw presses a gentle kiss to my lips, then pulls away. I open my eyes to see him looking at me with pure affection in his gaze.

"Tell me what to do, Jones," he says in a husky voice. "You're in control."

I take in a shaky breath, my mind a tangle of *what if's* and *should I's*. No one has ever cared enough about what I want, about *me*, to give me a moment like this.

"It's okay, love," he murmurs, giving me the courage to look into his eyes. "You don't have to overthink it, just tell me. What do you want?"

I brush my fingertips over the light stubble on his jaw. His eyes close and his throat constricts as he swallows.

"I want you to kiss me again," I whisper.

He doesn't laugh or tease me, he just slides one hand beneath my jaw and softly presses his lips against mine.

"Like this?" he murmurs before another soft kiss.

"More..." I search for a word, blushing as I come up short.

"I can do more," he says, his tongue flicking out against my bottom lip, making me gasp. "Better?"

I nod–too overwhelmed to speak–and he kisses me again, this time deepening the kiss. It's not frantic like before, but languid and rich. I take one of his hands and guide it to my hip. His thumb dips under my sweatshirt and traces circles on my skin. My hands find their way into his hair again and the low noise he makes in response has heat pooling in my stomach.

I tug on his hair to break our kiss, then brush my lips against his jaw.

"Put both your hands on my waist," I whisper, feeling bolder as we keep going. The hand that was holding my face slides down to rest in the curve above my hip, while the other continues tracing patterns on my hip bone.

I start to brush my lips over his jaw ever so slowly, exploring. He hums when I kiss down his neck, and digs his fingers into me when I dare to taste him.

I'm about to tell him to kiss me again when a loud rumbling sound from outside the room makes me jump. We freeze, listening to see if anyone is coming or something is happening.

After a moment, Shaw pulls me back in for another kiss, but I can't help but wonder what's happening out there. Is someone coming? What will happen if we get caught? Can I lose my job for making out with a player on the exam table? I press on Shaw's chest, getting him to stop.

"Relax, Jones, it's just the Zamboni," Shaw says with a chuckle, and I start to giggle.

It's only after he says it that I recognize the familiar sound. My panic dissolves into disbelief at the fact that I'm wrapped up in *Shaw Daniels'* arms.

"I can't believe we just kissed." I touch my lips with my fingertips, looking up at him.

"I've wanted to do that for a very long time, Sutton Rae Jones."

I dare to hope as I look into his eyes. "Was it worth the wait?"

Chapter Twenty-Eight

Shaw Daniels

"I don't know," I say with a smirk. "I think I need to kiss you again to make sure."

I lean down toward her, but she pushes my chest, laughing. Man, I love that sound. And I love *her* even more. I pull her in for a hug and kiss the crown of her head.

"It was worth it," I whisper into her hair. "But I wish I would have done it a lot sooner."

"You've really felt this way since before college?" she asks, pulling back to look up at me. Her fingertips toy with the collar of my t-shirt that I changed into after the game.

"Yes," I answer. "I know that's probably a lot to take in." She nods. "But I've been patient this long, I can wait for your feelings to catch up."

"What makes you think I'll fall in love with you?" There's a teasing glint in her eyes that has me smiling.

I shrug. "I'm irresistible."

"I think the word you're looking for is *insufferable*."

"Mmm is that why you were making out with me? Because I'm insufferable?"

"Shut up," she mumbles, her cheeks tinting pink.

"Is that the best you've got, Jones?" I tease, tickling her waist to make her laugh. "Did my kisses render you speechless? I've been known to have that effect."

"You're the worst," she says through giggles. I pepper her neck with kisses, feeling as though my life couldn't get any better.

She grabs my face and kisses me, successfully distracting me from tickling her. When we pull apart, we're both breathless. I press my forehead against hers, my mind emptied of everything except Sutton and this moment.

"We should probably go," she whispers. "Everyone is going to be wondering where you are."

She's right. I'm betting that I have plenty of texts and missed calls on my phone. I told everyone I'd be a little late to Sawyer's, but more than a little time has passed.

"Do you want to come to Sawyer's with me? I get it if it's too soon to be seen together." The last thing I want to do is push Sutton too much. Even if all I want to do is go find the tallest building in Huntsville and announce to the entire city that *I kissed Sutton Jones*.

"Everyone already thinks we're together," she says with a shy smile. "I don't mind keeping it that way."

"Are we together, then?" I tuck a strand of hair behind her ear, then cup her cheek with my hand. "I'm trying not to move too fast, Jones, I swear–"

She places her fingertips over my mouth, silencing me. "You're not moving too fast. I may not be at the level you are just yet, but I've had feelings for you for a while now, too. I was just fighting them." She drops her hand. "But now I'm not, and I don't do things halfway, you know that."

My chest warms. I'm convinced that by the end of tonight my face is going to be sore from smiling so much. I'd pictured this moment hundreds of times, but reality is so much sweeter.

"So when we go to this party, if a girl comes up to me, I can say I have a girlfriend?"

"If I don't tell her first, yes," she says, and I laugh.

"Good." I kiss her softly. "But tell me if you need to slow down. Just like earlier, you're in control here."

"Thank you." The gratitude in her voice is so sincere it steals my breath. It also assures me that making sure Mason regretted his words tonight was the right decision.

"Anything for you," I tell her. "Now, are you ready to go deal with a bunch of obnoxious and nosey hockey players?"

She laughs. "I'm ready."

·♥·♥·♥·♥·♥·

"I love this car," Sutton says in a dreamy voice, running her hands over the steering wheel.

I let her drive my red Lamborghini to Sawyer's since I know she's admired it for a while. It's the first time I've ever let anyone drive it. Thankfully, Sutton is a good driver so I wasn't too worried. Though I did grip the door when she took a turn faster than expected.

"It's yours if you want it," I say, and she looks over at me with wide eyes.

"You're joking."

I shrug. "A little, but I don't have to be. It's just a car."

"*Just a car?*" She shakes her head, unbuckling her seatbelt. "You're the gross kind of rich, aren't you?"

I snort at her wording. "What a wonderful response to a man trying to give you a car."

She laughs and opens the car door. "All I did was ask a question."

"What am I going to do with you?" I ask after getting out of the car. Sutton takes my hand and swings it as we walk up the driveway. The gesture comes out of nowhere and yet feels as natural as breathing.

"Kiss me?" she says. "Fall more and more in love with me each day?"

I stop and tug her to me, pressing my lips to hers for a quick kiss. "Done and done," I whisper.

She looks down. "I probably shouldn't tease you about loving me."

"If you didn't, you wouldn't be the woman I fell in love with." I tip her chin up and kiss her once more. "We need to hurry inside, before I give in to the temptation of just spending tonight together alone."

"I don't know, that sounds a lot better than being at a rowdy party…" she trails off.

The door to said party swings open to reveal Danny, shirtless with a beer in his hand.

"Look! It's the power couple of the Rockets!" he yells and a chorus of cheers breaks out. "Get in here, you two!" He gestures wildly, and Sutton shakes her head, looking amused.

"We can't back out now," I tell her. "Everyone will be disappointed that the *power couple* abandoned the party."

"I will come inside only if you never say the words *power couple* ever again."

I laugh and pull her into the chaos with me. We walk through the crowd of people, everyone patting me on the back or trying to give me a drink. The entire time, I can't get over the feeling of Sutton being by my side. I keep looking down at her, afraid I'm going to wake up and this will all be a dream.

It's not long before Liam's wife, Natalie, spots us and immediately starts gushing over the fact that Sutton and I are together.

"Liam said Shaw made it clear it was a rumor, but I guess Shaw was just protecting you." Natalie puts a hand over her chest like she might swoon at the thought, her large diamond ring glinting in the light.

"We wanted to announce things on our own terms, go at our own pace, you know?" Sutton says as if we didn't just start dating an hour ago. I'm both impressed and mildly concerned at how unrehearsed she sounds.

"I totally understand," Natalie says with a wide smile.

A few of the other couples make their way over, and I feel as though I'm having an out-of-body experience. I used to watch all of the "serious" couples talk to each other, feeling like I was an outsider. They all had their own get-togethers and inside jokes, while I spent my days with the bachelors of the team, pretending I liked watching them get drunk and flirt with a different woman in every city we went to.

Now, Sutton and I are a part of the couples group. Natalie invites Sutton to go for a pedicure and a few of the other women say they want to come too. The guys laugh and say we should all go throw axes or something while they get their nails done. It's a surreal feeling to be standing in the midst of a dream I've spent what feels like forever longing for. And while I couldn't care less about throwing axes or going on a double date, being included for once feels good.

Sutton lifts her hair off her neck with one hand while talking to Sawyer's girlfriend Maya about the game. Her face is flushed and she agrees when Maya says it's gotten warm in here.

"Here, Jones," I say in a low voice, pulling up the sleeve of my long sleeve shirt to reveal the hair tie I keep there for her.

"Thanks," she says with a smile as she takes it off my wrist and pulls her hair up in a high ponytail. All I can think about is how this new hairstyle will make it even easier to kiss her neck and hear that breathy little sound she made again.

I lean down to whisper in her ear. "You know, if you're uncomfortable, we could leave."

"I'm not–" Her sentence dies off when she meets my eyes. I raise my eyebrows and she bites her lip. "I think I'm starting to not feel well," she says just loud enough for the others in our group to hear.

They all start to say they're sorry, insisting that I take her home to get some rest and they hope she feels better. I bite the inside of my cheek to keep from smirking as we walk out of the party. It's only when the door closes behind us that I let out a laugh and pull her to me for a kiss.

"I could get used to this," I say.

"Me too," she replies, letting out a contented sigh when I kiss her temple.

And I hope we do get used to it. I hope the rest of our lives are sneaking out of parties and kissing in places we shouldn't. Whatever it is, whatever I'm doing, I just want Sutton there with me.

Chapter Twenty-Nine

Sutton Jones

"I don't want to call," I say to Shaw, laying my head on his shoulder. We're hanging out at his house after practice, snuggling while I procrastinate calling to tell my parents that we're officially dating.

I love my family, don't get me wrong, but they have a tendency to be overdramatic. When Shaw told Brock we were together yesterday, he asked if he was going to be the best man when we got married. It's only been a *week* since we kissed. Brock also spent half the call saying how he *called it* and *knew it all along,* which Shaw informs me was not the case whatsoever.

Considering how my mom acted after seeing a photo of me and Shaw dancing, I have a feeling her reaction to us actually dating is going to be soap opera level dramatic.

"It's not going to be that bad," Shaw reassures me, tracing patterns on my arm over the hoodie I stole from him. Though I don't know if it counts as stealing when Shaw told me I could have whatever I wanted from his house when he first brought me here. I jokingly asked for his college championship ring and he said if I really wanted it, he'd have a chain made for me to wear it.

"Okay, just press call." I groan and press my face into his neck. He chuckles at my dramatics–I come by it honestly–then I hear the phone beginning to ring.

"Hello?" My mom's voice comes through the phone.

"Hey Mama Jones," Shaw replies.

"Oh, hi Shaw. I was expecting Sutton. Is everything okay? Is she hurt?" Worry fills her voice.

"No, Mom, I'm not hurt," I say, lifting my head so she can hear me clearly.

"Then what's going on?"

I look at Shaw, and he gives me an encouraging nod. "Shaw and I are dating. We wanted to call and tell you before any news got out."

"Really? It's real this time?" she squeals into the phone. Shaw scrunches his face up at the high pitched sound, making me laugh.

"Yeah, it's real, Mom."

"Oh, that's wonderful news! I can't wait to tell your father when he comes back in. You know I've always hoped you two would get together."

"Yes, you've said that before."

"Shaw, did Sutton tell you about the hockey themed wedding cake I found?"

Shaw presses his lips together to keep from laughing, barely managing to reply, "No, ma'am, she hasn't."

My mother tsks. "These things are important to decide on early. Bakeries and venues book up fast–"

"Mom! Slow. Down."

"You sound like your father." She sighs. "He told me I was making a big deal out of all of this, but I'm just excited that one of my children is finally in a good relationship."

I see an opportunity to end the call, and I jump on it.

"Yep! I'm dating Shaw, but Brock was telling me the other day that he was feeling lonely. I think he might be ready for you to set him up with your dentist's granddaughter."

Shaw gives me an admonishing look. I ignore him and wait for my mom to take the bait.

"He said that? Dr. Paulson will be thrilled! She's been trying to get someone to date Layla for years now."

"You should call and set something up soon, for when Brock is back in town."

"Yes, yes you're right. I'll talk to you later! Love you, sweetie, be good."

She hangs up, and I place my hand over Shaw's mouth.

"Don't you say a word. Brock would have done the same thing to me." I let my hand fall into my lap.

"You're right, he would have." He pulls me into his lap and I straddle his legs. "You got through it. Your whole family knows about us. How do you feel?"

I place my hands on his chest, and his rest on my hips.

"Worried about coming home to a cake tasting," I say and he chuckles. "But other than that, happy. I'm really happy."

He smiles at me and it feels as if the sun has finally come out and melted a year long frost. Something bright and fresh is growing within me, blooming in the glittering light of his love.

"That's all I've ever wanted, love." His new nickname for me makes my stomach swoop.

"What about you? How do you feel?"

"Like the love of my life is in my house, wearing my hoodie, sitting in my lap." He lifts a hand and slides it under my jaw. "There's only one thing that could make this better."

"A hockey-themed wedding cake?" I joke.

"You shouldn't tease me about marriage, Jones. I'm not opposed to the idea of giving you more than just my championship ring." His thumb traces my bottom lip and my breath catches.

"We can't get married, we haven't even been on a date yet," I say, trying not to sound as breathless as I feel.

"It's a good thing I have a plan to remedy that. Are you free two nights from now?"

"I am."

"Then plan on spending your evening with me, on our first date."

"That didn't sound like a question," I say.

He smirks. "That's because it wasn't one."

"You have a lot of confidence, Daniels." My gaze falls to his lips.

"I'm not afraid to go after what I want."

"Which is?"

"You." His thumb caresses my cheek. "Always you. Only you."

I kiss him, because how could I not after he says something like that? He smiles into the kiss and while I'm not ready to say that I'm in love, there's a part of me that really likes the idea of doing this for the rest of my life.

· ♥ · ♥ · ♥ · ♥ · ♥ ·

I'm putting the last roller in my hair when someone knocks on my front door. I frown, placing the clip to hold it in place before wrapping my robe tightly around myself and heading to the door. Through the peephole I see a man carrying a large black box with a red silk bow.

I open the door and the older man's eyes widen, likely not expecting my hair to look the way it does. It's not my fault that he showed up in the middle of my hair and makeup routine.

"I have a date tonight," I blurt out and he nods slowly. I cross my arms over my chest. "Can I help you?"

"I have a delivery for Sutton Jones," he says, holding up the box.

"That's me." I take the box from him and set it inside the door, curious about what it could be. I don't remember ordering anything. After I sign for the package, I close the door behind me and take the box to my bedroom.

Once it's on the bed, I slowly unfurl the ribbon, wondering if I should even open it. There's no note to indicate where or who it's from. But I doubt anyone would go to such a length to hurt me in some way. Even Mason isn't that malicious. So the worst it could be is a prank from my brother. I shrug and open the lid. Black tissue paper is inside, with a white card on top. I pick up the small note, instantly recognizing Shaw's handwriting.

Wear this and your favorite heels. I'll see you at six. Yours, Shaw

I carefully move the tissue paper and gasp when I see a pool of red silk. The fabric is luxurious beneath my fingertips as I carefully lift the dress out and hold it up. It's reminiscent of the dress I wore to the charity event, but the deep cherry color takes the simple design to another level. I spread it across my bed, in awe that he would buy something so extravagant for our first date. He told me to wear something nice tonight, but this dress is *beyond* nice.

I walk to the bathroom and grab my phone off the counter, pressing call beside Shaw's name.

"This is too much," I say as soon as the line clicks.

"I take it your dress arrived safely?"

"Daniels–*Shaw*–you didn't need to do this. I have dresses."

"I know that, but I want you to wear that one. Do you not like it?" Uncertainty creeps into his tone.

"No," I reassure him, "it's beautiful. I just–"

"Jones, wear the dress. Let me spoil you. *I want to.*"

I walk back into my bedroom and gaze at the silk masterpiece. It's stunning, and I know it probably cost more than my monthly rent. I look for a tag to see the brand or price, but I don't find one.

"Okay," I finally concede. "I'll wear the dress, but only because it looks like you already took the tags off. What if it doesn't fit?"

"It will," he says and I roll my eyes at his confidence.

"What kind of date are we going on that I need a floor-length gown?

"The kind that's a *surprise.*"

"I don't like surprises," I say and I hear him chuckle.

"You love surprises, and you're going to love this one."

"How can you be so sure?"

"Because *I know you*. Now finish getting ready and try not to overthink this."

"Fine." I sigh. "I'll try."

"That's my girl. I'll see you at six, love."

"See you at six."

He hangs up and I stare at the dress for a moment longer before going back into my bathroom to do my makeup. I can't imagine what Shaw is up to, but I know I can trust him.

·♥·♥·♥·♥·♥·

An hour later, I open the door to find Shaw looking somehow both debonair and roguish on my front porch. He's wearing a pitch black suit, with a white dress shirt underneath of which he's left a few of the top buttons undone. His eyes rove over me, taking me in.

"You look..." he trails off, running a hand over his jaw. "Exquisite, ravishing, gorgeous beyond measure–there truly aren't enough words in the English language to describe how beautiful you are."

I wrap my arms around his shoulders and smile up at him. "You chose a beautiful dress."

"No," he says in a low voice. "I chose a beautiful woman." He kisses my forehead and steps back, holding my hands as he looks me over appreciatively once more.

I duck my head, only able to withstand so much of his affection before my face gets too hot.

"Are you ready to go?" he asks, and I nod. After I lock up, he leads me to a sleek black town car. A man in a suit opens up the back door, giving a polite nod before I slide inside. Shaw follows after me, leaving no room between us.

"You hired a driver?" I ask and he nods.

"I wanted to spend the whole night close to you." He places a hand on my bare knee that's poking out of the slit in the dress. A delicious warmth radiates from the spot.

His thumb traces circles over my skin, sending tingles down my leg as he tells me about his morning taking photos for Under Armour's latest campaign. I listen and enjoy the feeling of his touch, relaxing against him. I never thought being around Shaw could be calming, but it is.

The car comes to a stop, the driver opening the door on Shaw's side. Shaw gets out first, extending a hand to help me. I look up to find a quaint brick building with ivy climbing the walls and lit sconces on either side of the ornate door. The name above the door reads *Amoré*.

Shaw leads me inside and the scent of fresh basil and warm garlic greets me upon entrance. The inside of the restaurant is even more romantic than the outside, with candles everywhere and twinkle lights draped in rows across the ceiling. A hostess in a black cocktail dress steps out from behind a podium as we walk through the foyer.

"Mr. Daniels?" she asks, and Shaw nods. "Right this way."

We follow her to a table in the center of the dining area. As we walk, I notice that there's no one else in the restaurant. There aren't even place settings out on any of the tables except the one she's leading us to.

"Your waiter will be with you shortly," the hostess says with a smile.

"Thank you," Shaw says to her.

Once she's walked away, I look across the table. "Please don't tell me you rented out this entire restaurant."

"I did," he says, picking up the menu and looking it over.

"You didn't need to do this. We could have gotten regular reservations."

He looks up from the menu, a smile playing on his lips. "I know that."

"I'm not *this* high maintenance."

He reaches across the table and takes my hand in his. "Jones, did it ever occur to you that I wanted to be alone tonight?" He turns my hand over, running his fingertips over the inside of my wrist, making me shiver. "So that I could do whatever I wanted." In a flash, his lips are on my wrist. My toes curl as he trails kisses over my palm to my fingertips. "Without having to worry about a room full of people."

"There are still people here," I point out, barely able to form words as he kisses each one of my fingertips, grazing his teeth over the last one.

"I'm keeping an eye out," he says before pressing a kiss to the center of my palm and lowering our hands back to the table. "It's a lot easier to watch for one waiter than it is to have privacy in a full restaurant."

"We could have stayed at your place and ordered takeout if you wanted to be alone."

"But then I wouldn't have gotten to see you in this dress."

"I could have worn it." I'm grasping for straws, and we both know it. I don't know why I can't just accept his beautiful gesture.

"A dress like that isn't made for a night on the couch." He squeezes my hand. "What's going on? Tell me what's on your mind, love."

I look down, trying to find the words to convey how I'm feeling.

"I don't know how to accept what you're trying to give me," I say in a quiet voice. Shaw runs his thumb over the back of my hand in soothing motions. "I've always been the one to take care of myself. As soon as I was old enough to work, anything I wanted, I bought for myself."

"I know that, and I admire your independent spirit. But I want to take care of you, too."

I look up from the tablecloth to find him smiling gently at me. "It feels wrong to take from you without giving anything in return. But I can't give you anything you couldn't easily buy for yourself."

"You're looking at this all wrong. I don't want anything from you except to *be with you*. I bought that dress because I knew it would make you smile and you look amazing in red. I rented out this restaurant so I could be mostly alone with you while still having the kind of food we both like. And later on when I ask you to dance to your favorite music, it's so I have an excuse to hold you close." He squeezes my hand gently. "I told you before, you don't owe me anything, ever. That hasn't changed. I just want you."

Tears sting my eyes and I blink them away. I've always felt like I owed people something in return for whatever they gave or tried to give me. In relationships, I'd bend over backwards to become who they needed me to be, so that I didn't feel guilty during the rare moments I needed something from them. Mason was a prime example of that. I felt like the drinking and parties was my payment for when he would take me out. And he reinforced that by buying gifts after particularly rough nights.

But here Shaw is, in his suit, sitting across from me in a private restaurant telling me that I don't owe him a single thing. It's overwhelming and my heart is breaking, but it's like when you have to break a bone to set it properly. I healed the wrong way after Mason, and now with Shaw I have a chance to have a healthy, good relationship. I'm just experiencing a breaking down of my walls in the process.

"It may take me some time to come to terms with this," I say, my voice thick with emotion.

"That's okay, love. I'll be here helping you every step of the way."

"Thank you," I whisper, and it doesn't feel like enough. I wish I was ready to say that I loved him, but when I do I want to know with every fiber of my being that the words are true. After everything, Shaw deserves that level of love. And I hope to be able to give that to him some day.

Chapter Thirty

Sutton Jones

"I'm excited to officially meet the guys," I say as Shaw opens his front door for us. We just had lunch, and now we're back at his place. We're going to video chat a few of his friends to tell them we're together. I didn't know guys got so invested in each other's personal lives. Maybe most don't, but these ones definitely do. Shaw's phone started blowing up with texts when some photos of us walking into Amoré last night made it on a few gossip sites. Shaw ignored them, but when one of the guys, Jason Kingsley, messaged me on Instagram suggesting I formally meet Shaw's buddies over video chat, I couldn't resist.

"You've already met them, and in person too," Shaw says. "Which is why I don't think it's necessary to do this." He falls down on his couch, sprawling out with a sigh.

"I've only met them in passing," I say, looking down at him. "Plus, Jason seemed so excited to get to talk."

"He's excited to *embarrass* me."

I smile. "I know, that's why I'm excited too."

"I gathered that from your little maniacal laugh while you were messaging him this morning. Hence why I do not want to do this."

"It won't be that bad." I straddle his abdomen and he holds my hips. "And once we're done we'll have the rest of the day together."

"It's hard to say no to you like this."

I bend down, pressing my hands on his chest and hovering just above his mouth. "Why do you think I'm doing it?"

"You're not playing fair." His gaze snags on my lips.

"When have we ever played fair, Daniels?" I brush my lips against his.

"Never," he whispers before taking my hands off his chest and intertwining our fingers, then slowly moving them above his head. I sink against him. He kisses me, and stretches out his arms a little more so I can't sit up or move away easily.

Warmth spreads throughout my body as our kiss deepens into something more passionate. I melt against him, feeling both electrified and safe all at once. Being with Shaw, kissing Shaw, is like cuddling up in a warm blanket one second and jumping out of an airplane the next. It's a heady combination, and now that I've gotten a taste, I don't think I'll be able to give this feeling up.

Shaw's phone starts to ring in his pocket, but he doesn't stop kissing me. I'm tempted to ignore the call as well, but decide against it. I tug on his hands and feel him slowly, reluctantly, loosen his grip so I can sit up. By the time he's let me go, the phone stops ringing.

"You should call them back," I tell him.

"You might want to move before I do, unless you want to make all of them incredibly jealous. I'm okay either way." He smirks and I feel my face heat.

"Just let me fix my hair and then we can call."

I pull out my hair tie, then gather all my hair with one hand and smooth the edges with the other.

"You're torturing me, love," he says in a low voice.

I look down at him as I finish pulling my hair through the last loop. The desire in his eyes makes me bite my lip. His gaze dips to my mouth before his eyes fall shut, his jaw tight.

I lean back down, brushing my lips over his jaw. "I'm sorry."

"No, you're not," he rasps.

I smirk. "No, I'm not." I give him one more kiss before moving off of him. He pushes up to sitting, looking at me with a mixture of desire and frustration.

"You're going to pay for that, Jones."

"I'm looking forward to it," I reply without breaking his gaze.

He looks away, raking a hand through his hair.

"Let's make this call before my willpower is gone." I giggle and he shoots me a playful, faux angry look. He pulls out his phone and after a few seconds, it begins to ring. I move over so I can snuggle into his side and wait for the guys to answer.

Soon enough, the screen is filled with three mildly familiar faces. I've met them all briefly in the past, but not had a lengthy conversation with any of them.

"There's my favorite couple!" Jason says with a smile. "Why didn't you answer the first time? Were you two busy?"

I blush at his insinuation.

"Jason, don't be intrusive," Emmett says, surprising me. I remember first meeting him and he said maybe three words in the entire conversation.

"Don't be such a dad, ET, I'm just messing with them."

"We called to let you know we're dating," Shaw speaks fast, as if he's concerned he won't be able to get them out before someone interrupts.

"Congrats on finally speaking up, man," Miles chimes in with a laugh. "You should have heard him telling us about you, Sutton. He was crying over how much you didn't like him."

"I was not *crying*," Shaw says. "Remind me to never talk to y'all about anything personal ever again."

"Oh don't be like that," Jason says. "We can only have one gruff introvert in the group and that spot is taken by Emmett."

I laugh, thoroughly entertained by their bickering and Jason's big personality.

"Shaw did not cry," Emmett says. I watch a tiny smirk form on his lips. "He did however whine a little too much for my taste."

Miles and Jason lose it at this, laughing so hard they go out of camera frame. Even Shaw chuckles, though he's trying not to.

"You know it was bad if Emmett says something," Miles says through his laughter.

"Really, ET? Of all people, I didn't expect this from you." Shaw shakes his head.

"I might not have said it if you would have quit calling me ET when I asked."

"It's a nickname!" Shaw says in a tone that lets me know they've had this conversation before. "And a funny one at that."

"I disagree."

"Anyway, we just wanted to tease you a little," Jason says after he calms down. "We're happy for you, Shaw. She's way out of your league, you know that, right?"

Shaw smiles at me. "Yeah, I know."

"The whole relationship commitment stuff isn't my thing, but it looks good on you man," Miles says next. I resist the urge to frown at his words. I'll have to ask Shaw later why Miles is against relationships.

"Thank you," Shaw replies.

"I wish you both the best," Emmett says last and my heart warms. It feels as though we just received some kind of blessing from Shaw's closest friends. And while I know Shaw would choose me over everyone else–he's made that abundantly clear several times–it makes me happy to know that his friends seem supportive of our relationship.

"I appreciate it, you guys." He kisses the side of my head. "But, if you'll excuse us, I want to spend the rest of my day off with this angel."

"It was nice meeting you!" I say, realizing I haven't spoken at all. In the future I'll have to learn to be okay with interrupting or talking over someone to get a word in.

Everyone says their goodbyes before Shaw hangs up the phone. He turns toward me, and tips my chin up with a smirk.

"Now, where were we?"

·♥·♥·♥·♥·♥·

Two weeks later

Then sun shines down, warming my skin, while a cool breeze blows to ensure it doesn't get too hot. It's a *perfect* spring day. I feel as though I'm walking on clouds as I make my way through the farmer's market, Shaw's hand in mine. We have the morning off, and soon we'll be too busy with playoffs to do things like this. So, I'm cherishing this beautiful morning for the gift that it is.

"Oh!" I exclaim. "There's a flower truck, let's go build a bouquet for my place and one for yours." I veer off toward the airstream that has buckets of flowers attached to the front. Shaw lets me drag him along, like he's done the entire morning without complaint.

I greet the owner with a smile, then start to browse the flowers. I pull a few stems and hand them to Shaw, then a few more of a different flower. He holds them for me as I add to the bouquet little by little. Once it's fairly full, I tilt my head to the side, examining it. The muted blues and soft cream colors should go well with Shaw's modern home.

"What do you think about these for your house?"

"I think they're beautiful," Shaw says, "but I don't own a vase."

"There was a pottery studio selling them a few rows back. We could get one from there?"

He smiles down at me. "Perfect."

"Can you have her wrap them up for me while I make the one for my house?" I ask him and he nods. "Thank you."

He kisses my forehead, then walks over to the wrapping counter. It doesn't take long for him to return with the bouquet wrapped in butcher paper and tied with twine. He cradles the bouquet in a way that reminds me of a dad holding his new baby.

I smile as I picture him holding a tiny chubby baby that has his dark hair and my brown eyes. He would make such a good dad. I can see him teaching our child how to skate, me holding one hand while he holds the other and we slowly go around the ice rink. He'd be so patient and loving and protective ... *oh*.

I press a hand over my heart as it skips in my chest. *I love him. I'm in love with Shaw.*

"Is everything all right?" Shaw touches my arm. Concern furrows his brow.

"I-I'm fine," I stutter. He gives me a look that says he doesn't believe me. "Water!" I blurt out. "I think I'm a little dehydrated. Could you go get me a water?"

He eyes me for a second, but nods. "Sure, I'll go get you one. Stay right here."

"Will do," I say, sounding even more awkward than I already have. He walks off and I turn back toward the flowers so it looks like I'm doing something. Something other than spiraling, that is.

I didn't expect to feel this way so quickly, but I should have. Shaw has been the perfect boyfriend. He spoils me, supports me, makes me laugh, all without making me feel like I owe him anything in return. Each day we've been together, my defenses have come down brick by brick. They came down so slowly, in the little quiet moments with him, that I barely noticed it was happening. Until now, in a farmer's market on a Saturday morning, when he came and picked me up just because I said in passing that it sounded fun.

"Here you go, love." Shaw's voice comes from behind me and I turn back around. He hands me the cold bottle of water, the cap already off.

I take a sip then hand it back to him. He takes it and I spot one of my hair ties on his wrist as he twists the cap back on. Tears sting my eyes and I pretend to examine the half-formed bouquet in my hand to hide them. He loves me so well, and has for years now.

"How are you feeling now?" he asks.

"Perfect," I whisper. "Absolutely perfect."

Chapter Thirty-One

Shaw Daniels

First Round of NHL Playoffs, Game Six

I walk into the recovery center, smiling when I see Sutton pulling a jersey over the fitted athletic jacket she usually wears to work. Her hair is up, revealing my name on the back of the jersey. She wears my jersey every game day and it still doesn't get old seeing her in it.

She turns around, grinning when she sees me. "What are you doing in here? If Coach catches us we'll be in big trouble."

I wrap my arms around her waist, lifting her up slightly, and she throws hers around my shoulders. The rest of the staff is already in the arena, but I knew Sutton would be in here, putting on her jersey before we started.

"Coach sent me in here to get a kiss from my good luck charm," I say and she gives me a look.

"He did not."

"No," I say with a laugh. "He didn't. He did, however, tell me to get my wrist taped up."

She frowns. "Is it hurt? You said this morning you were feeling fine."

"I told him exactly what I told you, but he wants to take the extra precaution with us being this far into the playoffs." We're on game six against the Aspen Avalanches. If we win today, we go to the next round, but if not, we get one more game to make it to the championship series. I think we'll win today though. Our team is focused and ready to move to the next level.

"That's understandable," she says. "I'll get you taped up and ready to go, then."

I sit down on Sutton's exam table and push up the sleeve of my jersey.

"I'm surprised you didn't use this as an opportunity to take your shirt off," she says as she grabs the tape.

"Do you miss seeing my abs, Jones? You know all you have to do is ask," I tease.

She rolls her eyes. "It's hard to miss something I see every day."

"I *knew* you kept shirtless photos of me in your phone."

She hits my shoulder, and I laugh.

"The only shirtless photo I have of you is the one you made as my screensaver before we visited my parents. My relationship with my dad is scarred for life thanks to you."

"You love that photo. I bet you still have it as your screensaver."

Her cheeks flush. "I do not. My screensaver is a photo of me and Ariel."

"Where's your phone?" I ask her and she shrugs, but I can tell she's feigning nonchalance.

"I think it's in my bag, maybe? I don't know."

"Hand it over, Jones. Let's see if you're telling the truth."

"I don't have my phone on me."

"Liar," I say as I reach out and pull her to me. "Am I going to have to pat you down? Because I will."

"Shaw, someone might come in here and find us. I need to tape you up so you're ready for the game. Everyone is already out there."

"Hand over the phone, and I'll be on my way."

She sighs, pulling it out of her pocket and placing it in the palm of my hand. It immediately lights up to show that same shirtless photo of me that I put on there two weeks ago.

"Admit it, Jones. You *love* looking at me shirtless. It's like watching your favorite movie, it never gets old."

"How long does it take to tape up a wrist?" Coach Fowler yells, walking in the room. His eyes go from me to Sutton. He crosses his arms. "Do I need to ask Connor to come in here and do this instead?"

Sutton shoots me an I-told-you-so glare.

"No, sorry, Coach. It wasn't Sutton's fault, I'm the one who caused her to not be done. It won't happen again."

"I figured it was you causing problems. Miss Sutton is a wonderful physical therapist." Sutton's lips stretch into a smug grin. "Now quit bothering her so we can get out there and win this thing."

"Yes sir."

He walks out of the room and Sutton starts to laugh as she tapes my wrist.

"I can't believe he blamed me," I say.

"That was your karma for all of those years you sweet talked the teachers into thinking you were an angel. I am so glad I was here to witness that. I have to get Coach Fowler a present."

"I thought you were on my side now?"

"I am," she says with a saccharine smile. "But I'm also your former rival who quite enjoys seeing you finally get in trouble."

I shake my head. "I guess this is what happens when you fall in love with the enemy."

"I guess so," she says in a teasing tone as she finishes my wrist. "You're good to go. Play smart, don't lose." She kisses my cheek after saying what she's been telling me since the first game of the playoffs.

"I will." I give her a brief kiss. "I love you."

She smiles at me, and like every time I've said it since the first, I hold my breath for a second, waiting for her to say it back. When it doesn't come, I just kiss her again, tell her I'll look for her after I score, and walk out the door.

We haven't been dating for that long, but there have been a few times lately when it seemed as though she was on the verge of telling me. Maybe she is, but she's waiting for the right moment. Or she could be scared. No matter the reason, I'll continue to be patient, because that's what I promised her, and what she deserves.

・♥・♥・♥・♥・♥・

I race down the ice, the puck a few feet in front of me. An Avalanches player snags it, but I knock into him, stealing the puck back. It's almost the end of the first period and we're down a point. If I can score before intermission, the whole team can end on a high point. I speed toward the goal as fast as I can while keeping control of the puck. I'm almost there when suddenly, something strikes my ankle, hard. I take a fall to the ice, my ankle folding awkwardly underneath me. Searing pain shoots up my ankle and to my calf.

The ref blows the whistle, calling a penalty on the other team for slashing. I roll over on the ice, pushing myself up to a sitting position. Sawyer skates over and helps me up the rest of the way.

"You good, man?" he asks.

"Fine," I grit out.

I make it over to the bench and sit down, watching with a clenched jaw as one of my teammates, Mac, goes in to replace me. Coach doesn't let me go back in, and my frustration rises with each throb of my ankle. We end the period 1-1.

"Recovery center, now," Coach Fowler says as soon as we're in the tunnel. I don't respond, just head straight there.

"Are you okay?" Sutton asks when I walk in, slightly limping. I can see the worry in her eyes.

"Came down hard on my ankle, but I'm fine. Coach wants you to look at it."

She helps me get out of my skate so she can assess it. Every movement causes knifing pain, but I try not to show it.

"If you clench your jaw any harder you're going to break teeth," Sutton says as she prods my ankle and foot. "Quit pretending you're not hurting."

"It's a little sore, that's all."

She gives me a look. "It's no use lying to me. I watched the fall, and I can see that you're hurt."

"Just give me an ice pack for the rest of intermission, and I'll be good."

She raises a brow. "How about you let me make the medical decisions since I'm the one with the degree?"

I look up at the ceiling, taking a deep breath in and out through my nose. I don't want my frustration to get the best of me, but it's hard when the playoffs are on the line.

"I'm sorry," I say on a sigh. "You're right, do your job."

She continues examining my ankle, then takes a step back. I don't like the wary look on her face.

"You should get an X-ray, but it looks to me like a sprain. Recovery shouldn't take too long, but you can't go back on the ice today."

"It's game six, Sutton," I say and she gives me a sympathetic look.

"I know, I don't want to bench you, but I have to."

"I'm not sitting on the bench. I'll numb it with an ice pack and take a couple Tylenol. I'll be fine until after the game."

Her gaze hardens. "No, you're going to sit out. I won't let you be hurt for the championship."

"There might not be a championship if we don't win this!" I raise my voice and she looks over at Connor, who I didn't realize was in the room. He takes one look at us, then leaves. Smart.

"You're benched, Daniels." She crosses her arms. "You can go tell Fowler, or I will."

I white knuckle the table, wishing I didn't have to argue with her, but I do. This is too important. "It's just a little ankle injury. I'm not going out in *game six* for this."

"I don't care what game it is, you're not risking a more serious injury." Her voice goes up in both pitch and volume.

"I'll be fine. I'm going to play."

"No, you're not." She glares at me, her tone sharp, and I clench my jaw. "I'm done arguing about this." She turns like she's going to walk away.

"Players go out injured all the time, what does it matter if I do too?"

"Because I love you!" she yells, whipping back around. "And I couldn't bear it if I let you go out there and your season, or-or worse, your *career* ended because of me."

I stare at her, unable to speak or move. She wraps her arms around herself and looks off to the side, her jaw tight.

"You love me?" I whisper, reaching out and pulling her to me to close the distance between us.

"Yes," she says, her voice cracking. Her brown eyes are brimming with tears when she looks at me. "So please don't make me watch you get hurt."

"Hey, hey, don't cry, love." I brush her tears away. "I'm sorry. I won't go out there."

I hold her against my chest, swallowing down the emotions rising to the surface.

"Look at me," I whisper after a moment. She tilts her head up. "Do you really love me?"

"With all that I have." She gives me a watery smile. "And it's terrifying."

I press my forehead to hers, overwhelmed by the notion that after years of loving Sutton, *she loves me back*.

"It doesn't have to be scary," I tell her, and she laughs a little.

"It does, but that's okay. It's worth it, too."

I smile, joy bubbling up within me like a hot spring. The pain in my ankle, being benched, it all fades away.

"I'm sorry I blew up on you," I say, pulling my forehead back to look at her.

"It's okay, I love you anyway."

I kiss her, hard. She responds in kind, tangling her hands in my hair. Breathless, I trail my lips up her jaw to her ear.

"Say it again," I plead.

"I love you, Shaw," she whispers, tugging on my hair until I kiss her again.

Her words sink beneath my skin, past bone and marrow and burrow right into my very soul. They fill a void I've walked around with my whole life. I've always thought the notion of soulmates was foolish, that there's no one person for everyone. But as we kiss, it's clear that Sutton is the only one who fits the mold.

It's *always* been her for me, it could only *ever* be her.

Epilogue

SHAW DANIELS

Stanley Cup Finals, Deciding Game

I open the jewelry box, giving Sutton's engagement ring one last look. The five carat, oval cut diamond sparkles each time I tilt the box. Ariel helped me choose the perfect ring for her, though she just helped with the cut and style. I chose the carat size, and when I told Ariel over FaceTime at the jewelers, she was so shocked I thought my screen had frozen. But Sutton deserves nothing but the best. She's going to wear this ring for the rest of her life, it needs to be perfect.

I close the box, squeezing it in my palm as I take a deep breath. In the chaos of the locker room, no one notices my nerves because they're all so preoccupied with their own. Except I'm not only anxious for the game, but for what comes after. If we win, I'm proposing to Sutton tonight. If we don't, then I'll have to find another perfect moment, but I'm counting on my team pulling through.

THE GOLDEN GOAL

We've won three games against the Toronto Blizzards and they've won three against us. This is the final game, the one that determines the champion. I think we're the better team, but we have to show it.

I've been putting in the hours to do my part, and Sutton has been with me every step of the way. She's come to the arena with me on off days, walked me through extra mobility exercises, watched countless hours of game film dissecting each moment. She's the sole reason my ankle is back to a hundred percent. This win isn't just a Rockets' win, or my win, it's hers too.

"Hey, Phil," I call out, waving over one of our equipment managers. He sets down the water carrier he was holding and walks over to me. I lower my voice. "Are you still good to hold this for me?" I show him the ring box, and he nods.

"I'd be honored." He takes the box from my hand and puts it in the pocket of his Rockets jacket.

"Thanks, man. If we win, I'll skate over to the bench and grab it from you."

"There's no *if*. The Rockets have got this in the bag."

I smile at him and clap him on the shoulder. "You're one of the good ones, Phil."

"Good luck out there," he says, then walks off to finish filling the water bottles.

I shrug my shoulders up and down, stretching my neck to the left then right.

"All right, it's time to head to the tunnel," Coach Fowler yells out. My stomach feels like there's a tornado of nerves inside of it. "This is it. This is everything we've been working toward all season. Go out there, do your jobs, and let's take home a win." He hits the doorframe to punctuate his sentence, then walks out.

We make our way to the tunnel, and I can hear the fans chanting *Rockets, Rockets, Rockets* even over the pregame music. I suck in a breath and let it out in a whoosh. I wish I could see Sutton again. I got to talk to her this morning before warm ups, but with all of the press interviews and game day chaos, I haven't seen her since. I think we both thought I'd see her again before the game, because she didn't tell me her usual advice when I left the recovery center. Oh well, maybe I'll get to see her during the first intermission.

The countdown begins. Adrenaline buzzes in my veins. A deep voice announces our team, and I'm about to step onto the ice when I hear Sutton's voice.

"Daniels!" I turn around, the other guys moving past me onto the ice. My future wife runs and jumps in my arms, wrapping her legs around me. She pulls my helmet off and tosses it to the ground before her lips meet mine in a blazing kiss. I hold her up by the back of her thighs and tighten my grip when she quickly deepens the kiss. Her teeth graze my bottom lip as she pulls away, heat blazing in her warm brown eyes.

"Play smart, don't lose." She kisses me again, softer this time, but with no loss of passion. "I love you."

"I love you too."

She grins at me and jumps down. "I'll see you after you win."

The national anthem starts to play, so I don't have time to say anything else. Sutton gestures for me to go, so I do. I grab my helmet and skate out to stand beside my teammates, placing my glove over my chest and acting like I was there all along.

I can't help but smile to myself as the song continues. All my dreams are coming true. I'm playing in the finals, Sutton is my girlfriend, and if–no, *when*–we win, she'll be my fianceé, and then after that, *my wife*. It won't be just my name on our back anymore, but *our* name.

The pregame traditions end and it's time to play. I skate to center ice, staring down my opponent with a pounding heart. Another deep breath. The whistle blows. *Game on.*

· ♥ · ♥ · ♥ · ♥ · ♥ ·

Sutton Jones

They did it. They won. I scream, jumping up and down as the countdown clock hits zero. The team rushes to the center of the ice, slamming into a group hug. Tears fill my eyes and stream down my face as I watch them hug and celebrate. Confetti rains down on the crowd and celebratory music blasts through the arena, lights are flashing and everyone is shouting.

Brock throws his arms around me, yelling "He did it!" in my ear. I laugh, pure joy flooding me. I hug him back hard, then turn to my parents and hug them too. I'm so glad they were able to make it. I know it means the world to Shaw, especially since his grandmother can't travel.

The teams line up at center ice to do the traditional handshake line. I wipe my tears away, but they just keep coming. Brock grabs my arm and pulls me toward the stairs.

"Come on, let's get you to him."

We make our way through the arena and down the tunnel. I walk out onto the ice, being careful so I don't fall.

"There he is!" I say when I see a number ten jersey by the bench. Shaw turns around and spots me immediately in the crowd. A reporter tries to talk to him but he skates around her, coming straight for me with a smile on his face. His helmet is gone, so I'm able to kiss him when he sweeps me up into his arms. It's strange knowing all of those reporters are filming us together, but over time I've gotten used to it. Shaw always makes sure people respect my personal space and don't take any questions too far.

"I'm so proud of you," I tell him when he puts me back down.

"I love you," he says, and I smile up at him.

"I love you too, Daniels." I look around the ice, laughing in disbelief that I'm standing amongst a championship team. "This is incredible!"

"Sutton," Shaw says, drawing my eyes back to him. "There's no one else I'd rather be here with."

"I just stopped crying," I say on a sniffle. "No more sweet talk, Daniels."

"That's going to be kind of hard," he says, then he slides down on one knee. "Because I have something I need to ask you."

I gasp, my hands going to my mouth. He smiles up at me with tears in his eyes.

"Sutton Rae Jones, I love you. I think I always have. And if you'll let me, I want to spend the rest of my life loving you. Will you marry me?"

"Yes, *yes,* I'll marry you." He stands back up and pulls me into his arms, kissing me fiercely as everyone around us cheers. I don't know if they're cheering for us, but I don't care. All I care about is him.

He breaks the kiss, and with shaking hands, opens the ring box to reveal the most beautiful engagement ring I've ever seen in my life. I hold out my left hand and watch in awe as he slides it on, then kisses my hand the way a fairytale prince would.

As soon as the ring is on, we get bombarded by teammates. I giggle as I'm wrapped up in the center of a giant group hug. Danny yells out that they should lift and carry us off the ice and Shaw responds with an immediate, hard no. They settle for cheering *power couple* at the top of their lungs–which makes for a terrible chant–and squeezing us until I can barely breathe.

Shaw is laughing, looking happier than I've ever seen him, and it hits me that I'm the happiest I've ever been, too. And it's all because of Shaw. After years of taking care of myself and tamping down my own wants and needs, I've finally met a man who would do anything just to see me smile. A man who loved me for years and was still patient with me after he confessed his feelings that I didn't yet reciprocate on the same level.

If someone would have told me a year ago this would be my life, I would have laughed. And yet, somehow, deep down, I know it's always been Shaw. It was always going to be me and him in the end. Jones and Daniels. Except now, it'll be just Daniels. Sutton Rae Daniels does have a nice ring to it.

Keep reading for a BONUS EPILOGUE featuring Miles, the star of the next book!

And for a bonus scene showing Shaw and Sutton's wedding and honeymoon, sign up for my newsletter!

Bonus Epilogue

MILES DAY

The day before Shaw's game

I stare at the man working the airport ticket counter, opening my mouth, then shutting it again. There is no way I just heard him right.

"My ticket is for *where*?"

"Aspen, sir."

"That can't be right. I'm supposed to be going to Huntsville, Alabama."

"I'm sorry, sir. The ticket you purchased is for Aspen, Colorado." He points to the location printed on the ticket.

I pinch the bridge of my nose. "There has to have been a mistake." Suddenly, it dawns on me, and I slowly drop my hand from my face. "I'm sorry to have taken up your time. I just realized the problem."

The clerk eyes me like I've left my brain at baggage claim, and I don't blame him. Because I assumed the airport had gotten something wrong, when in reality I should have known it was Chris, my assistant who is about to be fired.

I pull out my phone and call Chris, trying to maintain my composure while I wait for him to answer.

"Hey, Miles! Aren't you supposed to be on a plane?" He laughs and I clench my jaw. The sound of loud music and laughter float through the speaker.

"I am, but my ticket is wrong. Why did you book me a trip to Colorado? I told you I needed one to Alabama."

"You said you wanted to meet up with your friend Hunter who lives in the Rockies. That's in Colorado."

"What?" I can barely form words right now, I'm so baffled and angry. "I asked you to book me a flight to *Huntsville*, so I could watch the *Rockets* game."

"Aw man, must have gotten lost in translation." He laughs, like it's funny that I'm going to miss one of my closest friends playing in the championship and proposing to his girlfriend.

I knew it was a mistake hiring Harold's grandson. He assured me when I talked to him on the course that Chris was a good guy, fresh out of college with a business degree and ready to work.

"Hey, do you need me for anything? Cause you told me I was off while you were gone, sooo I'm on my dad's yacht right now."

"No, I don't. And don't worry about coming in to work next week either."

"Cool! Are you going to extend your vacation?"

"Extend a vacation in the place I didn't even want to go?" I ask him, my voice taut. "No, Chris, I am not. You're fired." I hang up before he can say another word. Harold might snub me at the club, but I don't care. There's no way he actually thought his grandson could handle this job.

With a sigh, I call Shaw next.

"Hey," I say when Shaw answers, raking a hand through my hair. "I'm really sorry, but my assistant booked the wrong flight and there aren't any more heading there today. I can try to get one for tomorrow, but I don't know if I'm going to make it."

"That sucks. I was really hoping you'd be here," Shaw says and the disappointment in his voice makes my anger toward Chris worse.

"I'll try to get another flight," I tell him, hoping that I'll be able to.

"It's okay if you can't. It's not your fault."

"Still, I feel terrible."

I hear a feminine voice in the background, probably Sutton. Shaw repeats what I said.

"That's awful, Miles. We're going to miss you." Sutton's voice comes over the speaker. "It's really a shame since I was looking forward to hearing more stories about Shaw being hopelessly in love with me."

I smile, grateful that she's trying to lighten the mood.

"How tragic," Shaw mocks. I hear rustling over the phone and then deep laughter paired with girlish giggles.

"Uh, guys?" I say after no one says anything for a while.

"Sorry man." Shaw chuckles. "I was having to show someone who's boss."

Sutton says something I can't make out and I think I hear Shaw say *make me* in a tone I never wanted to hear from him.

"I'll let you guys go. I just wanted to tell you that I won't be there and I'm sorry."

"No worries, I knew you wanted to be here. And besides, I couldn't make the Masters for you either. I can come visit during the off season. Me and Sutton can crash at your beach house."

"That sounds like a great time. I *love* the beach," Sutton says.

"And I love the idea of you in a bikini," Shaw says, making me cringe. Sutton shushes him, giggling again.

"And *I* love not hearing my friend flirt with his girlfriend while on the phone." Shaw laughs at my words. "We'll plan something soon, good luck tomorrow."

"Thanks, Miles. Hope you find a better assistant."

Me too.

I hang up and catch myself rubbing at an ache in my chest. All of my friends have been single since I've known them. Sure, they all go on dates–except Emmett–but it's not been serious until Shaw started dating Sutton. I don't know why seeing photos of them and hearing that he's going to propose has me feeling weird, but it does.

I shake off the feeling and pick up my leather duffel bag. Whatever the feeling is, I'm sure it will pass.

To see Miles fall in love with his new assistant, Ellie, pre-order ***The Perfect Putt***, **a summer golf romance!**

For a bonus scene showing Shaw and Sutton's wedding and honeymoon, sign up for my newsletter!

Author's Note

Hello lovely reader,

I'm so happy you made it this far. I hope you enjoyed Shaw and Sutton's story. When I came up with the idea for this book, it was actually going to be a standalone. I saw that people were crazy about hockey, but that the closed door romance community didn't have many options. The more I thought about making this book a one time thing though, I couldn't shake the idea of it needing to be a series. But I didn't think I'd want to do a whole hockey series (now I can safely say I've become a little bit of a hockey fan, and could see myself writing one…maybe in the future!), so I decided to create a whole world of professional sports.

While the desire for more closed door sports romance is what inspired the creation of this series, my best friends who I dedicated the book to are what made it come to life. Over the course of our friendship they've given me ideas or funny lines or even just reels (*ahem, thirst traps*) with guys from sports or guys just doing romantic gestures. I can't even count how many times I've gotten a message in our group chat that's just a reel with my name in all caps, or *"Annah can you write this"*. And while I don't remember *every* time they said that, I did take inspiration from those messages and from their favorite things (like Anakin Skywalker). This whole series will have those kinds of details because when you're a writer everything is inspiration. So uh ... be careful what you say over the next year girls, hahaha.

All that to say, I'm grateful to my friends and to my readers who inspired me to write this. I had a blast with the banter and tension and learning more about hockey. I'm looking forward to writing the rest of the series! I hope you're looking forward to reading it.

Happy reading,
Annah

Acknowledgements

Thank you always and forever to my Lord, my King, Jesus Christ. I wouldn't know true love without You.

To my husband, Ryan, thank you for all that you did while I rushed against the clock to get this done. And for helping me make sure certain kiss scenes were ... *practical*. In a purely scientific, experimental, married kind of way. You're better than every book boyfriend to ever exist and I love you with all that I've got. *I belong to my beloved, and my beloved is mine.*

To my best friends, Baylie, Beth, and Kathryn, I can't thank you enough for the ways that you've blessed me through our friendship. I couldn't do this without your support, truly.

To Dulcie, thank you for always reading my work and helping me make it better! Also for talking me down whenever I panic. Which happens more often than it should, bless your heart.

To Amanda, thank you for taking time out of your schedule to read, especially while I'm rushing through at the end of manuscripts.

And thank you for your friendship. All of your gifts and kind words have blessed me so much.

To my assistant Beth, you get an extra thank you as always because you are an absolute rockstar. You've learned so much and come so far. I'm grateful to have you as a best friend and a person on my team!

To my editor Caitlin, I can't thank you enough for all that you do! We've been together since the beginning, and I can't see doing this process without you.

To my cover designer Stephanie, thank you for always creating the most beautiful illustrations that capture the essence of the book. You're amazing!

Huge thanks to my Insider Book Babes for creating STUNNING posts and content surrounding this book. You're all amazing and I can't wait to see where this team ends up!

Lastly, thank you to my ARC team and all my avid readers out there. I couldn't do what I do without you. Every day I wake up to a new message or comment or email and I can't believe that this is real, that this is my job. So, thank you for making that happen!

Also By Annah

Sweet Peach Series
The Love Audit
One More Song
Out of Office (FREE)
The First Taste
One Last Play
But He's a Carter Brother Series
But He's My Grumpy Neighbor
But He's My One Regret
But He's My Fake Fiancé (04/04/24)
More Than a Game Series
The Golden Goal
The Perfect Putt (06/06/24)

About the Author

Annah Conwell is an Amazon bestselling sweet romcom author who loves witty banter, sassy heroines, and swoony heroes. She has a passion for writing books that make you LOL one minute and melt into a puddle of 'aw' the next. You can find her living out her days in a small town in Sweet Home Alabama (roll tide roll!) with the love of her life (aka her husband), Ryan, and her two goofball pups, Prince and Ella.

She loves coffee, the color pink, and playing music way too loud in the car. Most of the time she's snuggled up under her favorite blanket on the couch, reading way too many books to call it anything other than an addiction, or writing her little hopeless romantic heart out.

Check out her website: annahconwell.com

Made in the USA
Thornton, CO
01/03/24 20:50:41

06f7c137-53c8-429d-be56-aafdaaae3d41R01